W9-BSB-841

Murder on
St. Nicholas Avenue

Berkley Prime Crime titles by Victoria Thompson

MURDER ON ASTOR PLACE

MURDER ON ST. MARK'S PLACE

MURDER ON GRAMERCY PARK

MURDER ON WASHINGTON SQUARE

MURDER ON MULBERRY BEND

MURDER ON MARBLE ROW

MURDER ON LENOX HILL

MURDER IN LITTLE ITALY

MURDER IN CHINATOWN

MURDER ON BANK STREET

MURDER ON WAVERLY PLACE

MURDER ON LEXINGTON AVENUE

MURDER ON SISTERS' ROW

MURDER ON FIFTH AVENUE

MURDER IN CHELSEA

MURDER IN MURRAY HILL

MURDER ON AMSTERDAM AVENUE

MURDER ON ST. NICHOLAS AVENUE

Murder on St. Nicholas Avenue

A Gaslight Mystery

Victoria Thompson

BERKLEY PRIME CRIME, NEW YORK

BERKLEY
PRIME
CRIME

An imprint of Penguin Random House LLC
375 Hudson Street, New York, New York 10014

This book is an original publication of Penguin Random House LLC.

Copyright © 2015 by Victoria Thompson.
The Edgar® name is a registered service mark of the Mystery Writers of America, Inc.
Penguin supports copyright. Copyright fuels creativity, encourages diverse voices,
promotes free speech, and creates a vibrant culture. Thank you for buying an authorized
edition of this book and for complying with copyright laws by not reproducing, scanning, or
distributing any part of it in any form without permission. You are supporting writers and
allowing Penguin to continue to publish books for every reader.

BERKLEY® PRIME CRIME and the PRIME CRIME design are trademarks of
Penguin Random House LLC.
For more information, visit penguin.com.

Library of Congress Cataloging-in-Publication Data

Thompson, Victoria (Victoria E.)
Murder on St. Nicholas Avenue / Victoria Thompson.—First edition.
pages ; cm.—(Gaslight mystery)
ISBN 978-0-425-27897-0
1. Brandt, Sarah (Fictitious character)—Fiction.   2. Malloy, Frank (Fictitious
character)—Fiction.   3. Women detectives—New York (State)—New York—
Fiction.   4. New York (N.Y.)—19th century—Fiction.   I. Title.
PS3570.H6442M878 2015
813'.54—dc23
2015021280

FIRST EDITION: November 2015

PRINTED IN THE UNITED STATES OF AMERICA

10   9   8   7   6   5   4   3   2   1

Cover illustration by Karen Chandler.

This is a work of fiction. Names, characters, places, and incidents either are the product of
the author's imagination or are used fictitiously, and any resemblance to actual persons,
living or dead, business establishments, events, or locales is entirely coincidental.

Penguin
Random
House

Wishing Liam, Ryan, and Keira
a wonderful Christmas!

MURDER ON
ST. NICHOLAS AVENUE

I

Maeve hurried to answer the door. Whoever was out there was getting impatient. Ringing the bell hadn't been good enough. Now they were knocking, too. Little Catherine had to practically run to keep up, but she wasn't about to be left behind by her nursemaid.

"Is it a baby?" Catherine asked, easily remembering how her mother would be summoned at all hours to deliveries when she was a midwife, since those calls had stopped only a few short months ago.

"I hope not," Maeve replied. "Your mama doesn't deliver babies anymore, and besides, she's too far away to help even if she did."

Maeve pulled open the door and found a middle-aged woman standing on the doorstep. Her hat was obviously the one she saved for "best," although her coat had seen better days. Maeve instantly classified her as one of the people who had started coming to the Malloy house looking for a handout as soon as they discovered her employer, Frank Malloy, had become a millionaire.

"Is this where the Malloys live?" the woman asked, looking up doubtfully at the imposing façade.

Malloy and his new bride had decided to wait until they returned from their honeymoon to hire servants, but Maeve was starting to think that had been a terrible mistake. Nothing like a snooty butler to send people on their way.

"Yes, it is, but—"

"I'm a friend of Mrs. Malloy. Mrs. Alma Malloy, that is, not the new missus."

"She's not—"

"Oh, I know she's not home now," the woman said, twisting her hands anxiously. "She's with the boy at his school, isn't she? I wouldn't know that if I wasn't really her friend, now, would I? But it's not her I was wanting to see, is it? No, it's himself, Mr. Malloy. Francis. I've known him from a boy, I have, and I . . ."

To Maeve's dismay, the woman burst into tears.

Maeve glanced up and down the street, checking to see if the woman had brought someone with her. She saw no one else lurking about. Briefly, she debated inviting the woman inside. She and Catherine were there alone, but the woman didn't look dangerous. Besides, how could she shut the door and leave someone sobbing on the stoop?

"Come in, please," Maeve said, taking the woman's arm and drawing her inside.

"Why is the lady crying?" Catherine asked.

The woman stopped dead at the sound of the child's voice and made a visible effort to recover her composure. "And who's this, now?" she asked.

"This is Mrs. Brandt's . . . I mean, Mrs. Malloy's daughter. The new Mrs. Malloy, that is."

"Francis's new bride," she said, nodding. "A sweet little thing she is, too."

"Mr. Malloy is my papa now," Catherine said.

"Of course he is," she said with a watery smile. "I don't suppose I could speak with Francis, could I? It's very important, you see. A matter of life and death."

It was always a matter of life and death when people wanted a handout, Maeve thought, but she said, "I'm sorry to say that he's not here, but I'll be happy to tell him you called."

"I can wait for him. I have to see him right away, you know."

"You'll have a very long wait, I'm afraid. He's still on his honeymoon, and we don't expect them back for several weeks yet."

"Several weeks?" she repeated, her eyes flooding with tears again. "But I can't . . . I have to see him. It's my daughter, you see. They've put her in jail, and they say she's done murder, but she never did. She's a good girl, my Una. She would never do what they said, but they're going to hang her unless Francis helps her!"

Oh dear, this wasn't at all what Maeve had been expecting. And not something Catherine needed to hear about either. She glanced down to see the child's eyes had widened in alarm.

"Mrs. . . . I'm sorry, I didn't get your name."

"Mrs. O'Neill, lass. I'm so sorry to bother you, but—"

"Not at all. Why don't we go into the kitchen, Mrs. O'Neill, and I'll make you a nice cup of tea, and you can tell me all about your daughter."

"I don't want to be any trouble now, miss."

"It's no trouble. Mrs. Malloy would never forgive me if I turned away an old friend in need," Maeve lied. Mrs. Malloy generally thought old friends in need were a lot of trouble.

Maeve would have to distract Catherine somehow first,

of course, but before she could come up with a plan, someone else rang their doorbell.

Wonderful, another visitor.

With an apologetic smile, she opened the front door again to find their neighbor Mrs. Ellsworth, smiling broadly and carrying a planter filled with sprigs of holly and trailing ivy.

"Maeve, dear, I've got this little planting for you and . . . Oh my, I didn't know you had company," she said, doing a much better job of lying than even Maeve herself could do, because of course she'd known very well that Maeve had company. Mrs. Ellsworth didn't consider it lying at all, though. People said things that weren't true all the time in polite society. It was just good manners, according to Mrs. Ellsworth.

Mrs. Ellsworth breezed right in without being invited, and Maeve did not object because they both knew she'd come to see if Maeve needed rescuing from an importunate beggar from the Malloys' old neighborhood. Nothing much happened on Bank Street that Mrs. Ellsworth didn't notice. She would have spotted the strange woman at the Malloys' door in a heartbeat.

Maeve introduced the two women.

"Are you quite well, Mrs. O'Neill?" Mrs. Ellsworth inquired, seeing the woman's red-rimmed eyes.

"Mrs. O'Neill has had some trouble, and she came to ask Mr. Malloy for help. It's detective business," she added, so Mrs. Ellsworth would understand that she didn't need assistance in running Mrs. O'Neill off. Frank Malloy had been a police detective until he came into money, and now he sometimes helped people in trouble. "I was just wondering if Catherine could visit with you for an hour or so while Mrs. O'Neill and I talk, at least until Brian and Mrs. Malloy get home from school."

"Of course, dear. You know little Catherine is always welcome. I'm just getting ready to make some pies for supper, and I know how she loves to make the lattice crusts. Would you like to help me with that?" she asked the child.

Plainly, Catherine wanted to stay and find out why this strange lady had been crying, but she was too well trained to refuse the invitation. "Yes, ma'am, I would."

"That's wonderful," Mrs. Ellsworth said, then seemed to remember the planter she still held. "And this is for your household, Maeve, for Christmas good fortune. The holly brings good luck to men and the ivy brings good luck to us females. We must always have them both together. That's only fair, don't you think? And let me know immediately if the ivy starts to wither. That's a very bad sign. And never burn the holly when it's still green. That's very bad luck."

Nearly overwhelmed by the detailed instructions while her mind was still on Mrs. O'Neill's problems, Maeve thanked her and took the planter and set it on a table in the hallway. A few moments later, after Catherine had been bundled into her hat and coat, she and Mrs. Ellsworth headed out and across the street to Mrs. Ellsworth's house.

"This house is . . . very nice," Mrs. O'Neill said, looking around in awe at the massive staircase and the chandelier hanging from the ceiling twenty feet above.

"Thank you," Maeve said. "I should probably take you into the parlor—"

"Oh no, the kitchen is fine for the likes of me, lass." She followed as Maeve led the way to the back of the house. "Alma must be very . . . comfortable here."

"She seems to be," Maeve said, biting back a smile. Mrs. Malloy wasn't the kind of person to let on if she was comfortable or not.

A few minutes later, Maeve had gotten Mrs. O'Neill to take off her coat and have a seat at the kitchen table while

Maeve set water to boil on the newly installed gas stove. It was one of only a few in the entire city, they'd been told. While she waited for the water, she cut a few slices of the pound cake left over from yesterday and arranged them on a plate. By the time the tea was steeping and the cake had been served, over Mrs. O'Neill's polite objections, her guest had calmed down quite a bit.

"I'm sorry Mr. Malloy isn't here," Maeve began, "but I would be glad to hear your story and help you figure out what to do."

She smiled sadly. "Oh, lass, there's nothing you can do, I'm sure."

Maeve smiled. "Don't judge me by my looks, Mrs. O'Neill. I've helped Mr. Malloy solve many a case." It was only a slight exaggeration.

Mrs. O'Neill frowned. "Oh, surely not."

"I've also done work for the Pinkerton Detective Agency, so even if I can't help you, I'll know someone who can. Now tell me, why on earth would someone accuse your daughter of committing murder?"

Her eyes filled with tears again, but she resolutely blinked them back. "I can't hardly believe it myself, but I saw her in the jail with my own eyes. Just sitting there staring at the wall, all covered with blood, she was. She wouldn't say a word to me, not a single word. They said she hasn't said anything at all since it happened."

"Since what happened?"

Mrs. O'Neill drew a deep breath and let it out on a shaky sigh. "It's a long story."

"I'm not going anywhere." Maeve picked up the teapot and poured them each another cup.

"Well, it all started . . . oh dear, was it only five months ago? Yes, just that. My Una, she's a pretty girl. I'm not bragging.

Everyone says so. And she's a good girl, too. Not vain like a lot of pretty girls are."

"I'm sure," Maeve said, doubting that but nodding her encouragement.

"She got a job at a factory about a year ago, sewing ladies' clothes. She'd give me her wages every week. I told you, she's a good girl."

Maeve nodded again.

"Then one day she came home that excited. A gentleman had seen her and offered her a job in his cigar shop."

"Seen her where?"

"Coming out of the factory. He was watching all the girls, and he picked her out special, because she's so pretty."

This sounded suspicious to Maeve. Men were always trying to take advantage of young women in the city. "Did he really have a cigar shop?"

"Oh yes. I can see what you're thinking, but I wouldn't let her get tricked into something bad. I went with her to see his shop. He was such a nice man. He liked to have a pretty girl to work behind the counter, he told us. It attracts customers. They come in to flirt with the girl and buy a cigar or two while they're there."

So long as cigars are all he's selling, Maeve thought.

"He'd just lost his counter girl because she'd gotten married. That happened to all the girls who'd worked there, he said. One of the customers would fall in love and off she'd go. So Una not only got a good job that paid more than she'd been getting at the factory, she also got a chance to meet a nice young man with prospects."

"And did she meet someone?"

"Oh yes. She wasn't there long before Mr. Pollock noticed her. He'd come in nearly every day, she said. Always polite, you understand. Mr. Winter didn't allow his girls to be treated rude. He told me that right off, or I never would've let her go there. And Mr. Pollock, he fell in love with my Una."

Which was, of course, what all men say when they want to have their way with a girl. Maeve's grandfather had told her that a million times when she was growing up, and in her limited experience, she'd found it to be quite true. "Did Mr. Pollock want to marry Una?"

"He did. At first she thought he was teasing. A lot of men teased her about getting married, but he was serious. He couldn't convince her at first, but then he asked if he could see her home one evening, to meet me. And when he did, he asked if he could marry my girl."

This sounded like a fairy tale, but unlike fairy tales, it probably didn't end happily. Something had obviously gone terribly wrong at some point, or Mrs. O'Neill wouldn't need help from Frank Malloy. "Did they get married?"

"Oh yes, and it wasn't one of those sham marriages either. I was there. I saw it happen. The priest said the words over them all right and proper. But this was only after I went to see his house. He has a beautiful house up in Harlem, on St. Nicholas Avenue. It's where all the rich people are moving. That's what he told us. He has a woman to cook for him and two more to clean and a boy to do the heavy work. And Mr. Pollock, he adored my Una. My girl was going to have the life I always hoped she would. It was like a miracle."

"But she didn't?"

"Oh, she did! Mr. Pollock, he bought her new clothes, and she lived in his beautiful house, and they were so happy. *She* was so happy. I know they were. He adored her."

She went still, staring off at something only she could see. Maeve waited, not wanting to rush her. Not really wanting to know at all, in fact.

"They came to me today. The police. Our roundsman, I

should say. He knows me, you see. His wife and I go to church together. He told me Una was in the jail and I should go down right away. He told me . . ." Her voice broke, and she covered her face with both hands.

Maeve waited, her stomach knotted, her fists clenched tightly on the tabletop.

Finally, Mrs. O'Neill lowered her hands. Her eyes were awful, full of despair. "They said she'd killed him. Killed Mr. Pollock. But how could that be? She loved him. He was her husband!"

Maeve knew lots of wives would happily murder their husbands and a few who actually had, but she didn't think that information would comfort Mrs. O'Neill. "What did Una say when you saw her in the jail?"

"Nothing. I told you, she wouldn't say a word. They told me she hadn't said anything at all since they found her."

"Where did they find her?"

"At the house. Mr. Pollock's house. She was . . . She was sitting on the floor in the parlor, holding his head in her lap."

"Who found her?"

"The maid, I think it was. He was dead, they told me, and she was just sitting there with his bloody head in her lap, stroking his hair."

"How did he die?"

"Someone hit him on the head, they said. Crushed his skull, they told me. Una must've found him or maybe she even saw it happen. She was in shock, I'm sure. That's why she couldn't tell them what really happened. So they put her in jail, and now they're going to hang her."

Maeve knew that New York no longer hanged murderers. They used the very modern electric chair instead, but Mrs. O'Neill wouldn't want to know that either.

"So you see, miss . . . Oh dear, I never even asked your name."

"I'm sorry. I should've told you. Maeve Smith. I'm the nursemaid for Mrs. Brandt's . . . that is, Mrs. Frank Malloy's daughter."

"A nursemaid who works with the Pinkertons?" she asked with a frown.

"No one notices a nursemaid. You'd be amazed at what I can find out."

Mrs. O'Neill smiled sadly. "I'm sure, my girl, but I don't think there's anything a nursemaid can do for my Una."

"You're right, at least at the moment. The first thing you need to do is hire an attorney."

"And how would I do that, miss? And what would I pay him with?"

This was a problem, of course. "Do you have any money at all?"

"I have a little put by, but not much."

"Would your daughter have any? Maybe she tucked away some housekeeping money or something."

"I don't know."

"Did she ever say anything about it? Her husband must've given her money for shopping and things."

"I . . . Well . . . That is . . ."

"What?" Maeve prodded when Mrs. O'Neill hesitated.

"I didn't . . . After they got married . . . Mr. Pollock, he didn't want me coming around anymore." She dropped her gaze, unable to look Maeve in the eye. "I haven't seen Una in . . . Well, since the day she got married."

That didn't sound like a man who adored his wife. Why would he have forbidden his mother-in-law from visiting his wife if he really cared about her? She couldn't think of any good reason, but she didn't want to go into that with Mrs. O'Neill just now. First things first. "Una should be able to spend her husband's money. She probably knows where he keeps it, at least, and if he has any in the house, we'll find it. I can help you with that."

"Wouldn't that be stealing?"

Of course it would, but Maeve said, "The money belongs to your daughter now that her husband is dead. You can use it to pay a lawyer."

"What good will a lawyer do?"

Maeve felt a stab of envy for someone who had never needed the services of an attorney. "He can figure out how to get Una out of jail, for one thing."

"Really?"

Maeve decided not to explain the concept of bail just yet. "Yes. I'll write down the name and address of an attorney I know. He can help you. Tomorrow you can visit Una and find out if she knows where her husband kept his money. In the meantime, I'm going to find out what the police know and why they think Una killed her husband."

"The police? How will you find out anything from them?"

Maeve smiled. "I'm just going to ask."

OFFICER GINO DONATELLI FOUND HIMSELF WHISTLING as he strolled down Bank Street and climbed the front steps to the Malloy house. He probably shouldn't feel so happy about being summoned, especially when he knew Malloy was still on his honeymoon so this couldn't possibly be an opportunity for him to work on a case, but he was whistling just the same.

He rang the bell and waited. Then the door opened and Maeve Smith was there and he couldn't hold back his smile.

"Miss Smith." He tipped his hat.

"Officer Donatelli," she replied. She wasn't smiling, but she usually made a point of not smiling at him. She stepped aside and motioned him in.

Before either of them could say anything else, two small bodies launched themselves at him, and he had to greet the children of the house. Catherine and Brian were both talking at once. Catherine used her voice and Brian used his hands, signing the way they had taught him at the deaf school he attended.

"What's he saying?" Gino asked Maeve, but Catherine answered.

"He's telling you we got a letter from Mama and Papa yesterday. They're in France."

"Are they now? And what are they doing in France?" Gino asked.

"Honeymooning," Catherine informed him.

"That sounds like fun," Gino said, grinning at Maeve, but she ignored him.

"Officer Donatelli and I need to talk," she said, signing for Brian's benefit.

The children tried to argue, but by then Mrs. Malloy had made her much more dignified way from the kitchen. Frank's mother was a formidable woman even though she wasn't quite five feet tall, and she tolerated no nonsense.

"Good evening, Officer Donatelli," she said. "Have you had your supper?"

"Yes, ma'am, I have, thank you."

"Maeve, take him to the kitchen and give him a slice of that pie we had," she said.

"I helped make it," Catherine said.

"Then I'm sure it's delicious."

"Come along, children," Mrs. Malloy said, taking them each by the hand.

"I'll see you later, after Miss Smith and I are finished talking," he promised them.

Maeve led him down the hall without speaking. He hung

his hat on the hall tree and followed her, silently admiring the shape of her as they went.

"Have a seat," she said, pulling a half-eaten apple pie with a lattice crust out of the pie safe and proceeding to cut him a generous slice.

"This is very nice," he said when she set it in front of him, "but I have to admit, I expected at least a kiss when I got here."

That finally got a reaction out of her. She reared back. "Why would you expect a kiss?"

"Because the message you left for me at Police Headquarters made everybody think you were my sweetheart."

"I never said any such thing!" Her cheeks had turned a becoming shade of pink, just as he'd expected.

"I took a lot of ribbing about it, too," he said as if he didn't notice. He'd also heard some speculation that she was going to tell him he was about to become a father, because why else would a girl go to the trouble of leaving an urgent telephone message for him at Headquarters? He decided not to mention that, though. Knowing Maeve, she'd hit him with the pie pan.

"It couldn't've been that bad. I see you managed to survive," she said with a smirk.

"Just barely. So what *was* so important that you had to see me tonight?"

She put some coffee on to boil, and while he ate his pie, she told him about the woman from Malloy's old neighborhood who had come looking for help for her daughter.

"I heard about it today, the murder. Everybody was talking down at Headquarters," he said.

"What did you hear?"

"Just that some woman bashed her husband's head in. It was way up in Harlem, so nobody from Headquarters was involved."

"Do you think you could get assigned to investigate?"

Gino frowned. "I'm not a detective, Maeve. Besides, they think the wife did it, so the police aren't investigating anything. But if she wants to hire a private investigator . . . ," he added with a hopeful grin.

"She doesn't have any money. She wasn't even sure she could hire a lawyer for her daughter."

Gino tried not to feel too disappointed. When he'd returned from fighting the war in Cuba last summer, he'd helped Malloy on a case. This wasn't unusual. He'd helped Malloy on several cases, but that was when they'd both worked for the New York City Police Department. When Malloy had come into some money recently, he'd lost his police detective's job, so last summer they'd both worked on the case as private investigators. Then Malloy left on his honeymoon to Europe, and as Malloy had advised him to do, Gino had returned to his old job with the police, even though he wasn't particularly happy to be back on the force. "Then there's not much I can do except ask around to see what I can find out."

Maeve sighed. "I wish the Malloys were back."

"So do I. Mr. Malloy would help, I know."

"Maybe we can help at least a little."

Excitement stirred at the thought of a real case, but he tamped it down. "I'll do what I can, but it'll have to be when I'm off duty."

"That's fine."

"Maeve?"

"Yes."

"What if you find out this Una really did kill her husband?"

"Then I'm sure she had a really good reason. Maybe she even did it in self-defense. A woman doesn't just bash a man's head in for nothing."

She was right, of course. A man might do something violent

just because he was drunk, but women—respectable women, anyway—usually got violent only as a last resort. "What are you going to do?"

"Tomorrow, Mrs. O'Neill will visit her daughter in jail to find out if she's got any money hidden away somewhere. Then I'm meeting her at her daughter's house. We're going to tell the servants that Una needs some clothes and things at the jail. That'll give us an excuse to go in the house and look around to see if we can find any money that Mrs. O'Neill can use to hire an attorney to help Una."

"Don't people like that keep their money in banks?"

"Sure, but they need cash to pay their servants and to buy things with. Mr. Malloy left us a lot of money for expenses while they're gone. We keep it in a safe. I figure Pollock kept at least a little money in his house, too."

"What if Pollock's money is in a safe?"

Maeve shrugged. "I'm hoping he kept his money in a drawer or under the mattress."

Gino hoped she was right. "What if the servants won't let you in?"

"What do you mean?"

"Servants are trained to keep people out. They won't know you at all, and if what you say about Mrs. O'Neill never being allowed to visit her daughter is true, they won't know her either. Who's to say you're not two strangers looking to rob the place?"

Maeve frowned. "You're right. Mrs. Brandt would know how to get them to let her in."

"Mrs. Malloy, you mean," Gino said with a grin. "And her mother would know even better."

"Her mother? You mean Mrs. Decker?" Maeve said, perking right up again.

"Can you imagine any maid refusing to let her in?" The

Deckers were descended from the original Knickerbocker families who had founded New York City. They'd had money—and servants—for generations.

"Of course! She'd be happy to help."

The sparkle in Maeve's eyes told him she knew exactly how happy Mrs. Decker would be, too. Rich ladies seldom got to do anything exciting. "Just make sure Mr. Decker doesn't find out."

P OOR MRS. O'NEILL NEARLY FAINTED WHEN MAEVE AND Mrs. Decker emerged from the Deckers' carriage in front of Pollock's house the next day.

"Miss Smith, is that you?" she asked a little breathlessly, warily eyeing Maeve's imposing companion.

"Yes, it is, and let me introduce Mrs. Felix Decker. She's Mr. Malloy's mother-in-law, and she has come to help us."

Mrs. O'Neill managed to mumble something appropriate in response to the introduction, although Maeve could see she was completely in awe of the finely dressed matron. Mrs. Decker's fur-trimmed coat and matching muff probably cost more than a cigar shop clerk earned in a year.

"I'm so pleased to meet you, Mrs. O'Neill," Mrs. Decker said as warmly as if she were meeting one of the Vanderbilts. "I was sorry to hear of your daughter's misfortune. I hope Maeve and I can be of some assistance to you."

"When I told Mrs. Decker what happened, she insisted on coming with me," Maeve explained.

"That's very kind, I'm sure," Mrs. O'Neill said faintly as Mrs. Decker swept past her.

"Is this the house?" she asked, indicating the gray stone, turreted row house behind Mrs. O'Neill.

"Yes, but . . ."

Mrs. Decker climbed the long flight of steps that led to the front door, located on the second floor. Maeve indicated Mrs. O'Neill should follow, which she did with obvious reluctance. Maeve brought up the rear after the driver, John, handed her the carpetbag Mrs. Decker had thought to bring along.

"I'm not sure we should be doing this," Mrs. O'Neill whispered to Maeve.

"You have every right to be in your daughter's house," Maeve lied.

Mrs. Decker used the brass knocker with what Maeve realized was authority. She would have to remember exactly how she did that. After what seemed like a long time, the door opened just a bit and a very uncertain face peered out.

"Good morning," Mrs. Decker said. "Mrs. Pollock's mother is here to gather some things for her. If you would be so kind . . ."

Maeve couldn't tell if Mrs. Decker actually pushed on the door or not, but the maid seemed to stumble a bit as she jumped out of the way when Mrs. Decker swept inside.

"There's nobody at home," the maid tried.

"Of course not," Mrs. Decker said. She was in the foyer now. Maeve gave Mrs. O'Neill a small nudge of encouragement to herd her into the house, too. "Mr. Pollock is unfortunately deceased, and Mrs. Pollock is being detained by the police. That's why we're here. Mrs. Pollock needs a change of clothing and some toiletries. Would you please take her mother, Mrs. O'Neill, up to her bedroom so she can pack them?"

Maeve didn't know who looked more astonished, the maid or Mrs. O'Neill.

Mrs. Decker gave the young woman a few moments to react, and when she just stood there, gaping, Mrs. Decker said, "Is it this way?" and started for the staircase at the end of the foyer.

The girl scrambled to catch up, and Maeve gave Mrs.

O'Neill another nudge. With a dismayed glance back at Maeve, she obediently followed the other two up the stairs. As she and Mrs. Decker had previously decided, Maeve remained downstairs, prepared to become inconspicuous until she was certain she was unobserved. This required a wait of only a few minutes, during which no other servant came to investigate and the maid who had gone upstairs with the others did not reappear. Mrs. Decker would be keeping her busy, as they'd planned.

When she was satisfied no one would notice, Maeve strolled down the hallway and glanced into each of the rooms. A small parlor to the right was the scene of the murder, according to what Mrs. O'Neill had told her. The room looked remarkably undisturbed except that the carpet had been rolled up and lay like a low barrier in front of the doorway. Maeve imagined it was bloodstained, and the servants hadn't wanted to look at it.

A long dining room lay to the left. Except for the rolled carpet, both rooms were well furnished, and everything in them was obviously brand-new if not of the very best quality. Beyond the parlor, behind a closed door, was what must have been Mr. Pollock's office or study. Judging from the lingering scent of tobacco smoke, no ladies would have felt welcome here. With another glance up and down the hallway to make sure no one was watching, Maeve stepped inside and closed the door behind her.

Only then did she realize she still held the carpetbag. Muttering an imprecation at her carelessness, she set it down and hoped her companions didn't send the maid back down for it before she'd finished exploring this room.

A walnut desk sat against one wall. Pollock was either very neat or he didn't really do any work at this desk. The top was bare except for an inkwell and a few knickknacks, and it had been polished to a shine. She checked the drawers but found nothing of interest there either. If Pollock kept money in the house, he probably had a more secure location than an unlocked desk. Two ugly landscape paintings hung on the walls, but neither concealed a wall safe. Pollock had no bookshelves to conceal hidden passages the way they did in novels, and the only other furnishings in the room were two comfortable-looking leather armchairs and the table between them.

Maeve sat down in one of the chairs and looked around the room again, wondering what she'd missed. That's when she noticed the table between the two chairs was rather oddly sized. The cube-shaped object seemed a bit too short for the job and, beneath a collection of singularly ugly knickknacks, was completely covered with what looked like a large silk scarf. The only reason you hid something with a scarf was because you didn't want anyone to see how old and battered it was, but everything else in this house was bright and shiny and new.

Maeve lifted the scarf and found a squat and ugly but very sturdy-looking safe.

Maeve sighed. Gino had been right about Pollock having a safe. He'd been concerned she wouldn't be able to open it, of course, and that was a legitimate concern. He probably couldn't imagine someone like herself being able to crack a safe either. That would, of course, be a valuable skill to have, especially at this particular moment. Her grandfather had taught her many things, but not that, unfortunately. He had, however, taught her another skill that might serve her even better. This time when she searched Pollock's desk, she checked his nearly blank appointment diary more carefully and found the series of numbers he'd written at the bottom of the very last page in pencil.

As she had hoped, they opened the safe on the second try—Pollock had been clever enough to list the numbers backward in case someone found them and guessed what they were. The safe opened with a satisfying click when she lifted the lever. She'd hoped to find a few hundred dollars inside that Mrs. O'Neill could use for a lawyer, but what she did find sent her rearing back with a most unladylike yelp.

2

POLICE HEADQUARTERS WAS UNUSUALLY QUIET WHEN Gino arrived that morning. Of course, he was early for his shift because he wanted to see what he could find out about the Pollock murder, and early morning was that calm period of the day when the drunks from the night before were safely locked up and sleeping it off and the evildoers of the daylight hours hadn't gotten started yet.

The desk sergeant gave him a knowing grin, obviously remembering the to-do about Maeve's phone message the day before. "So, when's the wedding?"

"Nothing so drastic," Gino said, grinning back. "She just missed me."

"Is she that girl what works for Mrs. Brandt?"

Everyone at Headquarters knew Mrs. Brandt. "She's Mrs. Malloy now," Gino reminded him. "And yes, Miss Smith works for her."

"Ah yes, Mrs. Malloy," the sergeant mused. "That lucky bastard Malloy."

Gino wasn't sure if the sergeant thought Malloy was lucky because of his sudden wealth or his marriage to Mrs. Brandt, but he said, "I don't know about luck. After what happened to that Pollock fellow yesterday, marriage isn't looking too good to me."

From his high desk the sergeant nodded at Gino. "You're right. Poor fellow. Although who's to say he didn't deserve it, eh?"

"Yeah, a woman doesn't usually bash her husband on the head for no reason. Did you hear anything about him?"

The sergeant shrugged. "Nothing special, but he's a bouncer. All them fellas is shady, you ask me."

"So he had money, did he?" *Bouncer* was a derogatory term for the newly rich who hadn't yet earned a place in society.

"He lived in one of them new houses up in Harlem. They don't come cheap, although why anybody'd want to live way out in the country like that, I don't know."

"It's pretty far, but it's not farmland anymore."

"I guess not, if bouncers are building houses there," the sergeant agreed.

"Did you hear what Pollock did for a living?"

The sergeant frowned down at Gino. "You're awful interested in this fellow."

Gino tried a shrug. "Just curious, I guess."

But the old sergeant wasn't fooled. "You ain't a detective, boy. Don't forget that. Nobody'll thank you for interfering in what ain't your business, and Malloy ain't here no more to cover for you."

"That's good advice," Gino said, giving the old sergeant a mock salute.

He was walking away, already trying to figure out how to

be more subtle in his inquiries the next time, when the sergeant called, "But if you want to find out more about Pollock, ask Broghan. His cousin walks the beat up there, and he was the first one in the house."

"Broghan, huh? I think he might still be mad at me about that case with the missing women."

The sergeant gave a bark of laughter. "Oh yeah, that was clever, but it's Malloy he's mad at. Besides, he's an Irishman. If you'll listen to him, he'll talk to you, mad or not."

"Thanks, Sarge."

Gino was whistling as he went to report for duty. Broghan wouldn't be in this early, but he'd be able to catch him later at his favorite bar.

MAEVE WAS SITTING ON THE BENCH IN THE FOYER, JUST where they'd left her and looking completely innocent, when Mrs. O'Neill and Mrs. Decker came back downstairs. The maid trailed behind them carrying a cheap suitcase that they'd apparently found upstairs. Thank heaven they hadn't needed the carpetbag, which sat at her feet.

"I hope you weren't bored waiting for us," Mrs. Decker said with a questioning look in her eye.

"Oh no, not at all. Did you get everything you needed for Mrs. Pollock?"

"Yes, and we also decided that we'll have my maid come back tomorrow and pack up all of Mrs. Pollock's things and take them to her mother's house. Under the circumstances, Mrs. Pollock will want to close up the house, I'm sure."

She didn't have to mention that with Pollock dead and Una in jail, there'd be no one to pay the servants and the other expenses of running a household.

"Oh, you might want to wait a week or two before doing

that," Maeve said. "Mrs. Pollock will probably be released, and she'll want to come home."

"She'll want to come home to *me*, I'm sure," her mother said. "She won't want to come back here, after what happened."

"But what'll become of us?" the maid asked. "There's nobody to write us a reference." Maeve had learned a lot about servants from Mrs. Decker, and she knew they changed employers frequently. The Pollocks' servants wouldn't have been with them long, so they'd certainly feel no loyalty to Una.

"I'll write all of you a reference, if it comes to that," Mrs. Decker said. "But don't go running off just yet. We'll see you're taken care of. And let me know if you need anything." She gave the girl her calling card. "Are we ready to go?"

Maeve said they were, so they filed out to the sidewalk, where the Decker carriage still waited at the curb. The driver hurried to assist the ladies inside, taking the carpetbag from Maeve and setting it by her feet at her instruction. He strapped the other suitcase to the back and then scrambled up to his perch after receiving instructions to deliver Mrs. O'Neill to the city jail first.

As soon as they were safely away from the house, Mrs. Decker said, "I assume your search was successful, Maeve."

"Yes, it was," she said, reaching into her pocket and pulling out a wad of bills. "Mrs. O'Neill, this should be enough to hire the attorney whose name I gave you and also to pay your daughter's bail, if he can arrange it."

Mrs. O'Neill stared at the money as if afraid it would bite her. "How much is there?"

"Five hundred dollars."

Mrs. O'Neill made a strangled sound. She'd certainly never seen so much money all at once, which would be more than a year's salary for an average person. "But I can't—"

"Of course you can," Maeve said. "It's your daughter's money, after all. You should use it to help her."

"I . . . What should I do with it?"

"Put it in your purse," Mrs. Decker suggested, but Mrs. O'Neill's horrified reaction clearly showed how dangerous she considered that idea.

"Put a couple hundred in your purse to pay the attorney," Maeve said.

"He'll want that much?" she squeaked.

"No, but you want him to see you've got more than what he asks for so he'll be willing to take the case. You can put the rest of it down in your corset, so you won't have to worry about losing it. I'll show you."

By the time Maeve had helped her hide the rest of the money, Mrs. O'Neill looked a little less terrified.

"What a good idea," Mrs. Decker said in wonder, having watched the whole thing with admiration. "Where did you learn that?"

Maeve didn't even consider answering truthfully. "I thought of it just now. It's clever, isn't it?" She turned back to Mrs. O'Neill. "The attorney's office is across the street from the jail, so go straight there after you take Una her things."

"She still wouldn't talk to me this morning. I tried everything I knew, but she wouldn't speak. I think whoever killed Mr. Pollock may have injured her, too, but how would we know, when she won't say anything?"

Maeve had no reply for that, but Mrs. Decker said, "Maybe she'll speak with her attorney. Sometimes it's easier to talk to a stranger about something so serious."

Mrs. O'Neill looked doubtful, but she wasn't going to disagree with someone like Mrs. Decker.

They rode the rest of the way in uneasy silence, in spite of Mrs. Decker's efforts to make small talk.

When they'd dropped Mrs. O'Neill at the jail, Mrs. Decker turned to Maeve expectantly. "All right, you obviously found some money, but what else did you find?"

"What makes you think I found anything else?" Maeve asked with a grin.

Mrs. Decker pointed at the carpetbag sitting on the floor of the carriage. "That bag is full of something, and you wanted to keep it close."

"I was so glad you didn't need it for Una's clothes." Maeve leaned over and opened it to reveal the contents.

Mrs. Decker clapped a hand to her heart. "Good heavens! How much is there?"

Maeve glanced at the stacks of cash. "I didn't take the time to count it, but it's thousands of dollars."

"That's why you said we didn't need to close up the house. Mrs. O'Neill thought Pollock was rich, but I'm not sure I really believed it before."

"I don't believe it now."

Mrs. Decker looked meaningfully at the carpetbag. "What do you mean?"

"I mean, Pollock had a lot of money, but rich people keep their money in banks."

"Maybe Pollock didn't trust banks."

"I guess that's possible, but thieves don't trust banks either."

"You think Pollock was a thief?"

"I have no idea, but he was a young man, from what Mrs. O'Neill told me, and she didn't seem to know exactly what he did for a living, and he's got thousands of dollars in a safe in his house. And"—she rummaged in the carpetbag and pulled out a book—"I also found this."

"What is it?"

"It's a ledger of some kind." Maeve opened it and showed her. "See, there's names and amounts of money."

"What does it mean?"

"I'm guessing it means these people gave him money, and he's keeping track of it in this ledger."

"Why would they have given him money?"

Maeve managed not to sigh. Mrs. Decker was hopelessly naïve, and Maeve didn't want her to know how much she knew about cheating people. "Probably some business thing, but we don't know enough right now to even make a guess."

"Maybe Mr. Decker could figure it out if he saw the ledger."

"Mr. Decker?" Maeve echoed in alarm. The last thing she wanted was to face him if he found out she'd involved his wife in all this.

"He's really not as terrifying as you seem to think, my dear," Mrs. Decker assured her. "We can't let him know that I helped you today, of course. You know how he worries about me. But you can just bring the ledger over to our house this evening and ask him for his advice. You can tell him everything that's happened except that I went with you to the Pollock house."

Maeve had to agree that this sounded like a good plan. "Should I bring the money, too?"

"Heavens, no. Doesn't Mr. Malloy have a safe?"

"Yes, he does."

"I thought Sarah told me he did. Do you know the combination?"

"Of course. Mr. Malloy left money for us to spend while they're on their honeymoon."

"Then put this money in the safe, too. Count it first, though. Mr. Decker will want to know how much you found. Was there anything else in the safe?"

"No, just the ledger and the money. I searched Pollock's desk, but I didn't find anything important in it except the combination to the safe."

"How odd that he would keep it so close."

"Lots of people write down the combination and keep it in a safe place in case they forget it."

"It doesn't sound like his desk was a very safe place if you found it so easily."

"Lots of people aren't very smart."

"So it seems," Mrs. Decker agreed with a grin.

Maeve was glad Mrs. Decker didn't think to ask her how she knew all this.

When they arrived at the Malloy house, Mrs. Decker came in for a short visit with Catherine, who had been visiting Mrs. Ellsworth again for a few hours while Maeve did her detective work. She couldn't stay long, though, because she had to be home when Mr. Decker arrived. She didn't want to have to lie about where she'd been this afternoon.

Maeve and Catherine started supper, and when Mrs. Malloy brought Brian home from school, they all ate together. Mrs. Decker had warned her that they ate supper late, so she shouldn't come until around eight o'clock, which left a long time for Maeve to wait. Luckily, Gino Donatelli arrived shortly after they'd finished eating. He also had to spend a little time with the children before Maeve could steal him away. Luckily, Mrs. Malloy was there to get them ready for bed while Maeve took him to the kitchen for a piece of cake.

"Did you have any luck at Pollock's house today?" he asked as she sliced the cake.

"You might say that. I was able to give Mrs. O'Neill five hundred dollars to hire a lawyer and pay Una's bail, if the lawyer can get it set."

He looked suitably impressed. "That's a lot of money. Where did you find it?"

She set the cake down in front of him. "In his safe."

"I was right about that, then." Men just loved being right, and Gino was no exception.

"Yes, you were," she said sweetly, more than happy to acknowledge it. She sat down at the table opposite him.

He started to take a bite, but stopped with the fork halfway to his mouth. "If it was in a safe, how did you get it out?"

She continued to smile sweetly.

He frowned. "You didn't . . . You don't know how to crack a safe, do you?"

How nice that he thought she might actually be able to do that. And how nice to see his various horrified reactions to that thought. "Of course not. He'd written the combination down, and I found it."

"Where?"

"In his appointment diary. In his desk. Really, he wasn't very good at this at all."

"Good at what?"

"Never mind. So were you able to find out anything about Pollock?"

He hesitated, as if he wanted to ask her something else, but then he sighed and said, "Not a lot about Pollock, but I found out more about the murder. Broghan's cousin was the first one in the house."

"Broghan? Mr. Malloy's friend?"

Gino grinned at that. "They aren't exactly friends."

"But he's a police detective, too, same as Mr. Malloy was?"

"Yes, although he's not the same as Mr. Malloy at all."

"Oh, I remember. He drinks, doesn't he?"

"All Irishmen drink. Broghan drinks a *lot*."

"Then I hope you waited until he was drunk to talk to him," Maeve said with a smile.

"He's always drunk, so that wasn't hard."

"And what did you find out?"

"Well, there was some kind of argument in the house. The servants were in the kitchen, and they claim they don't know who was there or what the argument was about. They just heard shouting, and they stayed where they were, trying to pretend they didn't hear anything because it was none of their business."

"Did the Pollocks fight a lot?"

"I didn't talk to the servants myself, so I don't know. And all this is secondhand, remember. Well, thirdhand, really."

"I just think it's funny the servants claim they don't know who was shouting. Servants know everything that goes on in their house."

"I know, which is why we need to question them ourselves. Anyway, after all the arguing, things got quiet for a while, and they thought it was safe to come out. That's when they found the Pollocks, both of them, on the parlor floor. He was all bloody, and she'd sat down with him and put his head in her lap."

Maeve tried to picture this in her mind. "Then what happened?"

"One of the maids ran out and found the beat cop, who is Broghan's cousin. He saw Una and Pollock in the parlor, then he sent for the ward detective, who decided Una did it and arrested her."

"That sure made it easy for him," Maeve said. "How is she supposed to have killed him?"

"Just like Mrs. O'Neill said, somebody hit him over the head."

"With what?"

"Broghan didn't know."

"That would make a lot of difference," Maeve said. "If it was something in the house, she might've done it, but if it wasn't . . ."

"I'm probably going to have to get Broghan's cousin drunk to find out more."

"Or maybe I can just ask the servants."

Gino raised his eyebrows. He had very nice eyebrows, she noticed. "When would you do that?"

"Tomorrow, when I go back to pack up all of Una's clothes. Mrs. Decker was going to send her maid to do it, but now I think I should."

"Why—?"

"Because Mrs. Decker thought they should close the house and let the servants go, since there's no one to pay them. That would mean selling everything except Una's personal belongings. Mrs. O'Neill wanted them taken to her flat so they'd be safe."

"That makes sense."

"But then I found the money."

"Five hundred dollars isn't going to pay the servants for long, especially if she has to pay the lawyer and bail money and—"

"I found more than five hundred dollars."

"How much did you find?" he asked with interest. He had nice eyes, too. She'd have to make a point of not noticing that.

"Thirty-seven thousand two hundred and seventy-six dollars."

Gino blinked his very nice eyes several times. "Thirty-seven *thousand* dollars?"

"And two hundred and seventy-six, not including the five hundred I gave Mrs. O'Neill."

"But what . . . ? Did you give it to Mrs. O'Neill?"

"Of course not. She almost fainted when I gave her five hundred. I didn't even tell her about it, but Mrs. Decker knows. She went with us to the house and kept the maid busy while I looked around."

"So Mrs. Decker took it?"

"No, I have it here, locked up in our safe. And I also found this." She got up and fetched the ledger book from where she'd left it on top of the pie safe.

"What is it?" he asked as she handed it to him.

"I think it's a record of the people who gave him the money. I added up all the entries, and it comes to a little over forty-five thousand. He probably spent some of it, so that would explain why there's only thirty-seven thousand left."

"Thirty-seven thousand two-hundred and thirty-six."

"*Seventy*-six," she said.

"I was just testing you," he said with a grin. She refused to notice his grin. "What are these other numbers?"

"I think the first column is dates. I don't know what the last column could be."

"But who are these people, and why would they give Pollock money?"

"I don't know, but Mrs. Decker thinks her husband might be able to figure it out."

"Mr. Decker?"

"He's helped us before," she reminded him. "Besides, Mrs. Decker says he's much nicer than we think he is."

"Did she actually say that?"

"Not exactly, but she could see I was afraid to ask him, so she was trying to encourage me."

"She thought you were *afraid* of something?" he said with mock amazement.

"You wouldn't want to talk to him either, if you didn't have to."

He didn't even bother to deny it. "But don't you know him pretty well? You've stayed at their house, haven't you?"

"That doesn't mean I know him. He's not real friendly."

Gino considered this a moment. "So what are you going to do?"

"I'm going to go to their house this evening and show it to him."

"You shouldn't be out alone at night."

"I'll take a cab."

"I'll go with you."

"Do you think I need help?" she said, managing to sound offended even though she wasn't.

"With Mr. Decker? Of course not, but a young woman isn't safe alone in the streets after dark."

She wasn't afraid to be out after dark, and he probably knew that. Still, his concern was gratifying. "Well, if you don't have anything else to do, that would be fine. You just have to remember that we can't tell Mr. Decker that his wife went with me today."

"I'm not going to tell him anything at all. I'm just going along to protect you."

THE MAID WHO ANSWERED THE DOOR AT THE DECKERS' house knew Maeve well and admitted them at once. After only a few minutes, Mrs. Decker sent word to bring them right in, and they were escorted to the rear parlor, which was the informal room the family used. Mr. and Mrs. Decker had obviously been relaxing after supper, and they greeted Maeve and Gino warmly.

"I hope nothing's wrong," Mrs. Decker said when they were all seated.

"Oh no, at least not with us. Everything is just fine at home," Maeve said.

"Then what brings you out so late on this chilly evening?" Mr. Decker asked. Even when he was being nice, Mr. Decker couldn't help being intimidating. Everything about his tall, slender frame was elegant, from his silvered hair to his well-tended hands, and his piercing blue eyes seemed to see right through a person. Fortunately, Maeve was only lying by omission today, so she had nothing to hide.

"It all started yesterday when a lady who had been a neighbor to the Malloys came to the house, looking for Mr. Malloy." As briefly as possible, Maeve told them about Mrs. O'Neill's visit.

"How awful," Mrs. Decker said, as if she were hearing this for the first time. She could have used a little practice with her lying, in Maeve's opinion, but it was probably good enough to fool her husband.

"That is an unfortunate situation," Mr. Decker agreed. "Are you by any chance involved in this investigation, Officer Donatelli?"

Gino sat up a little straighter. "Oh no, sir. Not at all. It happened up in Harlem."

"Then why are you here with Maeve?"

"I . . . When I found out she was coming here tonight, I didn't think she should be out alone, so I came with her."

"That was very gentlemanly of you," Mrs. Decker said. "I'm sure Maeve appreciates it."

Gino gave Maeve a questioning look that she refused to acknowledge.

"Yes, that was thoughtful of you, Officer Donatelli," Mr. Decker said, except he looked more amused than anything. "And since Officer Donatelli isn't involved in the investigation and Mr. Malloy is out of the country, I hope you told this woman you couldn't help her."

Maeve didn't have to pretend to be uncomfortable. She actually had to consciously not squirm under Mr. Decker's penetrating gaze. "I, uh, well, I did give her some advice. I told her she should hire an attorney for her daughter."

"That was excellent advice. Between him and the police, I'm sure they'll be able to sort this out."

"I'm sure they will," Maeve lied, "but Mrs. O'Neill didn't have any money to hire an attorney."

"Oh dear, of course she wouldn't," Mrs. Decker said. "Being a widow, she's probably very poor."

Mr. Decker gave her a curious glance, so Maeve hurried on before Mrs. Decker could say anything else to earn her husband's attention.

"I thought maybe Una's husband kept some money at his house, and since Una was his wife, it would be hers as much as his, so I offered to go to the house with Mrs. O'Neill to look. Mrs. O'Neill wanted to get some clothes for Una anyway, so we went there this afternoon."

"Isn't Mrs. O'Neill capable of looking around her own daughter's house by herself?" Mr. Decker asked.

"This Pollock fellow had told her she wasn't welcome there anymore after he and Una got married, so she was afraid the servants wouldn't let her in."

"But you thought they'd let you in," Mr. Decker guessed with a brief glance at his wife, who was trying to look as if butter wouldn't melt in her mouth.

"And they did," Maeve hurried on. "While Mrs. O'Neill was upstairs packing things for her daughter, I looked around downstairs and found a safe, and it did have money in it."

"Was the safe unlocked?" he asked.

"No, but Pollock had written the combination in his appointment diary, so I was able to open it without any trouble."

"How very careless of him," Mr. Decker said with a small smile.

"And how very lucky for Maeve," Mrs. Decker said.

This time Mr. Decker didn't even glance at her. "And did you find what you were looking for?"

"Like I said, I found some money, yes," Maeve said, "but it was a lot more than I was expecting. And I also found this."

She got up and handed Mr. Decker the ledger book. "I know it's a ledger, but I don't know what it means. I thought you might."

He opened it and flipped through. Most of the pages were blank, so he turned back to the first page, and they all waited while he scanned the entries. At last he looked up and said, "How much money did you find in the safe?"

"Thirty-seven thousand seven hundred and seventy-six dollars."

"Good heavens," Mrs. Decker cried, and this time she sounded genuinely surprised, probably because she was.

"And it was all in cash?" Mr. Decker asked.

"Yes, stacked very neatly and banded, the way they do at the bank, only with handmade bands."

"The ledger amounts come to about forty-five thousand three hundred," Mr. Decker said, impressing them all with his ability to total them in his head.

"Do you have any idea what it means?" Maeve asked.

"It's not a genuine accounting of anything. This isn't the format that a bookkeeper would use. It appears to be nothing more than a list that he kept for his own information."

"I thought the first column looked like dates," Maeve said.

"That would be my guess as well," he said, still studying the entries. "He only used surnames, probably because he knew who these people are, but it would be difficult for anyone else to identify them with any certainty."

"What do you think the numbers in the last column are?" Gino asked. He was leaning forward now, as interested as Maeve in the answers.

"There's no way to tell from this. As I said, it's not standard accounting, so it could mean anything, but . . ." They waited while he studied the numbers again. "They seem to total about half of the amount of the difference between the total of the one column and the amount you found in the safe."

"But you think the people listed there gave Pollock money?" Gino asked.

"That could be one interpretation, yes."

"But why would they give him money, especially so much?" Maeve said.

Mr. Decker carefully closed the ledger. "I doubt they *gave* him money. I suspect they would have expected something in return."

"You mean they were buying something?" Gino asked.

"More probably they thought they were investing in something."

"Like a business," Maeve said.

"What did this Pollock do for a living?" Mr. Decker asked.

"Mrs. O'Neill didn't know," Maeve said. "All she knew was that he lived in a nice house, so she thought he was rich."

"If he was spending this money, he would have given that impression, but judging from the amount you found in the safe, it appears he wasn't using it for anything other than his own expenses. He probably bought the house in Harlem, but he hasn't been squandering his money on much else." Mr. Decker tapped the ledger. "When they find out Pollock is dead, these men will be looking for their money. Did you give it to this Mrs. O'Neill?"

"No. I gave her five hundred dollars to pay for Una's lawyer and bail, but I didn't even tell her about the rest."

"That's good, because she's the first person the investors will go after if they find out she was in the house. Who else knows about the money?"

"Just us."

"And you left it where you found it?"

"Uh, no. I . . . I took it home. It's in Mr. Malloy's safe."

Maeve braced herself for his wrath, but Mr. Decker simply raised his eyebrows in surprise. "So long as no one thinks you stole it, that will be fine for the moment, and it's probably much safer there until we can get this all sorted out. Officer Donatelli, are you going to involve yourself in this matter?"

"I . . . I think I already am involved, although it's not official."

"At the very least, you can vouch for Maeve's intent to protect the money."

"And what should we do in the meantime?" Maeve asked.

"What were you planning to do?" he replied, raising his eyebrows again. She realized she wouldn't be able to fool him very easily.

"I was hoping we could help Mrs. O'Neill and her daughter."

"I think you've done everything you can for them, Maeve," he said. "Officer Donatelli doesn't have the authority that Mr. Malloy did as a detective sergeant, and you can't ask him to risk his job by getting more involved."

"But I did agree to go back to the house tomorrow and pack up the rest of Una's things," Maeve said, stretching the truth a bit, since Mrs. Decker had only promised to send her maid.

"I wouldn't want you to be there alone if someone came looking for this money," Mr. Decker said, tapping the ledger again.

He had a point. Maeve glanced at Gino, wondering if she dared ask him to accompany her.

"I could go with you after work tomorrow," he said.

"Or I could go with you in the morning," Mrs. Decker said, surprising everyone.

Her husband smiled at that. "And then we'd have two helpless females to worry about."

Maeve didn't like being thought of as helpless, but she wasn't going to contradict Mr. Decker. Men like him always had to believe they were right.

"And I know Maeve is anxious to get this taken care of," he went on, "and she can be impulsive, so she might not wait until you're available, Officer Donatelli. So why don't I go with her tomorrow morning instead?"

3

FELIX DECKER HAD NEVER CONSIDERED HIS LIFE BORING, at least not until his daughter Sarah had become acquainted with Frank Malloy. Even for some time after that, he had not been aware of her involvement with his work as a police detective. When he did become aware of it, he'd been furious and determined to remove her from the dangers of such involvement.

Seldom had he been quite so unsuccessful at something he'd set his mind to. Instead of removing Sarah from Malloy's influence, he'd seen his wife drawn into it—although she still believed he had no knowledge of her participation. And now here he was, serving as a bodyguard to his daughter's nanny while she visited a home where a murder had taken place.

Without a doubt, his life used to be extremely boring.

"Is something wrong?" Maeve asked.

"Of course not," he said, squinting to see her expression

in the shadowed interior of the carriage. He had insisted on traveling to Harlem in his carriage, even though she'd pointed out they could travel faster on the elevated train. He had won the argument when his wife reminded her they would be bringing back a trunk full of Una Pollock's belongings. "What could be wrong?"

She smiled with what he thought was sympathy. "I know this is an unusual situation for you."

"But not for you?"

"I've helped Mrs. Brandt before. I mean Mrs. Malloy. I keep forgetting her new name."

Felix did, too, but he saw no need to mention this to Maeve. "Mrs. Decker told me you played an important role when they discovered the identity of the man who killed Sarah's first husband."

"I was happy to help," she said with appropriate modesty. She was, except for his own daughters, the most self-possessed young woman he had ever met. Even still, she managed to maintain an air of femininity that compelled a man to offer his assistance. Which probably explained why he was on this fool's errand.

"Do you have family, Maeve?" he asked, realizing how little he knew of her.

"Not anymore. I lost my parents when I was little. My grandfather raised me, but he died a few years ago."

"Was that how you came to the Mission?" he asked, remembering now that Sarah had first met her at the Daughters of Hope Mission.

"Yes. I was lucky they took me in."

How true, he thought. The streets of New York were a dangerous place for a girl alone. "Are you happy working for Mrs. Malloy?" he asked, glad he had remembered to use her new name.

She looked surprised at the question. "Of course."

But he hadn't asked the right question, he realized, because that really wasn't what he wanted to know. "What I mean is, will being a nanny satisfy you?"

Some girls her age would have lied and said yes, just because he would expect that answer. Others would have coyly replied that they hoped to marry someday and raise their own children. Still others would have been dismayed by this question, knowing the world did not approve of girls having ambitions. Maeve simply said, "No, sir, it won't."

"I didn't think so." He studied her for a moment as the carriage rattled through the streets. She met his gaze unflinchingly, something even some of his longtime employees could not do. "Do you have any idea what you'd like to do?"

"You mean besides helping Mr. and Mrs. Malloy in their new detective agency?" she asked with a sly grin.

Outrage stung him. "Do they have a detective agency?" And why had no one told him?

"Not yet." Her sly grin widened. "But they'll have to, won't they? I mean, people aren't going to stop needing help that the police won't give them, and the Malloys won't be able to refuse to help, especially now that they're rich and don't even have to worry if people can pay them or not."

"But Malloy will be too busy for that kind of thing," he protested.

"Busy doing what?" Her dark eyes were wide and apparently innocent, so why did he feel she was challenging him? Girls like her didn't challenge men like him.

"He'll have . . . other interests," he tried.

"Like what? Going to his club? Even you have your business, Mr. Decker. Mr. Malloy is used to working and feeling useful, too. And how is he going to refuse when somebody asks him for help?"

"Or more to the point, when someone asks *Sarah* for help," he said, seeing it very clearly now. "He might be able to refuse, but she'd never allow it."

"Besides, helping people is fun."

"Fun?"

"Oh, not fun like going to Coney Island, but it's . . . I don't know, interesting, I guess."

"Are you serious?" he asked, incredulously.

"Of course I am. That's why you're going with me today, isn't it?"

"I'm going to protect you," he protested.

She seemed unconvinced. "You could've sent one of your servants with me. In fact, the coachman would probably do just fine."

He tried frowning at her, which usually worked beautifully when he wanted to silence an annoying subordinate, but she just smiled knowingly. Yes, his life truly was no longer boring.

And Harlem was no longer farmland, Decker observed as the carriage delivered them to St. Nicholas Avenue. New houses had sprung up here like some modern crop of bricks growing in neat rows along freshly paved streets. Who lived here, he wondered, besides men like Pollock who had needed a respectable home from which to operate?

He helped Maeve down when the carriage stopped in front of a turreted stone house. It was, he saw, a double house, and he caught the twitch of a curtain on the front window of the house next door. The neighbors must surely be wondering who was driving up to a house where the master had been murdered and the mistress was in jail. At least no one here was likely to recognize him.

Maeve preceded him up the front steps, and he took a moment to glance around the neighborhood. Although he felt they were being watched, he saw no one on the street and no visible faces pressed to window glass to observe them. He actually heard a bird singing somewhere, reminding him of how far they were from the heart of the city.

No one answered Maeve's first knock, even though she'd worked the brass knocker with some authority. "I wonder if the servants decided to leave after all," she said with a frown, and tried the knocker again.

"Surely they wouldn't go off without a reference," he said. "Or did you give them one?"

"Not yet," she said. Then the door opened a crack to reveal part of a face and a maid's uniform. "Do you remember me? I was here yesterday."

The door opened wider, and the maid's face reflected relief. "Yes, miss, I remember you."

"We're here to pack up the rest of Mrs. Pollock's things."

"Oh, miss, I don't know about that," the maid said in some distress. "We've had some trouble here."

"What kind of trouble?" Decker demanded, startling the maid, who backed up a step, her eyes widened in alarm.

"This is Mr. Decker," Maeve said quickly, taking advantage of the maid's retreat to move into the foyer. "He came along to help. What's happened?"

"Oh, miss, we don't have no idea. It was like this when we come down this morning."

"What was? Show us," he said.

With an uncertain glance at him, the maid indicated they should follow her down the hallway. He closed the door behind them and caught up with Maeve. The maid led them to a door that stood open. Maeve got there first, and her surprised gasp almost prepared him for the sight of the room.

It was, he saw at once, an office of sorts, with a desk and some upholstered chairs. Or it had been. Now it was a mess.

The desk drawers had been pulled out and dumped, their contents scattered on the floor. The chairs had been over-turned and their cushions slashed open. The stuffing lay in heaps. But the centerpiece of the mayhem was the squat little safe with its door hanging wide open.

He caught Maeve's eye. "Did you . . . ?"

She shook her head, then turned to the maid. "Who did this?"

"We don't know," the girl cried, wringing her hands. "We was all asleep. Or at least we figure it must've happened in the night sometime. Everything was fine when we went to bed, and it was like this first thing this morning."

"Didn't anyone hear something?" he asked.

"No, sir. We never heard a thing."

"Have you sent for the police?"

"Oh no, sir! We was scared to do that!"

"Were any of the other rooms disturbed?" Maeve asked.

"No, miss. Not that we could tell. What should we do?"

Maeve gave him a questioning look.

"Let me check this room, and then we'll decide what to do. Maeve, why don't you pack up Mrs. Pollock's things while I look around?"

"Come along," she said to the maid, ushering her out. "Mr. Decker will take care of everything," she added, glancing back to give him a little grin. He wasn't sure he appreciated her confidence in him.

Mrs. Decker had told Maeve that they'd found an empty trunk in Una Pollock's bedroom, so she hadn't brought one with her. Sure enough, the small trunk sat in a corner of the bedroom that Una had apparently shared with her husband.

"We need to pack up all of Mrs. Pollock's belongings," Maeve told the maid. "We can put them in this trunk, and we'll get the coachman to carry it downstairs for us."

"Yes, miss. I guess Mrs. Pollock won't be coming back, will she?"

"I can't imagine she'll want to live here after what happened, can you?"

"Oh, I . . . I guess not. But I was thinking she'll be in jail."

Maeve had pulled open one of the dresser drawers to begin gathering the clothes, but she stopped and turned to look at the girl. "Do you think Mrs. Pollock killed her husband?"

The girl's eyes widened in alarm. "Oh, I . . . I wouldn't want to say, miss. I'm sure I don't know anything about it."

And Maeve was sure she knew a lot about it. "I understand you heard an argument before Mr. Pollock was killed. Did the Pollocks argue a lot?"

The girl glanced anxiously at the open bedroom door. Maeve hurried over and shut it. "It's important to find out exactly what happened to Mr. Pollock," she said. "It would be horrible if the wrong person were punished for killing him, wouldn't it? Not to mention how awful it would be for a killer to get away."

"Oh, I never thought of that, miss."

"That's why we need to find out the truth of what happened that day."

The maid frowned. "But how can you help, miss? You're not with the police, are you?"

Smart girl, Maeve thought. "No, but I work for a private investigator that Mrs. Pollock's mother has hired to help her."

"A private investigator?"

Plainly, this was a new concept to the girl. "Yes, we help the police in situations like this." The girl didn't look as if she really believed Maeve's lie, but she also had no reason to doubt it either. Maeve decided that was good enough. "So, did the Pollocks argue a lot?"

"Not what you'd call arguing, no," she said with a frown.

"Then what would you call it?"

The girl's frown deepened.

"It's all right to tell me," Maeve said. "I won't tell anybody where I heard it."

"Well, Mr. Pollock, he was very particular about . . . about everything."

"What do you mean, particular?"

"He liked everything just a certain way, and if it wasn't that way, he . . . Well, he got real mad."

Maeve carefully schooled her expression so her excitement didn't show. "Did he get angry with the staff?"

The girl wrung her hands and wouldn't meet Maeve's eyes.

"Did he hit you?" Maeve asked.

"Oh no, miss, not me," she said quickly.

"Did he hit someone else?"

She hesitated, chewing her bottom lip as if uncertain how to reply. "He never hit the staff. Not once."

Maeve saw it then, the whole ugly picture. "But he did hit Mrs. Pollock, didn't he?"

"Only when she deserved it, miss," she hastily explained. "I told you he was particular, and she tried, she really did, but she couldn't always please him. She wasn't brought up in a nice house, and she didn't know how to conduct herself, you see."

Fury roiled in Maeve's stomach, but she kept her voice level. "Is that what he said?"

"Yes, miss. We could hear him, you see. He'd tell her how . . ." She caught herself and stopped, dropping her gaze to the floor.

"How stupid she was?" Maeve guessed. "And worthless and ugly?" How often had she heard men shouting those words in the tenements? And how silly she'd been to think that men who lived in houses like this would be gentlemen and treat their women with respect.

The girl looked up in surprise. "How did you know?"

"And did he hit her?" Maeve asked.

She nodded jerkily, then lowered her gaze again.

"Did he hit her that day? The day he died?"

She looked up in surprise. "I don't know."

"But they were arguing . . . or at least he was yelling at her that day."

The girl bit her lip again. "I don't know. I mean, yes, he was yelling, but I don't know if he was yelling at her or not."

"Why not, if you could hear him?"

"We were downstairs in the kitchen. That's where we always went when it started. We just wanted to stay out of his way, I guess. And we didn't want to know about it."

"So you didn't actually see him hitting her?"

"I . . . I saw him slap her once, but after that, he was more careful. I guess he saw how shocked I was. He never did it in front of us again."

"How do you know he hit her, then?"

"Because . . . I was her maid. She never had a lady's maid before, so she had to get used to me helping her dress, and . . . after a while, she tried to dress herself and tell me she didn't need me, but sometimes she did, and then . . ."

"Then what?"

"I'd see the bruises. He didn't hit her in the face, except for that one time I know of. He didn't want the marks to show."

Maeve sighed. Men in the tenements didn't care if the bruises showed. They thought beating up their women made them more manly or something. That was a difference between uptown and the tenements, she supposed. "Did Mrs. Pollock ever fight back?"

The girl seemed shocked. "Why would she do that?"

Why, indeed? That was only asking for a worse beating, Maeve supposed. "Did you hear anyone else come into the house the day Pollock was killed?"

She hesitated again. Was she trying to remember or trying to decide what to say? "I always open the door for visitors. I didn't open the door that morning. Please, miss. We're scared to stay here now. When can we get paid and leave?"

"I'll see what I can do for you. In the meantime, let's get Mrs. Pollock's things packed up."

WHEN MAEVE AND THE MAID WERE GONE, DECKER TOOK the precaution of closing the door behind them, then looked around again at the damage. Whoever had broken in last night had been thorough. They must have also known that Pollock kept his money and his records in this room, which explained why they had confined the search here. He would have to compliment Maeve for having the foresight to remove the money and the ledger yesterday, or whoever had broken in would have it all now.

The safe was empty, of course. Maeve had cleaned it out herself, but the thief hadn't known that. Did he know the combination or had he discovered it the same way she had? He found an appointment diary on the floor beneath some of the scattered stuffing from the chairs. Flipping through, he saw the combination written just as Maeve had described it. The thief must have also found the diary in the desk, located the combination, and then dropped the diary here. Finding the safe empty, he had then ransacked the rest of the room.

He went to the pile of papers that had been dumped from the desk drawers and quickly went through them. Maeve was right, he found very little of importance until he came to a packet of papers that he recognized as copies of a prospectus for an investment opportunity. They had been professionally printed on expensive, watermarked paper. He slipped one of them out of the packet, folded it carefully, and tucked it into his pocket.

Only when he was finished with his search did he realize he had made a neat stack of the desk's contents, which he probably shouldn't have done. Of course, he shouldn't have even come here today, but since he had, he felt obligated to do as little damage as possible, so he rearranged the papers to look as much like they originally had as he could.

When he was satisfied with his efforts, he opened the office door to find the remainder of Pollock's servants standing anxiously in the hallway. A middle-aged woman in an apron, who was probably the cook, another maid, and a handsome youth of about sixteen gaped at him.

"Can I help you?" he asked, recognizing the irony of asking if he could help servants.

"Oh, sir," the older woman said, "we can't stay here, not with people breaking in all hours of the night. You can't ask us to do that!"

"You're certainly free to leave if you want to," he said.

"But what about references?" the maid asked. "Mrs. Decker said she'd write us references."

This was interesting. "When did Mrs. Decker say that?"

"Yesterday, when she was here."

Yes, this was very interesting. No wonder Elizabeth had been acting so oddly last night. He should have known she'd never let Maeve come here alone.

"And our pay, sir," the boy added. "She said we'd get our pay."

"And you shall. I'll see that you have it all by tomorrow." He couldn't wait to see Elizabeth's face when he told her. "In the meantime, let's take a look around and see if we can figure out how the intruder got in last night."

"Dɪᴅ ʏᴏᴜ ғɪɴᴅ ᴀɴʏᴛʜɪɴɢ?" Mᴀᴇᴠᴇ ᴀsᴋᴇᴅ Mʀ. Dᴇᴄᴋᴇʀ when they were back in the carriage and driving away.

"I found a broken window in the basement."

"That explains how the burglar got in, I guess."

"And I found this." He pulled a piece of paper out of his pocket and handed it to her.

She unfolded it and tried to read it, but it didn't make much sense to her. "What is it?"

"It's a proposal to build a railroad across Panama."

"Where's that?"

"It's in Colombia."

"Is that in New York?"

She thought he was trying not to smile at her ignorance. "No, it's in South America. Well, really, Panama is in Central America. It's on the narrow strip of land that connects North and South America."

"Why would someone here want to build a railroad all the way down there?"

"According to this explanation, the railroad would carry goods and passengers across this area of land where the distance between the Atlantic and the Pacific Oceans is the shortest. It would save time and money because the goods wouldn't have to be shipped all the way around the tip of South America, the way they are now. They could just be unloaded from a ship on one side, carried across the land by train, then loaded onto a ship on the other side. The railroad would be enormously profitable."

"What's this about a canal?" She pointed to a paragraph that talked about a canal across the Isthmus of Panama, whatever that was.

"The French have been trying to build a canal in that area for years."

She hated showing her ignorance again, but she said, "What's a canal?"

This time he didn't smile. "It's basically a huge trench that runs through the land from one ocean to the other so ships could just sail right through."

"That sounds like a better idea. Then they wouldn't have to load and unload the ships."

"Exactly, but the company trying to build the canal went bankrupt because the land is all jungle, and their equipment kept rusting in the tropical climate and their workers kept dying from tropical diseases. According to this"—he pointed to the paper she still held—"the canal will never be built, so the railroad is the best solution."

"So Pollock really did have a good plan for people to invest in," she said in surprise.

"Yes, it's an excellent idea, except for one small detail. The French built this railroad fifty years ago."

"Oh!"

"Yes, oh."

"And people are using it?"

"Yes, as they have been for fifty years."

"Then wouldn't everybody know about it?"

"You didn't."

"I'm just a nursemaid," she reminded him. "You knew about it."

"Because I own a shipping company. I'm guessing the men whose names are in Pollock's ledger do not."

"But they must have lots of money."

"That doesn't mean they're knowledgeable about these things."

"Oh, you mean they're bouncers."

He did smile at that. "They may have made their fortunes recently, yes, but whatever their circumstances, they most likely don't know a lot about transporting goods around the world. They may also have just moved to New York from the western United States, where people are more . . . trustworthy."

Maeve knew exactly what he meant. Her grandfather had made his living cheating bumpkins who came to New York expecting to outsmart the city slickers. Pollock, it seemed, had simply discovered a new way to do it.

"One of these men must have heard about his murder," he was saying, "and come to the house last night in search of his investment."

But that didn't sound right to Maeve. "If they thought he was investing their money in a railroad, they wouldn't expect to find it in his house, would they?"

He stared at her for a long moment, obviously impressed by her reasoning. "You're right. If he'd invested their money, it would still be safely invested, even if Pollock died. They'd just be trying to find out who was managing the scheme with Pollock dead."

"But somebody knew the money was at the house, and they came for it," Maeve mused. "They came for it in the middle of the night, too, when nobody would see them. Who would've known the money was there?"

"Maybe Pollock had a partner," Mr. Decker said.

"A partner who wanted to get the money and disappear before anybody else found it and started asking questions."

"How did he find out Pollock was dead, though?"

Maeve thought this over. "I don't know. It hasn't been in the newspapers yet. Someone must have told him. Or . . ."

"Or what?"

"Or maybe the person who killed him is the one who came back last night for the money. That person wouldn't need anybody to tell him Pollock was dead."

"No, he wouldn't," Mr. Decker said. "So all we need to do is find out who this person is."

Maeve decided not to point out to Mr. Decker that he had just included himself in the investigation.

DECKER HAD FULLY EXPECTED TO GO STRAIGHT TO HIS office after dropping Maeve and the trunk full of clothing at his daughter's house. After learning of his wife's involvement, however, he decided he couldn't wait to discuss that with her, so he returned to his own home instead. Elizabeth was at her desk, writing letters, when he found her.

"Felix, is something wrong?" she asked, rising instantly and coming to greet him.

He kissed her cheek. "Why would something be wrong?"

"I didn't expect you back here until this evening."

"And I thought you might like to find out how we fared at the Pollocks' house this morning."

She smiled with delight, reminding him of how much he loved to see her smile. "How very thoughtful of you, because of course I've been dying to hear."

"And this will save you the trouble of going all the way down to Bank Street to ask Maeve," he said, making her happier still.

"How well you know me. Now sit down here and tell me everything." She drew him over to the sofa, where they sat down side by side.

He told her about finding the office in shambles and locating the proposals for the Panamanian Railroad.

"Would people really invest in something like that without investigating it first?" she asked.

"People sell the Brooklyn Bridge to unsuspecting immigrants every day."

"They do?" she asked in surprise. "I thought the government owned that bridge."

"It does," he said gently.

She needed only a moment to figure it out. "Oh! Good heavens, that's horrible! Those poor people."

"Exactly. New York is teeming with crooks, and fortunately for them, it is also teeming with fools."

"And this Pollock fellow apparently found some of them."

"He found some with a lot of money, too."

"But what was he planning to do? Sooner or later, his investors would expect to see some progress on the railroad and eventually some return on their investments."

"I'm sure he explained to them that this project would take years to complete, and the beauty of it is that it's so far away. They wouldn't be traveling down to Colombia to check on the progress, and Pollock could invent all sorts of setbacks and problems to delay them even longer."

"But wouldn't they expect to see something in the newspapers about it? And there's always the danger that someone would find out the railroad had already been built."

"I doubt Pollock intended to keep things going for long. As you say, he couldn't take the chance of someone finding out the truth. He probably intended to leave town at some point and simply not return."

Elizabeth seemed intrigued by the thought. "He could have told them he was traveling down there to take care of some business and then have someone notify them that he died down there. By the time they got it all sorted out, he'd be long gone."

"Elizabeth, I had no idea you had such a nefarious imagination," he said with unfeigned amazement.

"It's only common sense, Felix," she protested.

"Common sense if you're a criminal."

She stared back at him with guileless eyes and then distracted him with a change of subject. Or so she thought. "Did Maeve get all of Mrs. Pollock's belongings packed up?"

"Yes, and she took the trunk home with her. She'll contact Mrs. Pollock's mother about what to do with it."

"It sounds as if you had a productive morning, Felix. I'm sorry you had to deal with the results of the burglary."

"I also had to deal with the servants."

"The servants? Oh yes, I'm sure they must have been upset. First a murder and then someone broke in the house."

"They want to leave."

She frowned. "Oh dear. I guess no one can blame them for that, but is it wise? To leave the house empty, I mean?"

"I didn't think of that, but when I told them they could go, they said they hadn't been paid, and then there's the issue of references, I understand."

"I don't suppose Una Pollock is in any position to write them either, is she?"

"I don't suppose she is."

"What did you tell them, then?"

"I told them you'd write them references."

"Me? Why did you tell them that?"

"Well, actually, I didn't tell them that at all, but when they said you'd already promised to do it, I simply assured them you would."

Her expression was priceless, everything he'd imagined, but it lasted only a moment before fading into an annoyed frown. "Felix, you are infuriating."

Now he was the one surprised. "How am I infuriating?"

"You've been teasing me all this time. Honestly, how can I take any pleasure at all in defying you when you turn it into a joke?"

"I hope you don't think I was making a joke. Really, Elizabeth, you had no business going to a house where a murder had been committed, you know."

To his amazement, she smiled in delight. "Thank you, dear. That's the reaction I was expecting. So, are you saying it was all right for Maeve and poor Mrs. O'Neill to go there but not me?"

"I'm not saying that at all, but they had business there. You did not."

"You're absolutely right, my dear, but neither Mrs. O'Neill nor Maeve could possibly deal with the servants. And as you point out, someone must see to getting them positions else-where. They shouldn't have to suffer for the sins of their employer just because he had the bad judgment to get himself murdered."

"Bad judgment?" he echoed, a bit confused.

"And when am I supposed to write these references?"

"I . . . uh, I may have indicated they would have them tomorrow."

"Tomorrow? I'm flattered that you think I could accomplish that in one afternoon, and I probably could, if necessary, but now we're back to leaving the house empty. If I give them their references—"

"And their pay," he added. "They apparently are owed some salary."

"Of course they are, and we can certainly pay them from the funds Maeve found. If I give them their letters and their salary, however, they will leave within the hour. How will we then keep track of who comes and goes at that house?"

"Who would be coming and going?"

"I don't know and neither will anyone else if the house is empty."

"But why would we need to know at all?"

"How else will we find out who Pollock's partner was and who the investors are and who might have killed him?"

Decker had so many objections to make that he hardly knew where to begin, but before he could decide, a maid knocked on the door and stuck her head in when he impatiently replied.

"Excuse me, sir, but there's a gentleman here to see Mrs. Decker."

"Me?" Elizabeth asked. It was much too early for morning calls, which didn't begin until after luncheon.

"Yes, ma'am."

"Who is he?" Decker asked.

The maid stepped into the room and handed him a calling card for someone named Adam Yorke from Chicago. "He said to tell you his sister was Randolph Pollock's wife."

4

MAEVE LEFT THE TRUNK SITTING IN THE FOYER. THEY'D probably be moving it somewhere soon, but she didn't have time to think about that now. After a quick trip across the street to make sure Mrs. Ellsworth was willing to watch Catherine for the rest of the day—which of course she was—Maeve pulled a dress and some undergarments out of the trunk. She folded them carefully and put them into a market basket.

Then she went to the kitchen and wrapped up the leftover cake she found there. Prisoners in the Tombs were allowed not only to bring their own clothing into the prison, but they were also allowed to have food brought in to them.

When she had packed the cake into the basket, she went to the safe and got out a hundred dollars of the Pollock money, which she hoped was far more than she would need. She hid half of it in her corset and put the rest in her purse.

After slapping together a cheese sandwich and wolfing it down as her noon meal, she headed out for the Tombs.

The New York City Halls of Justice and House of Detention had been designed to resemble an ancient Egyptian mausoleum and had consequently been nicknamed "the Tombs" at some point. Built on the former site of the Collect Pond, which had once provided water for the city, the structure had almost immediately begun to sink into the marshy ground and crack. Repairs had kept the place functioning for over sixty years, although no one had been able to eliminate the creeping mold and the stench from the seeping groundwater. The city had finally decided to tear the place down and rebuild it. For a year now, they'd been doing just that while leaving the prisoners inside as the work went on around them.

Maeve identified herself as Una O'Neill's cousin, and after making her way carefully around scaffolding and construction debris, she finally arrived at the women's section of the prison, where a female guard admitted her after checking the contents of her basket for anything untoward.

"Somebody already brought her clothes," the guard said.

"I know, but this is her favorite dress. She wanted it special."

The guard made a rude noise. "Special for what?"

Maeve shrugged. "Where is she?" she asked, suddenly realizing she didn't have any idea what Una looked like. How would she explain her failure to recognize her own cousin?

"In her cell. She never comes out." To Maeve's relief, she pointed to one of the cubicles that lined the large central gathering area. All the cell doors stood open at this time of day, so most of the inmates were sitting at tables or gathered in groups to sew or knit or just gossip.

The buzz of conversation noticeably silenced as Maeve crossed the room and entered Una O'Neill's cell. Most of the women jailed here would be prostitutes or thieves, so an accused murderess would be something of a celebrity. Her visitors would certainly be objects of great interest to the other inmates.

Maeve paused in the doorway of the tiny cell. The Tombs had no proper windows anywhere, and the narrow, foot-long slit in the outside wall in each cell admitted little light and less air. Gaslights burned in the gathering area, but their feeble glow barely reached here. After a moment, Maeve could make out the figure lying on the bunk, curled into itself as if for protection.

"Una? Are you awake?"

Maeve had to step closer to see that her eyes were open. She met Maeve's gaze fearfully.

"Una, my name is Maeve. I'm here to help you. I brought you some things." She held up the basket. "I have some cake. Would you like some?"

"She don't eat nothing," someone said.

Maeve looked back to see a woman standing just outside the cell. She wore a flashy dress cut just a little too low in front, and her hair was a shade of red not found in nature, with black roots starting to show. "Who are you?"

The woman raised her chin defiantly. "Her friend."

"And I'm her cousin," Maeve said. She glanced meaningfully around the cell. "I think her mother brought some of her clothes over yesterday. I wonder where they could be?" She looked back at the red-haired woman, giving her the look her grandfather had made her practice in the mirror until she got it just right. "If they've been stolen, it'll go hard on that person."

The woman's chin dropped instantly. "I been keeping her stuff for her so nobody else would take it."

"You can bring it back, then. Right now," Maeve added when the woman didn't move.

The woman's mouth twisted with fury, but she scurried off.

Maeve turned to Una, who stared back with wide-eyed amazement. "You need to sit up."

Without bothering to get consent, Maeve set down her basket and lifted Una to a sitting position, swinging her feet down to the floor so she sat on the side of the bunk.

"Have you eaten anything today?" Maeve asked.

Una continued to stare at her, and for a moment, Maeve was afraid she wouldn't reply, but at last she shook her head.

"I brought you some cake." Maeve pulled the bundle from the basket and carefully unwrapped it. She'd scraped off the frosting, as the trip had caused it to crumble a bit, but she knew that wouldn't affect the taste. She broke off a chunk. "Here."

She held it to Una's mouth, but the woman just continued to stare at her.

"You need to eat. If you don't, you'll get sick and die. Is that what you want?"

The fear-filled eyes flooded with tears, and she nodded.

"Oh, for heaven's sake! Don't be a goose. Do you think you're the only person who ever had some trouble in her life? Do you think you're the only woman whose husband died? Life is hard, Mrs. Pollock, and bad things happen. If people rolled over and died every time they did, there wouldn't be a single person left in this city. Somebody killed your husband, Mrs. Pollock. Don't you want to see that person punished?"

Una blinked, sending the tears rolling down her cheeks, but she nodded.

"So do I. Now eat this cake. It's delicious."

Una obediently opened her mouth, and Maeve fed her the chunk of cake.

After the second bite, Una took the remaining cake from Maeve and began to feed herself. Maeve stepped back to watch.

Una was almost finished when the red-haired woman

returned with a hastily wrapped bundle. She stopped dead in her tracks. "She eating?"

"Yes, she is." Maeve took the bundle from her. "This better be all of it."

"I ain't no thief," she protested with creditable outrage.

"You're in jail," Maeve reminded her.

The woman chose to ignore that. She studied Una for a moment. "She won't last long in here."

"I know that, but she won't have to."

"Says you. She done for her old man."

"Says you," Maeve snapped. "Get out of here."

"I don't have to take orders from you."

"Then take a suggestion, if you know what's good for you, and leave me alone with my cousin."

Maeve's glare worked once more, and when they were alone again, Maeve found Una staring up at her in awe. She'd eaten all the cake, so Maeve took the napkin from her and folded it up.

"Who are you?" Una asked.

"Your cousin Maeve," she replied with a grin. "Your mother sent me to help."

Una continued to stare at her, and only then did Maeve really look at her.

When Maeve had packed up the remainder of Una's belongings, she'd noticed the quality of her clothes. Mrs. O'Neill had said Mr. Pollock had bought Una all new things, and he obviously had. Every garment in Una's wardrobe was practically brand-new and expensive-looking. They weren't custom-made, but she wouldn't have expected that. The dress Una wore now was of the same quality except that the entire front of it, bodice and skirt, was stiff with a brownish stain.

Blood.

Sweet Lord in heaven, she was still wearing the blood-stained dress she'd been arrested in. Why hadn't anyone changed her clothes?

"Stand up. You need a clean dress."

"No!" she said, her voice little more than a rusty whisper. Maeve remembered that Mrs. O'Neill had said Una hadn't spoken since the murder. Could she have really remained silent until now?

"Why not?"

Una opened her mouth but nothing came out.

"Don't you want the world to see what happened to your husband?" Maeve said. "We can show them your dress. We can show them what they did to him."

Una's face crumpled, and for a horrible moment, Maeve thought she was going to cry. Instead she pushed herself unsteadily to her feet and began to unbutton the dress. Maeve had to help. Dried blood made the buttonholes nearly unyielding, but they finally got them all free. Maeve peeled the ruined bodice off her and held her hand while she stepped out of the skirt.

Her underclothes were stained as well, and Maeve helped her strip off her chemise and petticoat. She pretended not to see the bruises. Some were freshly dark while others had faded to green or yellow or even rose. Just as the maid had said, he'd hit her only where the marks wouldn't show. Maeve was afraid to see what might lurk beneath her corset and drawers so she quickly dug out a clean petticoat and slipped it over Una's head before she could think to remove the rest of her clothes.

"What dress would you like to wear?" Maeve asked. She only had the choice of the one her mother had brought yesterday and the one Maeve had randomly chosen to bring today.

"I should wear black," she said.

"I don't think you have anything black," Maeve said as matter-of-factly as she could manage. "You'll have to order something. In the meantime, why don't you wear this?"

She chose the darker of the two dresses, a royal blue that would bring out the blue in Una's eyes. She was, Maeve had to admit now that she'd gotten a good look at her, a truly beautiful young woman. Or she would be under other circumstances. Her haunted expression gave her a helpless air that Maeve didn't like at all. Men might find it attractive, or at least some men might. Not Frank Malloy, of course, and she hoped not Gino Donatelli. Randolph Pollock probably would have found it irresistible, along with her raven black hair and her bright blue eyes.

When Una was decently clothed again, Maeve sat down on the bunk beside her.

"Has your attorney been to see you?"

"Attorney?"

"Yes, your lawyer. Your mother hired him."

"Why would she hire a lawyer?"

"The police think you killed your husband."

For the first time, a spark of spirit flared in her lovely blue eyes. "I wouldn't kill Randolph! He's my husband. I love him!"

"You were the only one there when they found him, and you had blood all over you." Maeve nodded to where she'd dropped Una's ruined dress on the floor of the cell.

"I don't remember that."

"Do you remember if your lawyer came to see you?"

"A man was here."

"What did you tell him?"

"I don't . . . Nothing. He asked me some questions, and then he went away. I didn't talk to him, though. I didn't know what he was asking me."

Maeve knew the attorney well. He'd know what to do about the bruises. People might feel sorry for Una if they knew her husband beat her, but that also gave her a reason to kill him. Maeve wasn't going to tell anyone else about it until she'd talked it over with the attorney.

"What happened that day?"

"What day?" Una asked. She seemed perfectly sincere.

"The day your husband died."

She winced. "I don't know."

"You don't know or you don't remember?"

"I don't remember."

"The servants said someone was arguing with Mr. Pollock."

"Really? I don't know who that could have been."

"Did he have a business partner?"

She frowned. She looked even more helpless when she frowned. Maeve would never understand the appeal. She wanted to slap Una. "He had business *associates*."

"That's what he called them?"

"Yes. He would tell me he was meeting with his associates and I wasn't to bother him."

"Do you know their names?"

"I met a few of them. We had them to dinner sometimes. He wanted them to see what a lovely wife he had."

She seemed proud of this, although Maeve found it disturbing. Had Pollock literally shopped around until he found a woman who would look nice sitting at the dinner table? He'd hardly known Una when he proposed to her, so he couldn't have chosen her for any other reason.

"Was there anyone in particular who was . . . ?" How could she phrase it? "Who was there more often? Or who was more important than the others?"

"I don't . . . Well, maybe Mr. Truett."

"Who was he?"

"He was . . . I guess you could say he was more like Randolph's friend. He never came to dinner, but he would visit Randolph in his study. He came almost every week."

"Do you know his first name? What did Randolph call him?"

"He called him Truett. He was very nice to me. Randolph didn't want me to talk to him, but sometimes I would see him, and he always had a kind word to say."

"That's nice," Maeve said, although the words wanted to stick in her throat. Who was Pollock to tell her she shouldn't talk to someone? "Did he visit Randolph the day he died?"

Una stared at her with sad eyes. "I don't remember."

"I'm sure it will come back to you. Now I'm going to talk to your attorney, and he'll come to see you again. This time, you need to answer his questions and do whatever he tells you to do."

"Are you going to leave me here?" she asked in alarm.

"I have to. You'll be safe here."

"But these other women—they don't like me."

"Don't worry about that. They don't like anyone."

"But they're mean to me."

Maeve felt a small stab of pity, although she knew it was wasted. Still, she couldn't leave Una here unprotected. "If anyone tries to hurt you, call out for the matron."

"But she doesn't pay any attention to me."

"She will now." Maeve knew exactly how to get her to protect Una. "And you have to eat. Eat everything they bring you, no matter how much you might not want to. You have to keep up your strength."

"All right." She didn't look happy about it, though.

Maeve had one more question. "Why did you talk to me when you wouldn't talk to anyone else?"

She looked up in surprise, her blue eyes so wide and innocent that Maeve believed her. "Because I was afraid of you."

"Good," Maeve said, meaning it completely. "Now do what I tell you. I'll be back when I can."

She found the matron dozing in a corner of the gathering room. The woman jolted awake when Maeve bumped her chair.

She looked like a weasel in a uniform, and she glared up at Maeve suspiciously. "What do you want?"

"I want you to look after Mrs. Pollock. Make sure she eats and don't let any of the others bother her. The redheaded woman stole her clothes. That better not happen again."

"I can't watch them all the time," she said and settled back into her nap.

"You can watch Mrs. Pollock all the time," Maeve said, slipping five dollars out of her purse and holding it up. This was more than the woman earned in a week, Maeve was certain.

The matron's eyes widened. "Well, she does seem like a decent sort."

"Nobody hurts her or bothers her or steals from her. If she calls for help, you see that she gets it. If she gives me a good report, you'll get more."

The money disappeared into the weasel's claw. "You can trust me."

Maeve was sure she could.

FELIX DECKER LOOKED AT HIS WIFE FOR AN EXPLANA-tion, but she was as puzzled as he.

"Did this Mr. Yorke say his sister is Mr. Pollock's wife?" Elizabeth asked the maid.

"Yes, ma'am, he did."

"But why is he *here*? He's come all the way from Chicago. And why would he want to see you?" Decker asked his wife.

"Because I gave the servants at Pollock's house my card

in case they needed anything. I suppose they sent him here. What confuses me is how could Una O'Neill be his sister?"

"Why don't we ask him?" Decker said, knowing full well they should send this Yorke fellow on his way and not get more involved in this than they already were. But common sense was no match for curiosity, he was learning.

"Bring Mr. Yorke up, will you?" Elizabeth asked the maid, who hurried to obey her.

"Who could this man possibly be?" he asked when they were alone.

"Perhaps he's one of the people listed in Pollock's ledger."

He hadn't thought of that. "I don't recall that name."

"We should have copied the names so we'd have a list."

"In case one of them happened to show up on our doorstep?" he asked.

"When you're working on a case, you must be ready for any eventuality, Felix."

He was still gaping at her when the maid announced Mr. Yorke.

He was a respectable-looking man in his thirties. His waistline was still trim, although his hairline had begun to retreat. His clothes were well tailored, but his face was haggard. "I'm sorry for bursting in on you like this, missus—" he began as if reciting a speech he had prepared, but the sight of Felix, whose presence he could not have anticipated, stopped him. "Sir," he said with a curt but uncertain nod.

"This is my husband, Mr. Yorke," Elizabeth said. "He just happened to be here and is as interested as I in learning your business with me."

"I'm pleased to make your acquaintance, Mr. Decker, and I must apologize to you both for my intrusion, but it is a matter of some importance, and I didn't know where else to turn."

"Then by all means have a seat and tell us why you're here," Decker said, indicating a chair.

"May I offer you something, Mr. Yorke? Some coffee perhaps?" Elizabeth said.

"Thank you, no. I don't wish to inconvenience you." He sank down into the chair as if he were grateful to rest. Now that Felix had had an opportunity to study him for a moment, he realized the young man appeared to be under a great deal of strain. His hands gripped the arms of the chair and his lips seemed nearly bloodless.

"So tell us, Mr. Yorke, what brings you here today?" Elizabeth said.

"I need to see Randolph Pollock, but his servants told me he wasn't available and I would have to speak to you. Please, if you'll just tell me where I can find him, I'll be on my way."

"I'm afraid Mr. Pollock really is unavailable, but if you'll tell us what your business is with him, we'll assist you in any way we can."

He drew a breath as if to calm himself before he replied. "As I said in the message I sent with your maid, my sister is married to Randolph Pollock."

"Your sister is Una O'Neill?"

"No. My sister is Cecelia Yorke."

Felix and Elizabeth exchanged a startled glance. "We were under the impression that Pollock was married to a young woman named Una O'Neill," Elizabeth said.

"Yes, it is my understanding that he has married a second time."

"While he was still married to your sister, Mr. Yorke?" Felix said.

Yorke hesitated. "Pollock claims that Cecelia . . . that she died."

"I'm so sorry," Elizabeth said.

"You sound as if you doubt that claim, Mr. Yorke," Felix said.

Yorke closed his eyes for a moment and sighed deeply, as if reaching for some inner strength. "We haven't seen Cecelia for almost two years. Since right after she married Pollock."

"Why not?" Elizabeth asked when he didn't go on.

"It wasn't our choice, if that's what you're thinking. My parents approved of the match, and even though Cecelia hadn't known him very long, he seemed genuinely devoted to her. But shortly after they were married, Cecelia stopped visiting our parents, and when any of the family tried to visit her, they were turned away. She wrote us a letter, telling us that Pollock didn't think our family was a good influence on her, and he preferred that she not see us."

"Not a good influence?" Elizabeth echoed. "In what way?"

"She didn't say, and our family is perfectly respectable, so there was no legitimate reason to cut off contact. I think Pollock just didn't want us knowing what was going on."

"And what was going on, Mr. Yorke?" Felix asked.

"I don't know, but I do know Cecelia wasn't herself. Occasionally, she'd send a brief note to let us know she was fine and we weren't to worry, but I could tell that she wasn't fine at all. She seemed frightened, but I never could find out of what."

"And then Pollock told you she died?" Elizabeth said very gently.

"Only after we finally ran him to ground," he said bitterly. "We hadn't heard from Cecelia for several months, so my father and I went to the house. We were going to demand to see her, but the place was empty. They'd moved out. It took us several more months to find Pollock, and when we did, he was living alone in some rented rooms. When we confronted him, he told us Cecelia had died. In childbirth, he said."

"How tragic," Elizabeth said.

"Except her death was never reported in the newspapers, and he wouldn't tell us where she was buried. My poor mother was hysterical. She just wanted to be able to mourn her daughter properly, and that cad wouldn't even tell us where her grave was. This led us to suspect he'd lied to us about Cecelia and that perhaps she was still alive. We were afraid he might have turned her out and she'd been too embarrassed to return home. But when we went back to try to find out, he'd vanished again. It's taken months, but we finally traced him to New York."

"And what do you want from us, Mr. Yorke?" Felix asked again.

"I just want to know where Pollock is. I confronted him the other day, and that's when I found out he'd remarried, which was a shock, as you can imagine. He still refused to tell me anything, and he threw me out of his house, but we still hope to find my sister or at least find out where she's buried if she truly is dead. But when I tried to call on Pollock again today, the servants said he wasn't home and I'd have to speak with you, Mrs. Decker."

Felix exchanged another glance with Elizabeth and saw her distress. "The servants didn't tell you what happened?" she asked.

"What do you mean, what happened?"

"Mr. Pollock is dead. Someone murdered him."

HENRY NICHOLSON, ESQ., HAD HIS OFFICE ACROSS THE street from the Tombs, which was convenient for him and his clients. Maeve climbed the stairs to the second floor, where his name was stenciled on the glass window of one of the doors along the long, dusty hallway. Inside, half a dozen clients waited in wooden chairs lined up against the walls—gang members, madams, and bunco artists—while several young men escorted them in and out of the adjoining offices of the various partners. A harried-looking fellow in a green eyeshade sat at a desk, and he looked at Maeve suspiciously as she entered.

"May I help you, miss?"

"I'd like to see Mr. Nicholson. He's an old friend of my family's. Tell him Maeve is here."

Frowning doubtfully, he went into an inner office, and in a moment, Henry himself bustled out of his office, his fleshy face wreathed in smiles. As usual, he wore a too-flashy vest and violently checked pants that made him look even fatter than he was. His vest was stained with whatever he'd had for lunch, and his shirt needed a fresh collar, but a solid gold watch chain stretched across his broad belly, and enormous diamonds flashed from every finger on his hands.

"Maeve, my darling girl! How wonderful to see you." He took both her hands in his and squeezed them tightly as he looked her over. "I see you're doing well. I'm so glad of that."

"I'm doing very well, and I'll be happy to tell you all about it."

"Then come inside and do it. Freddy, don't disturb us," he added to his clerk, who plainly disapproved of this disruption to Henry's schedule.

Henry escorted her into his office and sat her down in one of the worn client chairs placed in front of his battered desk. Henry, she knew, could have afforded an elegant suite of rooms in the most expensive building in the city and he could have worn tailor-made suits of the finest fabrics, but fancy lawyers got fancy clients, and Henry didn't like fancy clients. His bread and butter were the successful criminals who considered competent legal assistance a necessary business expense. These men weren't impressed by fancy offices. They needed a smart lawyer who knew how to maneuver the system and keep them out of jail. For that they were willing to pay handsomely.

"What have you been up to, girl?" he asked when he'd taken his seat behind his bare desk. Henry kept no paper in the office. He'd been raided by the police more than once, and they'd found not one scrap of incriminating evidence against any of his clients. "I hope you aren't here because you need my services."

"I do, but not for myself. I'm the one who sent you Una Pollock."

"Oh, that unfortunate Irish girl who smashed in her husband's skull."

"She didn't do it," Maeve said.

"Of course she didn't, if she's my client. But I don't know how I can help her. I went to see her yesterday, and she wouldn't say a word to me. I could probably get her out on bail if she'd tell me what happened . . . or at least give me a good yarn to spin to the judge."

"She's talking now, or at least she was when I saw her a little while ago. She claims she doesn't remember what happened, but I'm sure you can coax it out of her."

"And just how did you get yourself mixed up in a murder, Miss Smith? Your grandfather wouldn't be pleased."

Maeve smiled. Her grandfather would never have understood her involvement in any of this. "I'm not mixed up in it at all. After the old man died, I went to stay at a mission."

"You? At a mission? Did they make you go to church?"

"Of course they did, but they kept me off the streets. The old man didn't want me in the game, so I was trying to stay honest. Then a lady offered me a job taking care of her little girl, so that's what I've been doing."

"Not the lady who killed her husband, I hope."

"I told you, she didn't kill him, and no, this lady was a widow. She had a gentleman friend who was a police detective, though—"

"Police! Good God, Maeve. Don't tell me you've taken up with the police."

He looked so horrified, she had to smile. "Not anymore. He got fired."

"Well, that's something, I guess."

"Mr. Malloy was too good for them. He solved several really tough cases, and Mrs. Brandt would help him when she could, and so did I. Then he came into some money, and they got married. They're on their honeymoon now, but when they get back, Mr. Malloy is going to open a detective agency." She didn't mention that Malloy didn't know this yet.

"Malloy, you say? Wait a minute, is this the copper who inherited all that money? The one in all the newspapers?"

"I'm afraid so."

Henry seemed to sag. "Are you working a con on him, honey?"

"Oh no! I told you, the old man didn't want me in the game, and Mr. Malloy wouldn't be a good mark anyway. He's too smart."

"The old man used to say the smart ones were the easiest to fool."

"I told you, he was a copper. He's seen it all."

Henry shrugged. "So if you're not running a con, what are you doing?"

"I told you, I have a job as a nursemaid, but sometimes I help out when Mr. Malloy is working on a case."

"So you think you're going to work in his detective agency?"

"Yes, and in the meantime, we're helping Una Pollock. Her mother is a friend of Mr. Malloy's mother from their old neighborhood."

"Who is this 'we'?"

"Me, of course. And Mr. Malloy's in-laws, and a policeman named—"

"Wait a minute. Who are these in-laws?"

"Mr. and Mrs. Felix Decker."

"And who are they when they're at home?"

"They're society people, but—"

"Rich?"

"I suppose."

Henry's frown frightened her. "Are you sure you aren't running a con?"

"No, I told you! The Deckers are just helping out because they're nice people. Well, Mrs. Decker is nice, and Mr. Decker likes to be in charge."

"So who's paying my fee?"

Another question Maeve didn't particularly care to answer. "Mrs. Pollock is paying it herself. Her husband had some money that she inherited when he died."

"How much money?"

"Enough. More than enough, actually."

This pleased him. "And what do you mean she inherited it?"

"I mean he's dead and now it's hers."

"And where is it?"

"In a safe place."

Henry studied her for a long time, but she knew her face gave nothing away. "The old man trained you well, my girl."

"Yes, he did. I thought Mrs. O'Neill gave you some money."

"She gave me a retainer."

"Then why are you worried?"

"I guess I'm not. And she's got money for bail?"

"Yes, she does. I just wanted you to know that we're trying to find out who really killed Pollock, and when we do, Mrs. Pollock will be off the hook. In the meantime, I know she'd like to be out of jail."

"I'll see what I can do about that."

"Good, and if you need anything, just let me know. Here's where I live." She gave him one of Malloy's calling cards.

"That's not a very fancy address for a millionaire," Henry observed.

"Mr. Malloy's not a very fancy man. There's something else I need to tell you about Una Pollock."

Henry folded his hands on his desk and leaned forward. "And what's that?"

"Pollock used to beat her."

"Who told you this?"

"One of the maids. She said the servants heard an argument the day Pollock was killed, but they claim they didn't see anything. They thought it was Pollock shouting at his wife like he did when he was beating her up, so they went down to the kitchen and hid out until it was over."

"And do you know for sure that this is true?"

"I don't know if it was true the servants heard shouting the day Pollock was killed, but I don't think they have a reason to lie about it. I do know that somebody was beating Una Pollock. I helped her change her clothes today at the jail and she's covered with bruises."

"Maybe the killer beat her up."

"Some of the bruises were new, but some were old and fading. Whoever beat her did it regularly."

"Why didn't the police notice the bruises?"

"Because he never hit her anyplace where it would show, so they wouldn't have seen the marks."

"This is all very interesting."

"Yes, it is," she agreed. "The question is, what do you want to do with that information?"

"I want to keep it to myself for the time being."

"Because it gives her a reason to kill Pollock?"

"It would seem like that to most people, yes. I happen to

know from years of experience that these women hardly ever kill their husbands, though. Just the opposite. They spend their miserable lives trying desperately to please them and never succeeding and then mourning them when they do die. They hardly ever even try to defend themselves. You can't convince a jury of twelve good men the truth of that, though. They either believe the fellow beat his wife because she deserved it and don't consider the beating an excuse for killing him, or they think the woman made it up as an excuse for killing an upstanding pillar of the community. Either way, they find her guilty and send her off to prison for the rest of her life."

"And if a man kills his wife when he's beating her?"

"Which is what usually happens, in my experience. Like as not, they'll decide he didn't mean to and let him off. Unless he did something unspeakable, like cut her up into little pieces and feed her to the dog, in which case they'll send him to Old Sparky. But not many men are that imaginative."

"So I guess I shouldn't tell anyone about the bruises."

"No, my dear, you shouldn't, but feel free to find out who really did kill Pollock, if you can. Even if Mrs. Pollock did it, it will be helpful to know how it came to pass so we can explain it in just the right way to the jury."

Maeve frowned at that, but she said, "I'll do my best."

5

GINO WAS PLEASED TO SEE MAEVE OPEN THE DOOR AT
the Malloy house that evening. Of course the children were
with her, eager to see who their visitor was, and he had to
greet them properly before he could turn his attention to her.
But still, he'd been looking forward to seeing her all day.

After he'd done his duty with Brian and Catherine, Mrs.
Malloy took them off, ordering Maeve to feed him.

"I just had supper at my mother's house," he said. "I couldn't
eat another bite."

"Then let's go into the parlor. The children aren't allowed
in there," she added with a conspiratorial grin. She slid open
the pocket doors to the large, elaborately furnished room.
He'd expected it to be chilly, but then he remembered the
house had central heating. "Did you have an interesting day?"

"No," he said, watching her turn on the electric light. "Just the usual shoplifters and drunks. Walking a beat is dull work when you've been a detective."

"I had an interesting day." She sat down on one of the sofas, and he sat down beside her.

"Tell me everything."

She started with her visit to the Pollock house and the break-in.

"I hope you didn't tell any of the servants that you'd taken the money."

"Of course not," she said. "If they knew it was there, they must think the burglar got it. And he's the only one who knows he didn't, of course."

"Why didn't they call in the police?"

"They're scared, and they're just servants. They don't think it's their place to make decisions like that."

"The police should know, though, in case the person who broke in is the one who killed Pollock."

She frowned at this. "They think they already know who killed Pollock, and they aren't going to change their minds unless we make them."

He wanted to argue with her, but she was right. "All right. I guess that trunk in the hall is Mrs. Pollock's clothes."

"Yes. I'm not sure what to do with it, but we should probably go see Mrs. O'Neill soon and she can decide. Maybe I should've asked Una when I saw her today, but I didn't think of it."

"You saw Una? You went to the Tombs?" he asked in amazement.

"Of course. I packed up some of her clothes to take to her and pretended that's why I was visiting her. Can you believe it? She was hiding in her cell, all curled up on her bed, and still wearing the dress she had on when they found her. It was covered with blood."

"You mean the police didn't take it for evidence?"

"Obviously not. I made her change into something clean, though."

"What happened to the bloodstained dress?"

"I've got it. I'm not sure if it proves anything one way or the other, but I figured it should be someplace safe. But the best news is that I got Una to talk."

"How did you do that?"

"She said I scared her, but I can't imagine I scared her any more than the police or the guards at the prison or even the other inmates. I think she was just waiting for the right person to talk to."

"What makes you say that?"

"I don't know, but have you ever seen anybody so scared they couldn't talk?"

Gino thought back to his limited experience in police work. "Once or twice, when something awful happened."

"And how long did it last?"

"A few minutes or maybe even the better part of an hour."

"But not days. They said she couldn't speak, but I think she just didn't know what to do so she kept her mouth shut."

"That was probably a good idea, at least with the police."

"Maybe, but she wouldn't talk to her lawyer either, so he didn't even try to get her out on bail."

"Who's her lawyer?"

"Henry Nicholson."

Impressed, Gino gave a low whistle. "He's the best defense attorney in the city. How did she get him?"

"I told her mother to hire him."

"You did? How do you know about Henry Nicholson?"

"Everybody knows about him. Like you just said, he's the best defense attorney in the city," she said, mocking him.

He decided not to point out that a nursemaid shouldn't

have any reason to be familiar with defense attorneys. Maeve had led an interesting life in the years before they'd met, though, and she plainly wasn't ready to share it with him yet. He was pretty sure she'd never needed Nicholson's services herself. At least he thought he was sure.

"Anyway," she continued, "I asked him to get her out on bail."

"Nicholson? Was he at the jail when you were there?"

"No, I went to his office after I saw Una."

"You went to his *office*?"

"Of course. How else was I going to see him? Anyway, I wanted to ask him about something else, too, and he told me not to tell anyone, but I don't think he meant I shouldn't tell you and the Deckers. I did tell him we were trying to find out who really killed Pollock, and he said we should keep doing that."

"How generous of him."

She smiled at the bitterness in his tone. "You have to stop thinking like a policeman, Gino."

"I *am* a policeman."

"And so you hate Nicholson because he defends the people you arrest."

"And he gets guilty people off."

"Everyone in America is entitled to a legal defense."

He knew Maeve hadn't just thought that up. That was what defense attorneys always said when they got a guilty person sprung from jail, so she'd heard it from one of them. Probably from Nicholson himself. Maybe it was good Gino didn't know much about Maeve's past. "So what did you find out that Nicholson told you to keep secret?"

Before she could reply, the doorbell rang.

Maeve jumped up to answer it. "That's probably the Deckers. They telephoned to say they're coming over. They have something to tell us."

The next few minutes were chaotic as the children had to greet the Deckers and the Deckers had to greet Gino and Mrs. Malloy had to insist they all needed coffee. Then she finally took the children off with her to make some.

"I'm glad you're here, my boy," Mr. Decker said when they were back in the parlor and Maeve had closed the pocket doors behind them. "We're hoping you can help out at the Pollock house."

"I'd be happy to, sir," he said, a little disconcerted that Mr. Decker had a particular job for him.

"Oh yes," Mrs. Decker said, taking one of the chairs while her husband took the one next to it. "We weren't expecting you to be here, but I'm delighted that you are. It will make everything much simpler."

Maeve sat on the sofa and Gino happily sat next to her again.

"What will it make simpler?" he asked.

"The Pollock servants, you see," Mr. Decker said.

"They're afraid to stay in the house because someone broke in last night and ransacked Pollock's office," Mrs. Decker said.

"They want to quit, but they need references. Mrs. Decker promise to write them, but—"

"But we decided we shouldn't leave the house empty, in case someone comes by looking for Pollock or the money or something," she said.

"So Mrs. Decker isn't going to give them their references—"

"Or their back pay," she added.

"—until we're satisfied we can abandon the house. We don't think the servants will leave without their pay or their references—"

"But just in case they're too afraid to stay there alone, we were hoping you could spend your nights at the house, Gino."

"To provide some protection," Mr. Decker said.

Gino needed a minute for his brain to catch up with them, and when he looked at Maeve, she was smiling.

"That's a wonderful idea," she said, "and while you're there, you can charm the maids into telling you all about the Pollocks."

"How clever of you, Maeve," Mrs. Decker said, also smiling.

"What do you mean, 'charm the maids'?" Gino asked, not certain he liked this plan at all.

The two women exchanged a knowing glance that made Gino even more uncomfortable.

"Just be nice and chat them up," Maeve said. "Pretend you're interested in them and listen to what they say. Ask questions."

"That's what I'd normally do," Gino protested.

"Of course it is, dear," Mrs. Decker said. "And you can't help being charming."

Was that true? Did Maeve think he was charming? He'd be sure to ask her that very thing the next time they were alone.

"Would you be willing to spend a few nights at the Pollock house to make the servants feel more secure?" Mr. Decker asked. "We'd pay you for your time, of course."

"Out of Pollock's money," Maeve added.

That didn't sound right to Gino. "What if that money belongs to someone else?"

"Of course it belongs to someone else," Maeve said, "and they wouldn't be getting a single penny of it back if we'd let somebody steal it. They also wouldn't be getting all of it back ever, because Pollock already spent some of it. So if we spend a little more helping save his wife and finding out who really killed him, then they should be grateful to get anything at all instead of nothing."

"How very sensible, Maeve," Mrs. Decker said.

"Well, it doesn't matter if it's sensible or not, because you don't need to pay me," Gino said. "None of you are getting paid." While they were all gaping at him, he added, "Of course I'll stay at the house and question the maids. What should I tell them about the reference letters and their salaries?"

"Tell them we will have it for them in a few days," Mrs. Decker said. "And if they have any concerns, they can come to me."

"That should eliminate any complaints," Mr. Decker said slyly.

"And another reason we're glad you're here, Gino," Mrs. Decker said, "is because we had an interesting visitor today and we need to tell you both about him."

"Somebody on Pollock's list?" Gino asked.

"We don't think so," Mr. Decker said. "But we couldn't remember for sure. We need to make a copy of the list."

"We should have thought of that before," Maeve said. "I'll get the ledger and make a copy before you leave."

"Two copies," Gino said. "I may come across some of these people."

"Good idea," Mrs. Decker said.

"So who was your visitor?" Maeve asked.

"A Mr. Yorke, from Chicago," Mrs. Decker said.

"Apparently, Pollock was in Chicago before he came here. Yorke says his sister was married to Pollock," Mr. Decker said.

"*Was* married?" Maeve asked. "Why isn't she married to him anymore?"

"Because Pollock claims she's dead," Mr. Decker said.

"But Mr. Yorke doesn't want to believe she is," Mrs. Decker said. "Pollock claimed she died in childbirth over a year ago, but he never notified the family, it was never announced in the newspapers, and he wouldn't tell them where she's buried."

"Do they think Pollock murdered her?" Maeve asked.

"Oh dear, no," Mrs. Decker said. "They think he put her out, and she was too ashamed to come home."

"You mean that's what they *hope*," Gino said. Everyone turned to him in surprise. "As long as they don't know for sure that their loved one is dead, people will believe all kinds of things."

"So you think she's dead?" Mr. Decker asked.

"I think there's a good chance. Maybe she did die the way he said and maybe he killed her. We don't really have any reason to think he did, but—"

"Yes, we do," Maeve said. This time everyone turned to her. "It's what I was going to tell you just when the Deckers arrived," she told him. "I found out from the maid today that Pollock used to beat Una."

Mr. and Mrs. Decker were shocked, but hardly anything shocked Gino anymore. "Are you sure?" he asked.

"I saw the bruises when I helped her change clothes today."

"You saw her?" Mrs. Decker asked.

"Yes. I went to the Tombs after Mr. Decker brought me home."

"Why didn't you tell me you were going to do this?" Mr. Decker asked.

"Because I was afraid you'd try to stop me. Then after I left Una at the Tombs, I went to see her lawyer."

"Her lawyer? Whatever for?" Mrs. Decker asked.

"Because if Pollock was beating her, it was a reason for her to kill him."

"And what did Nicholson say?" Gino asked.

"Who's Nicholson?" Mrs. Decker asked.

"Henry Nicholson, her attorney," Maeve said.

"She hired that scoundrel?" Mr. Decker asked.

"Maeve told Mrs. O'Neill to go see him," Gino explained, earning a black look from Maeve.

"Mr. Nicholson said not to tell anyone about the bruises," Maeve said, still glaring, "but I thought all of you should know. It's important that it doesn't get out, but I knew I could trust you not to mention it to the press."

"The press?" Mrs. Decker said. "What do they have to do with it?"

"Nothing yet," Gino said, "but sooner or later they'll get wind of the case. Probably when Nicholson asks for a bail hearing."

"The mere fact that Nicholson is involved will attract the press," Mr. Decker said.

"Who is this Mr. Nicholson?" Mrs. Decker asked.

"I'll explain it to you later, my dear," Mr. Decker said. "In the meantime, we have Mr. Yorke and his family to deal with."

"I don't see why we have to deal with them at all," Maeve said.

"But if we can help them find out what happened to Cecelia, shouldn't we do that?" Mrs. Decker asked.

"I doubt we can help with that," Gino said. "It happened in Chicago, after all. But if we can show that Pollock's first wife disappeared under mysterious circumstances, we could make a case for self-defense if Una really did kill him."

"Do you think she did kill him?" Mrs. Decker asked.

"If he was beating her, she might've fought back," he said.

"And she's saying she still doesn't remember what happened," Maeve said. "I guess it's possible she doesn't, but if I'd killed my husband, I'd probably say I didn't remember what happened, too. Just remember, we're not supposed to know Pollock beat her or say anything about it."

"What are we going to do about Mr. Yorke?" Mrs. Decker asked.

"Wait a minute," Gino said, wondering why he hadn't thought to ask this before. "Why did Yorke go to you in the first place?"

"He went to Pollock's house and asked to see him. The servants didn't know what to do, so they sent him to Mrs. Decker," Mr. Decker said.

"He didn't know Pollock was dead?" Gino asked.

"No, he was very surprised when we told him," Mr. Decker said. "Although . . ."

"Although what?" Maeve asked.

"He did say he'd been to see Pollock once already. Did he say exactly when he'd been there, Elizabeth?"

"No, I don't think he did."

"So he might've been there the day Pollock was killed," Gino said. A frisson of excitement skittered across his nerve endings. "He might be the killer."

"But he didn't even know Pollock was dead," Mr. Decker said.

"And he was very upset when we told him," Mrs. Decker said. "Nearly in tears, in fact. You see, Mr. Pollock is the only one who knows what happened to Mr. Yorke's sister. Now he's afraid they'll never find her."

"Or maybe he just acted like he didn't know Pollock was dead," Maeve said. "If he'd killed Pollock, that would be a good way to prove he had nothing to do with it. You two would make excellent witnesses about how surprised he was to hear the news."

"How very clever," Mrs. Decker said. "I must remember that."

"Why?" her husband asked. "Are you planning to murder someone?"

"One never knows what might happen, dear."

Gino had to cough to cover a laugh and Maeve covered her mouth with both hands, while poor Mr. Decker just stared at his wife, dumbfounded.

Mrs. Decker acted like she didn't notice their reactions.

"On the other hand, if Mr. Yorke killed Mr. Pollock, why didn't he just go back to Chicago? No one would have ever known he was here."

"Indeed," Mr. Decker said, regaining his composure. "I suppose someone should go see Mr. Yorke, then, and ask him some pointed questions. Gino, perhaps you would be the best one for that."

"It would have to wait until I'm off work tomorrow evening."

"That should be fine," Mr. Decker said. "He gave us the name of his hotel so we could contact him if we learned anything about his sister. You can find out from the servants when he actually visited Pollock before you see him."

"Is there anything else we need to know?" Gino asked.

"Oh, I almost forgot," Maeve said. "Una told me that Pollock had a special friend named Truett. She said he had other men come for dinner, but this Truett just came over to meet with Pollock and they didn't socialize."

"Did she tell you his first name?" Mr. Decker asked.

"She said she didn't know it, but it sounds to me like he might be Pollock's partner."

"So that's something else to ask the servants about, Gino," Mr. Decker said. "Is that all?"

Everyone looked at everyone else, and no one had anything to add.

"I'll get the ledger and we can drink Mrs. Malloy's coffee while we make copies of the names," Maeve said.

THE DECKERS HAD OFFERED TO TAKE GINO TO POLLOCK'S house in their carriage, but he had to go home and pack some things first. He could, he pointed out, travel faster on the elevated train in any case. The Deckers decided to drive up to Pollock's house in the meantime and inform the servants in person that Gino would be guarding them for the next few days, until they could get things sorted out. He was glad he didn't have to be present for that conversation. Dealing with the aftermath was going to be bad enough.

Harlem had pretty much settled in for the night when he arrived at Pollock's door, but lights still burned in the front hallway of this house, at least. Gino climbed the front steps and the door opened before he could knock. An anxious-looking female peered out at him.

"Are you Officer Donatelli?"

He'd decided to wear his uniform in hopes of reassuring them. "Yes. Did Mrs. Decker tell you I was coming?"

"Oh yes, sir, she did." She swung the door wide and welcomed him inside.

He was surprised to see three other people in the hallway, obviously waiting for him. The woman who had admitted him appeared to be in her thirties and was dressed like a maid. The others were another woman, younger than the first and also dressed like a maid; an older, stouter woman in a plain dress and apron who must be the cook; and a skinny boy of about sixteen.

"Sorry I'm so late," Gino said. "I hope I didn't keep you up."

"We couldn't've slept a wink until you got here anyways," the cook said. "Eddie, you take Officer Donatelli's bag up to his room," she added to the boy. "Officer, you come right on into the kitchen. I've made you some supper."

Gino had already had supper and then Mrs. Malloy had insisted he eat some pie while they were copying the names in the ledger, but he figured he could eat a little something more to please the cook. She might want to chat, and he figured eating her food might charm her, whatever that meant. He only wished Maeve was here to see it.

To his surprise, the two maids followed them down the

hallway and downstairs to the kitchen, while the boy carried Gino's carpetbag to some destination upstairs. The boy was back by the time the cook had pulled a covered plate from the warming oven and set it before him. He joined the others in standing there, staring at him, although Gino thought he looked more angry than the others. Gino felt awkward eating while they watched him, wide-eyed.

The room was warm from the stove, and except for his dishes, everything had been put to rights and scrubbed clean for the night. After he'd complimented the cook on the beef stew and the lightness of the biscuits, he said, "You folks can go on to bed, if you like, but at least sit down if you're going to stay here."

"Sit, sit," the cook said, motioning them to the other chairs at the table. "I'm Velvet, by the way. And that's Hattie." She pointed to the older maid. "And this here's Jane. The boy's name is Eddie."

"I'm pleased to meet all of you," he said between bites. "How long have you worked for Mr. Pollock?"

"We all started about six months ago, I reckon. When he first moved into the house. He got an agency to find him some staff, so we all started at the same time."

"Was he a good man to work for?"

Silence greeted his question, and when he looked up, none of them would meet his eye.

"Did he mistreat you?" he asked.

"Oh no, sir, nothing like that," Velvet said.

"But maybe his wife wouldn't say the same thing," Gino tried.

More silence and averted gazes.

Velvet jumped up. "Let me get you some more coffee."

As she refilled his cup, Jane said, "It was her own fault."

"You hush," the boy snapped. "It wasn't any such thing."

"It was," Jane insisted. "He said so."

"Don't pay her no mind," Velvet said to Gino.

Gino turned to Jane. "That was just an excuse. It wasn't her fault that he hit her. It was his fault. He hit her because he wanted to be mean to her."

Jane looked like she wanted to argue.

"Jane, you go on to bed now, you hear?" Velvet said.

Jane pulled a face. "I don't wanna go upstairs by myself."

"Eddie, you go with her."

When Gino looked at them, he saw Eddie and Hattie were no longer avoiding his gaze. Something had changed. Even the air in the room felt a little different. Jane rose slowly and headed for the stairway. "Come on, Eddie."

The boy followed with obvious reluctance, and he paused at the foot of the stairs. "What's going to happen to Mrs. Pollock?"

"I don't know, but we're trying to get her out of jail on bail."

"Will she come back here then?"

Gino didn't think so, but he said, "That's up to her."

That seemed to please him. "Will you be here in the morning?"

"I'll have breakfast, but then I have to go to work. I'll be back tomorrow night, though."

Jane took Eddie by the ear and gave him a tug.

"Ouch! I'm coming," he snapped and followed her up the stairs.

When their footsteps had died away, Velvet said, "He's right fond of Mrs. Pollock."

Gino nodded. That would be understandable. He started eating again. "How long have the Pollocks been married?" he asked, trying to make it sound like idle curiosity.

"About three months, I'd say," Velvet said.

"Going on four now," Hattie corrected her.

"Is it? Time does fly."

So Pollock had moved to New York, gotten himself a nice house, and then within just a few months had gotten himself a pretty wife, too. She wasn't a society girl, but no society girl would've married him on such a brief acquaintance, especially since he was new in town and no one knew who his people were. Gino would never be in society himself, but he'd learned a lot about it from working with the Deckers and their daughter, Mrs. Brandt. Or Mrs. Malloy now. Would a society girl have put up with being beaten? Would her family have tolerated being shut out of her life? Cecelia Yorke had endured both of those things and had even disappeared without notice. But she probably wasn't a society girl either.

"Would you like some more, Officer?" Velvet asked, bringing Gino back to the present. "There's plenty. Or I've got some white cake you might enjoy."

"The cake sounds good," he said with a smile. "That was delicious, ma'am. Thank you. What's Mrs. Pollock like?" he asked while Velvet cut him some cake.

"She's all right," Hattie said after Velvet offered no opinion.

"Don't know nothing about running a house, poor thing," Velvet said.

Gino didn't expect she did. "She was working in a cigar store when they met, I heard."

"Is that so?" Velvet said with interest, setting the generous slice of cake down in front of him.

"We knew she wasn't quality," Hattie said. "You could tell that right off."

"She tried real hard, though," Velvet said. "She did everything Mr. Pollock told her."

Hattie sniffed derisively. "She never pleased him, though. She just wasn't quite good enough for him."

"Nobody was good enough for that man."

Gino finished up his cake without comment, giving the women every opportunity to continue, but they'd exhausted their gossip for the moment. "Thank you for the supper, Miss Velvet. It was delicious."

"It's a pleasure to cook for a man who enjoys good food," she said with a grin. She cleared the dishes and dropped them into the pan of soapy water she'd prepared for them.

"If you don't mind, I'd like to take a look around and check the house before I go to bed," he said.

"Hattie, you show the officer around while I clean up. Soon as he's done, take him to his room, and you can go to bed yourself."

Hattie didn't look too pleased at this assignment, but she said, "Where do you want to start?"

"Let's start in the basement, where the burglar got in last night."

Like most basements, this one was dark and dreary. The house was wired for electricity, and a lone bulb hanging in the center of the space cast dark shadows in the corners. The area was oddly empty, though. A few boxes were stacked against one wall, but the place had a deserted feel to it. Gino supposed Pollock hadn't lived here long enough to accumulate a lot of stuff.

"This here's the window where he came in," Hattie said, pointing. "Broke the glass. We cleaned it up and nailed the board over it as best we could."

They'd done a good job. The board seemed secure, although there were other windows that could be broken. High up near the ceiling, the windows were at ground level outside and easily accessed. A grown man would have no trouble lowering himself to the floor. When they'd climbed back up the stairs, Gino checked the door at the head of the stairs. It had no lock.

"Can you get me some pots?" he asked Hattie.

"What you need pots for?" Velvet asked. She was drying his dishes and putting them away for the night.

"I'm going to put a chair under the handle on this door, in case somebody tries to get in again. It won't stop a burglar, but it'll slow him down. If we stack some pots on the chair and he does force the door open, the pots will fall over and I'll hear them."

The two women looked at him like they thought he'd hung the moon, and he wondered if they thought he was charming or just smart. Maybe he should ask them.

When they'd fixed up the basement door, he checked the bolt on the back door and found it adequate. Then he made sure all the downstairs windows were locked, particularly the one in Pollock's office. They hadn't cleaned up the mess, just in case they decided to call in the police, so Gino could easily see what had happened.

When they reached the front parlor, he pulled the door open without thinking, and only when he found the light switch and illuminated the electric chandelier hanging in the center of the room did he realize the women had stopped halfway down the hall and let him go on alone. Of course. He should have remembered this was where Pollock was killed.

The place looked harmless enough and perfectly ordinary except that the carpet had been rolled up and lay in front of the door. "Is this where you found him?" he asked the women.

"I found him," Hattie said. "Them, I mean. She was here, too, with him."

"Can you tell me how it was?"

She came forward slowly, every step a silent protest that radiated through her body. She stopped in the doorway, obviously unwilling to go any farther. "They was over there." She pointed to the left-hand wall.

"Can you tell me how they were when you found them? Sitting, standing, or what?"

"He was laying down. He was already dead. Anybody could see that. So much blood . . ." She shuddered.

"I'm sorry to make you remember it, but it's important."

She glanced back at Velvet, who said, "Tell him, Hattie. The truth never hurt nobody."

Gino wasn't sure about that, but he didn't contradict her. "What was Mrs. Pollock doing?"

"She was sitting there." With a resigned sigh, she lifted her skirt and stepped over the rolled carpet, then walked to the spot she'd pointed to before. "She was sitting right here, her legs straight out, and she had his head . . ." Her voice broke, but she cleared her throat. "She had his head in her lap, even though it was all busted and bleeding. She had blood all over her dress."

"What was she doing?"

"Doing?"

"Yes, was she crying and upset or—"

"She was humming."

"Humming?"

"I think, or maybe singing real soft-like. And rocking a little. Back and forth like this." She moved the upper part of her body forward and back. "Like he was a baby and she was trying to soothe him or something."

This was good to know, because this was not at all a typical reaction. Surely, Mrs. Pollock had been in shock. Shock would be the natural reaction of a female to finding her husband bludgeoned to death on her parlor floor. "Was anybody else in the room?"

"Oh no, just the two of them."

"And the parlor door was open?"

"Yes, sir. About like it is now."

The door hung wide, as if someone had opened it and left.

But it wasn't pushed up against the wall, the way it would have been if someone had just intended to leave the room open.

"What did you do when you saw them?" he asked.

"Oh, Lordy, I screamed something awful. Jane and Velvet come running."

"What about Eddie?"

"He was out, running an errand for Mr. Pollock."

"And then what happened? Did Mrs. Pollock say anything?"

"Oh no, sir. She didn't say a word. She just kept singing. Didn't even act like she heard me screaming or even notice I was there."

"What did you do when you saw him?" he asked Velvet.

"I sent Jane out to find the police. We know where they go."

Gino didn't question her about that. She probably meant they knew where the beat cops went to catch a nap or cadge a drink. "And she brought back Officer Broghan?"

"How did you know that?" Velvet asked.

"I know his cousin. What did he do?"

"He took one look around and ran off to find a call box. Then the rest of the police come, and they took Mrs. Pollock away, and they took Mr. Pollock's body away, and they didn't tell us anything."

They probably hadn't asked them any questions either. They'd decided Mrs. Pollock had killed her husband, and she hadn't denied it, so they'd bundled her off to the Tombs and closed the case. If he'd never met Frank Malloy, he might've done the same thing. "I guess they took the weapon."

"What weapon?" Hattie asked.

"Whatever the killer used to bash his head in."

"Oh yes. It disappeared, so I reckon they took it."

"What was it?"

"It was a frog."

6

GINO WAS SURE HE HADN'T HEARD HER RIGHT. "A FROG?"

"Wasn't no frog at all," Velvet said.

"That's what it looked like to me, and I'm the one dusted it every day."

"You dusted a frog?" Gino asked.

The two women frowned at him.

"Not a real frog," Velvet said.

"It was a statue," Hattie said.

Oh, this was making more sense. "A statue of a frog?"

"It weren't no frog," Velvet insisted. "More like a lizard, and it had a lady's face."

This must have been a very ugly statue. "How big was it?"

"About so big," Hattie said, holding her hands about six inches apart. "But heavy."

"What was it made of?"

"Some kind of stone, looked like," she said. "All carved up to look like a frog."

"It was a lizard," Velvet said.

"I never seen no lizard."

"Well, if you did, you'd know it was a lizard. Some heathen foreign thing," Velvet added in disgust.

"And you're sure that's what the killer used on Pollock?"

"Oh yes," Hattie said. "It had blood all over it, and it was laying on the floor right near him."

"It used to sit on that table over there." Velvet pointed to a small table sitting beside an upholstered chair just beyond where Hattie indicated the body had been found.

So the murder weapon was conveniently to hand for anyone who might have had a sudden urge to bash Pollock's head in. That didn't help Una, but it did mean just about anyone else could've killed him just as easily. And now he was very curious to see this "statue" of a frog or lizard or whatever it was.

"Did Mr. Pollock have a visitor named Yorke recently?" Gino asked as he escorted Hattie out of the parlor and turned off the lights.

Hattie frowned. "Yes, sir. He come the day Mr. Pollock died."

Gooseflesh rose on Gino's arms. "How long before Pollock died was he here?"

"I don't rightly know, not exactly, because I don't know just when Mr. Pollock died, you see. It was maybe two hours before I found them in the parlor, though."

That might mean he was long gone when Pollock was killed, but the fact that he was here at all would help Una's case. "Was Mr. Pollock happy to see him?"

"I wouldn't say happy," Hattie said. "But he wasn't mad neither."

"Did he ever get mad when he had other visitors?"

She shrugged. "Sometimes he wasn't too happy to see Mr. Truett."

"Who's Truett?" Gino knew, but he wanted to see what they'd say.

"Just a friend of Mr. Pollock's."

"He wasn't no friend. He never once stayed for dinner, did he?" Velvet said.

"But he and Mr. Pollock always visited a good long time whenever he'd come," Hattie said.

"He visited pretty often then, I guess," Gino said.

"Yes, at least once most every week," Hattie said. "They had a lot of business to talk over, or at least that's what Mr. Pollock would always say."

"That's what he would say to Truett?" Gino asked.

"Yes, he'd say something like, 'We have a lot to talk about,' or 'A lot has happened since you were here.' Things like that."

Which sounded to Gino like Truett was working with Pollock on the railroad swindle. "Do you know where this Truett lives?"

They just stared blankly back at him. Of course they wouldn't know that.

"Do you know his first name, by any chance?"

"Mr. Truett is all I ever knew," Hattie said. "But I could ask him next time he comes."

"Has he been around since Pollock died?"

"No, sir, but sometimes I didn't know when he came unless I saw him leaving. Sometimes Mr. Pollock would let him in, you see."

"Well, Mr. Pollock isn't going to be letting him in any-more, so when he comes, tell him Mr. Decker would like to speak with him and find out where he lives, if he'll tell you."

From the way Hattie was scowling, she didn't like that assignment at all. Servants weren't in the habit of interrogating visitors or giving them instructions. Then Gino thought of something to sweeten the pot, at least for Truett. "He and Mr. Pollock were business partners, and Truett is going to be looking for his share of their profits."

"You mean he has money coming?" Velvet asked.

"He probably thinks so, yes."

"But that burglar got all Mr. Pollock's money out of his safe."

"Truett won't know that, though, and we . . . we think we know who has it." Which was the God's truth. "If we're right, we can get it back. That's why Mr. Decker wants to talk to him, to explain it."

They still looked uncertain, but he felt more confident that they would at least send Truett to Decker.

After Gino had checked the lock on the front door and found it suitable, the women took him upstairs. He was disconcerted to discover that they had put him in the master bedroom. When Hattie took him to the rest of the rooms on that floor, however, he understood why. None of the other rooms were furnished.

"Mr. Pollock said there was no sense wasting money on furniture for this part of the house," Hattie explained while Gino checked the window locks. "Nobody but us and the family ever comes up here."

"I hope the servants' rooms have furniture," he said.

"Oh yes, sir. We got everything we need. Mr. Pollock, he saw to that, at least. When do you think we might leave here? For good, I mean. We're awful scared now to be here by ourselves."

"I don't think you've got anything to be afraid of, and I'll be here every night until you're gone. Just remember, you don't have to let anybody into the house. Just tell them to go see Mr. Decker."

That seemed to reassure her a little, and she didn't offer any more complaints while he finished checking that floor.

"Do you want me to check upstairs?"

"No need for that. Nobody could get in up there. We put clean sheets on your bed and everything," Hattie said. "And you just tell me if you need anything."

Gino wished her good night, and gratefully made his way to his quarters. The room was comfortably furnished and the bathroom just outside in the hallway was far more luxurious—and a whole lot cleaner—than the shared facilities at the tenement where he lived with his parents. He could get used to living like this.

The furniture, like all the furniture in the house, was new. The four-poster bed was plain, not like the ones he'd seen in houses where the people were really rich, with carvings on the headboard and on the posters. The wood was poor quality, too, like the furniture people in the tenements had. He checked the twin wardrobes. The one was empty, probably because Maeve had packed up all of Una Pollock's clothing. The other one still held Pollock's things, and Gino started going through them methodically, the way Frank Malloy had taught him.

Pollock had several suits, all tailor-made and good quality. His shoes were expensive, too, and polished to a gleaming shine. He even had a suit of evening clothes and a silk top hat. Somehow, Gino couldn't picture Pollock taking a girl like Una out to the opera or wherever men wore suits like that. He searched all the pockets of every article of clothing and found nothing but a few ticket stubs and flakes of tobacco. The bureau drawers held piles of silk underdrawers and blindingly white shirts. On the top lay silver-backed brushes and a glass dish holding pearl shirt studs and gold cuff links engraved with Pollock's initials.

Two small drawers flanked the top of the bureau, too tiny to hold clothing or much of anything else, but when Gino pulled the first one open, he found exactly what he'd been looking for: a small black address book. Inside were the same names they'd just copied from the ledger, along with addresses. Truett was in there, too. Gordon Truett.

When he'd finished searching the room, finding nothing else of interest, he pulled out the pencil he always carried and carefully copied all the addresses over to the list of names he'd made at Malloy's house. Then he put the address book back where he'd found it. If the police had to come back looking for new evidence because he and his cohorts had cleared Una Pollock of a murder charge, they'd find it waiting for them.

At last, Gino washed up and turned out the lights. He lay down, still wearing his uniform pants just in case some intruder knocked over the booby trap he'd set downstairs and he had to go running.

Mrs. Malloy and Brian hadn't even left for school when someone started ringing the doorbell the next morning. Brian couldn't hear the doorbell, of course, but he was always willing to go running after Catherine, who raced to the front door. She knew better than to open it herself, though, so Maeve had to shoo them out of the way so she could do so. She found Mrs. O'Neill standing on the stoop, much as she had a few days ago when she'd come the first time to beg for help.

She looked a little less frazzled this morning, but still a bit desperate. "Oh, Miss Smith, I'm that sorry to bother you again, but I don't know what to do. That lawyer you told me to hire, he's taking Una to court. He sent me word, but I've never been to court and I don't know what I'm supposed to do."

"Don't leave her standing in the cold," Mrs. Malloy said, having followed the rest of them to see who the visitor was. As usual, her wrinkled face was pinched into a disapproving frown, but Maeve noticed she seemed a little more disapproving than usual today.

Maeve obediently invited Mrs. O'Neill inside.

"Oh, Alma, it's good to see you. How have you been keeping?" Mrs. O'Neill asked.

"Not too bad," Mrs. Malloy said. "The boy keeps me busy."

"He's growing like a weed," she said, smiling fondly at Brian. "Looks more like his father every day."

"Yes, poor thing," Mrs. Malloy said. Maeve bit back a smile.

"I guess you heard about my troubles," Mrs. O'Neill said.

"Maeve told me. Such a tragedy."

Mrs. O'Neill's eyes filled with tears. "I thought I had my girl all settled."

"Why don't you come into the kitchen and have a cup of coffee to warm you up," Maeve said quickly, knowing Mrs. Malloy's store of sympathy for other people's misfortunes was rather small. "Don't you have to take Brian to school?" she added to Mrs. Malloy.

"Indeed I do," she said without a hint of regret to be leaving her old friend. "Please give Una my condolences on the loss of her husband."

"That I will," Mrs. O'Neill said. "Such a fine man. I can't imagine why anyone would harm him." She was dabbing at her teary eyes, so she didn't see Mrs. Malloy rolling hers.

The children had already lost interest in their visitor and wandered off. "I've got to get Brian ready. Maeve will take good care of you." With that, Mrs. Malloy slipped away, leaving Maeve to escort Mrs. O'Neill to the kitchen.

"Women with sons don't know what it's like," Mrs. O'Neill said as they walked. "You try to do what's best and you pray every night that your daughter finds a good husband, because otherwise, what's to become of her?"

She was right, Maeve knew, although she hated every word of it. Opportunities for women in this world were few, and most of them weren't worth contemplating.

When Mrs. O'Neill was seated at the table, Maeve poured her what was left of the breakfast coffee. "What did Mr. Nicholson's message say?"

"He said to come to the courthouse and to bring some money for bail and I could take Una home."

"Did he say how much money?"

"No. Do you know?"

"No, I don't. How much do you have left?"

"Four hundred dollars. He only asked me for a hundred dollars, but what if I need all of the rest of it for bail money? He said he'd need more money for his fees if Una went on trial, but if I need it all for bail, how will I pay him?"

"Don't worry about that. I don't think Una is going to trial. Just take what you have, and if you need more, send me word. We'll figure something out."

"Oh, I couldn't take money from you, Miss Smith. How would I ever pay you back?"

"I said not to worry. Just let me know. We don't want Una sitting in that horrible jail, now do we? They're practically tearing it down around the prisoners' ears!"

"Oh, and those women who are in there with her, well, they looked like they would cut your throat for a nickel."

Maeve thought she was probably right, but she didn't want to scare Mrs. O'Neill any more than she already was. "Do you know where the court is? In that building across the street from the Tombs?"

"Which one? There's so many of them, and I'm too afraid

to ask anyone where to go. Everyone down there is so rude and mean."

Maeve sighed. "Would you like for me to go with you?"

Mrs. O'Neill visibly sagged with relief. "Would you? I don't want to inconvenience you, but I don't know where else to turn."

"I'll have to see if my neighbor can watch Catherine," Maeve said. "Just wait here while I make arrangements."

Mrs. Malloy was buttoning Brian into his coat when Maeve reached the foyer. Catherine stood by, watching forlornly as she always did when her brother left for school.

Seeing Maeve was alone, Mrs. Malloy said, "So you're going with her to the court, are you?"

"How did you know?" Maeve asked in surprise.

"She's a sly one," Mrs. Malloy said. "Plays all helpless to get people to do what she wants."

Was that true? And if it was, why hadn't Maeve recognized it at once? She was usually very good at getting people's measure.

"And that Una, she's twice as bad," Mrs. Malloy continued. "Pretty girls always are. Acts like butter wouldn't melt in her mouth, but she always manages to get her way."

Except with Randolph Pollock, Maeve thought, remembering the bruises. "She'll have to do more than that to get out of a murder charge."

"Will she?" Mrs. Malloy said. "We'll see."

"Hello, there, and who might you be?" a voice called as Gino reached the bottom of the Pollocks' front steps. He looked up to see the beat cop approaching. The fellow was young and Irish, around Gino's age with reddish blond hair, but his uniform wasn't nearly as neat as Gino's. He'd managed to grow a sparse mustache, although his cheeks still looked too smooth to need shaving. He didn't seem pleased to see a copper he didn't recognize on his beat.

"Good morning to you," Gino said, smiling as broadly as he could manage. "I'm Gino Donatelli. How are you this fine morning?"

The fellow had reached him, and Gino noticed he had his nightstick in his hand. He glanced up suspiciously at the house and back at Gino. "What were you doing in there?"

"I spent the night. Mrs. Pollock is worried about somebody breaking in, with only the servants there, so she asked me to guard the place."

The cop frowned. "I thought she was in jail."

"She is."

"And how would you be knowing Mrs. Pollock for her to ask you for help?"

"My girl is a friend of hers," Gino said, the lie coming easily to him. Maeve would spit nails if she heard him claim she was his girl.

"Are you claiming Mrs. Pollock is friends with some Italian girl?" he scoffed. He pronounced it "Eye-talian."

"My girl's Irish. Prettiest red hair you ever saw." That part wasn't a lie, at least. "Say, you wouldn't be Broghan's cousin, would you?"

"And what if I am?" he asked, surprised.

"Then I'd be pleased to meet you. He's been bragging about how you solved this case even before the detectives got here."

This obviously placated the fellow, at least a little. He slipped his nightstick back in its loop at his belt. "It wasn't hard. The wife was right there with blood all over her."

Gino nodded encouragingly. "The maid showed me where the body was, but she didn't know much. What was it like?"

Broghan shrugged like he found murdered men on his beat every day. "It was pretty gruesome."

"The maid said the wife killed him with a frog."

"A frog? Is that what it was? I never saw nothing like it. Somebody said it was Egyptian or some such."

"I'd like to buy you a beer and hear all about it, but it's a little early."

"No, it's not. I know a place," Broghan said, finally returning Gino's grin.

Elizabeth Decker was examining the latest batch of invitations she and Felix had received and trying to decide which events to attend and which to decline, when her maid tapped on the door.

"There's a man to see you, missus."

Elizabeth noted that she had not said a "gentleman" was here to see her. She took the calling card the girl had carried up. It said, GORDON TRUETT.

Elizabeth's heart gave a little lurch when she realized Randolph Pollock's partner was downstairs, the very man they'd all decided they needed to find. She dearly wanted to see him, but when she thought of how angry Felix would be if she saw him alone and how disappointed Maeve and Gino would be if she somehow mishandled this meeting with him, she hesitated. She couldn't send him away, though. He might never return.

"Polly, if you would, please telephone Mr. Decker at his office and ask him to come right home because Mr. Truett is here to see him. Be sure to speak with him directly. Then tell Mr. Truett I am occupied and ask him to wait. Then you may send him up in, oh, say, fifteen minutes."

Polly frowned a little at such a complicated request, but she said, "Yes, ma'am," and hurried off to do her bidding.

Elizabeth looked at the card again. It simply gave Mr. Truett's name and an address that looked like it might be one of those bachelor apartments in the apartment hotels that were springing up all over the city. She used the time she spent waiting to jot down a list of questions she wanted to ask Mr. Truett, although she wasn't at all sure they were the questions that Sarah or Frank Malloy would have asked him. She'd helped them on cases before, but mostly by collecting gossip from society matrons like herself. Truett certainly wasn't a society matron, and she didn't think he'd be very interested in gossiping, at least about himself.

This detecting business was much more complicated than she'd realized.

After what seemed like an hour, the maid tapped on the door and announced Mr. Truett. He came in looking uncertain. He was a youngish man, probably in his early thirties, a bit stout but pleasant-looking, or at least he would have been if he hadn't been wearing an unfortunate plaid jacket and matching pants and had his hair pomaded to within an inch of its life. If he'd been an actor, he would have played the ne'er-do-well friend of the hero.

"Mr. Truett," she said as graciously as she would have greeted the son of her dearest friend. "How kind of you to come. Polly, bring us some tea, please."

"Oh no—" he tried, but Elizabeth ignored him and waved Polly out.

"Please sit down. I'm so sorry to have kept you waiting."

"That's all right." He sat, as ordered, on the sofa, but he perched on the edge, prepared to make a hasty exit if necessary.

She sat down beside him, as if they were old friends, which seemed to disconcert him even more. "You're a friend of Mr. Pollock's, I understand."

"Uh, yes, I am," he said, apparently surprised that she knew this.

She instantly changed her expression to the somber one she used when comforting the bereaved at funerals. "I'm so sorry. Have you heard what happened to poor Mr. Pollock?"

"I, uh, yes. I mean . . . Do you mean that he's dead?"

"Yes, of course. I didn't know if you knew."

"I . . . the servants told me when I . . . That is, I went to meet with Pollock this morning. We're business associates, you see, and they, well, they told me he's dead."

"It hasn't been in the newspapers, so I wasn't sure if you'd heard. What a terrible thing, and how sad for you to find out from servants."

"Yes, a . . . a very terrible thing," he said, although he didn't look as if he really thought so.

Elizabeth smiled gently, pretending she believed he really mourned the death of his associate. This seemed to confuse him even more. "Is something wrong, Mr. Truett? I mean something besides your friend's death?"

"Yes, I mean, no, but . . . Well, I'm a little confused. I told Pollock's servants I needed to get some papers from his office. About our business dealings, you understand. But they told me they had instructions not to let anyone inside, and they sent me here."

"Oh yes. We told them to send any visitors to us, you see."

"But . . . I don't mean to be rude, Mrs. Decker, but what is your relationship with Pollock?"

"Relationship? Why, none at all. I've never even met Mr. Pollock."

He looked so bewildered, Elizabeth almost felt sorry for him. As she had planned, however, a tap at the door announced the arrival of the tea tray she had ordered, which put a temporary stop to their conversation while Polly brought in the tray and Elizabeth served him.

When Truett had a cup of tea that he probably didn't want and a slice of cake he probably did, he said, "If you never met Pollock, why are you . . . ? I mean, why am I here?"

"I don't know why you're here, Mr. Truett. Perhaps if you tell me, I can help you."

He was still gaping at her in confusion when the door opened and Felix stepped in. Elizabeth gave him a welcoming smile, even though his expression was thunderous. "Felix, dear, this is Mr. Truett. He's a business associate of Randolph Pollock."

Truett jumped to his feet and shook hands with Felix, who cast her a look that told her he would deal with her later, before greeting Truett with appropriate courtesy.

Elizabeth poured a cup of tea for Felix without asking and handed it to him when he'd sat down in the chair opposite the sofa. "Mr. Truett went to see Mr. Pollock this morning. The servants broke the news to him about Mr. Pollock's demise and sent him here."

"I see," Felix said. "And you had no idea Pollock was dead?"

"Of course not," Truett said. "I went to see him this morning as usual. We're business associates, you see."

"So my wife just said. I assume you are involved in the Panamanian Railroad scheme."

Truett's eyes widened in surprise, but he said, "Yes. Yes, I am. It's a wonderful investment opportunity for a few discerning individuals."

"I'm sure," Felix said dismissively. "And when was the last time you saw Mr. Pollock?"

He had apparently pegged Felix as a potential investor and needed a moment to catch up. "The last time? Well, uh, last week. Thursday, I believe."

Felix nodded, as if this were important information, which it was if he was telling the truth. "So exactly what can we do for you today, Mr. Truett?"

"Oh, well, as I said, Pollock and I are . . . were business associates. On the Panamanian Railroad project, as you say, Mr. Decker. Pollock's death complicates our dealings, of course, but I'm perfectly able to take over management of the project. I just need to collect the documents from Pollock's office."

Elizabeth noted that Truett was becoming ever so slightly agitated. She almost felt sorry for him again.

"Documents?" Felix said, although Elizabeth was sure he understood, as did she, that Truett wasn't at all interested in mere documents. He most certainly knew about the thousands of dollars Pollock had stored in his safe.

"Yes. Contracts and the official, uh, deeds, and what have you, authorizing the building of the railroad. And the agreements with the investors, of course."

"I'm afraid I have some bad news for you, Mr. Truett," Felix said.

Truett grew a little more agitated. "Bad news?"

"Yes, you see, someone broke into Pollock's house the night before last."

"Broke in?" Truett echoed in alarm.

"Yes, and made rather a mess of Pollock's office."

"What do you mean, a mess?"

"The contents of his desk had been emptied onto the floor and the furniture had been sliced open and the stuffing scattered around. We can't know what, if anything, is missing, of course, but we found the safe empty as well."

How clever of Felix not to claim the safe had been robbed, she thought. He was such a stickler for telling the truth.

"The safe was *empty*?" he asked weakly.

"Yes, and I'm afraid I didn't find the documents you are describing among the papers that had been left behind either. I'm sure it can all be replaced, but I know such things take time, especially when you're dealing with a foreign country."

Truett seemed not to have heard him. "But who could have broken into the house? Who even knew?"

"Who knew Pollock was dead, you mean? We've been wondering that ourselves," Felix said.

"The person who killed him knew, of course," Elizabeth offered.

"But the servants told me she's in jail," Truett said.

"Mrs. Pollock, you mean?" Elizabeth said in surprise. "That's a terrible mistake. She didn't kill him."

"But I thought . . ." Truett apparently decided not to tell them what he thought.

"So how may we help you, Mr. Truett?" Felix asked after an awkward silence.

"I . . . I don't think . . . But tell me, why are you involved in all this? Mrs. Decker said she didn't know Pollock, but surely you must have, Mr. Decker."

"No, I never met the man."

"Then why . . . ?"

"We are friends of Mrs. Pollock's family," Elizabeth said, proud that she could be as careful with the truth as Felix.

Truett blinked several times as he took in this information, but he couldn't seem to summon a reply.

"If you think of anything we can do to help, please don't hesitate to contact us," Felix said.

Poor Truett looked almost ill. He stared at Felix for a long moment and then turned to Elizabeth, but he didn't have anything to say to her either.

"And we will certainly contact you if we learn anything about your documents," she said. "Is this the address where we can find you?" She pulled his calling card from her pocket and held it up.

"Yes," he said, his voice little more than a whisper.

"I know this has been a shock to you," Felix said. "Losing a friend is always difficult, especially under such unpleasant circumstances. Let me show you out."

Truett was too stunned to thank his hostess, but he allowed Felix to escort him from the room. Elizabeth poured herself another cup of tea while she waited for her husband to return. When he did, he carefully shut the door behind him, but before he could speak she said, "He showed up here unannounced, and I was afraid if I sent him away, we'd never see him again."

This took a bit of the wind out of his sails, but he was still upset. "You could have waited until I got here to see him. For God's sake, Elizabeth, the man could be a murderer."

"After what he said, I don't think so, but even if he is, I can't think why he'd want to kill me, especially in my own home, which is full of servants who saw him come in. At any rate, I kept him waiting for fifteen minutes so we were only alone a very short time when you arrived. You made very good time, by the way."

"I ran practically the entire way." He did not sound happy about it either, but his admission made Elizabeth smile.

"Rushing to my rescue. Felix, I'm touched."

He sighed and sank down into his chair. "I forbid you to frighten me like that again."

"I will do my best to obey you, but we must expect other visitors like this. Those men who gave Pollock money will hear about his death, and they'll eventually come here. What shall I do when they arrive, lock them in the cellar until you get home?"

"Don't be ridiculous."

"I'm not being ridiculous. I need to know."

He sighed again. "Perhaps I will have to stay home until this is settled."

Broghan took Gino to a bar a couple blocks away. It wasn't open this early in the morning, of course, but the proprietor let them in at Broghan's knock. He didn't look happy to see them, but he wasn't going to offend the cop to whom he probably paid protection money. He gave them each a beer before going back to sweeping the floor.

They settled at a table in the corner.

"So how did you come to find the body?" Gino asked, not having to feign his interest.

"One of them colored maids come running out of the house, screaming her head off. I was just around the corner, so naturally, I went to see what was happening."

"Did she have blood on her?"

Broghan frowned at the question. "Why would she?"

"You didn't see any then?"

"I didn't look." Gino's questions annoyed him. "I followed her back to the house and went inside. That's when I saw the two of them."

"In the parlor?"

"Yeah, in the parlor. She was sitting on the floor and had his head in her lap, of all things. That awful, bloody thing, and she was all red with it."

"And he was dead?"

"As dead could be. His eyes was open, like he was surprised or something. Never saw anything like it."

"What was she doing?"

"Her?" He wrinkled his forehead with the effort of remembering. "Just sitting there. Singing or something."

"Singing?"

"Yeah. It was the damnedest thing. She didn't even look up when I come in, just kept singing to him."

"She was probably in shock."

"I guess she was. Isn't every day a woman smashes her husband's head in."

"What made you think she did it?"

"Who else was there? The servants said nobody else was in the house, and the two of them was fighting. They was always fighting, from what they said. I guess she just finally had enough."

"And it was the back of his head that was bashed in?"

"Yeah, she come up behind him with the . . . frog, did you say it was?"

"That's what one maid said. The other said a lizard with a lady's face."

Broghan shrugged. "I didn't look at it real close. It was green. Some kind of stone and just the right thing for smashing a head, if you ask me."

"What did she say happened? The wife, I mean."

"She never said nothing at all. I told you she was singing, and when I talked to her, she just ignored me, like I wasn't even there."

"She must've said something."

"Not a word. Not a peep. Not even when the detectives got there and started shouting at her. When they took Pollock away, she started crying, but she still wouldn't talk."

"So they took her to the Tombs," Gino said.

"Yeah, because she must've done it," Broghan said. "Who else could it have been?"

7

"THANK YOU SO MUCH, MR. NICHOLSON," MRS. O'NEILL said after the hearing, when she and Una were safely ensconced in his office and his clerk had brought in an extra chair for Maeve. Maeve had decided she needed to hear what Nicholson had planned. "That was so kind of you to get my Una out of the jail."

"Just doing my job, Mrs. O'Neill," he assured her. "And you're the one to be thanked since you paid the bail."

"What happens now?" Una asked. She'd fixed herself up real nice for the bond hearing. Her hair curled prettily around her lovely face, and she'd managed to get all the wrinkles out of her dress. It fit her well, too, showing off her shape. No wonder the man who owned the cigar store had picked her out of all the girls at the factory. No wonder Randolph Pollock had married her. And no wonder the judge had melted like butter on a hot stove when Nicholson claimed she was no threat to anyone.

"In a few minutes, you can go home, but I wanted to speak with you about the case. After today, the newspapers will have discovered you. Up until now, the police assumed you'd confess and there would be no trial, but now, it's clear there will be."

"But I didn't kill my husband," Una said. "Why do I have to go to trial?"

"Because the police think you did, and the district attorney thinks he has the evidence to prove it. The trial will be of great public interest because people are always interested when a woman kills her husband."

"But I didn't kill him," she repeated. Maeve would've been angry by this point, but Una just pouted prettily.

"Of course you didn't," Nicholson said. "Tell me, Mrs. Pollock, do you have a lover?"

"A lover? What are you talking about? I'm a married woman."

"Lots of married women have lovers, and if you do, the reporters will find him, so it's better if you tell me about him now."

"The *reporters*?" Mrs. O'Neill said. "You mean newspaper reporters?"

"Yes, they'll be investigating you, Mrs. Pollock, because the reporters are much better at investigating than the police are. They have more manpower, for one reason, and more money to spend, for another. Hearst at the *Journal* will probably put the whole Wrecking Crew on this."

"What's a wrecking crew?" Una asked in alarm.

"That's what they call the group of reporters they send out to cover a big story. It's dozens of reporters and sketch artists and photographers. They'll talk to everyone you ever knew and uncover every secret you ever had."

"I have no secrets and I have no lovers," Una said. "I'm a

respectable married woman who has been falsely accused of murder."

"It would help," Maeve said, surprising everyone because they had obviously forgotten she was even in the room, "if you could tell us who did kill your husband."

For a moment, annoyance flickered across Una's lovely face, but only for a moment. She turned back to her attorney. "I'm sorry, Mr. Nicholson, but I still can't remember anything about it. I remember getting up that morning and having breakfast, but then I don't remember anything else until I was at the jail." She slipped a handkerchief from her sleeve with practiced ease and dabbed at her eyes. "I still can't believe dear Randolph is gone."

"The servants said you were arguing," he said, unmoved. He'd seen gallons of tears shed in this office.

"But we never argued, so that can't be true. Perhaps he was arguing with someone else, the person who killed . . ." Her voice broke, and she pressed the handkerchief to her lips as she fought back more tears.

"Maybe you can tell me if he had any enemies, Mrs. Pollock. Anyone who'd want to harm him."

"Heavens, no. Everyone liked Randolph. He was such a pleasant man. We often entertained his business clients, and they always enjoyed his company."

"What kind of business was your husband in, Mrs. Pollock?"

"I don't know. He said it was too complicated for me to understand, and he never discussed business in front of me. I only know he was very successful and that his clients were very happy."

Maeve wondered how happy they were going to be when they found out there was no railroad in Panama. "What about Truett?" she asked.

Una looked at her in surprise again. She was probably *trying* to forget Maeve was there. "I can't imagine Mr. Truett would have any reason to harm Randolph."

"Who is this Truett?" Nicholson asked.

"A business associate of my husband's," Una said sweetly. Plainly, someone as pretty as she could know nothing of business.

"And how about Adam Yorke?" Maeve asked when Una would have dismissed her again.

"Who?" Una asked, but she didn't fool Maeve. She knew who he was, all right.

"The brother of Pollock's first wife," Maeve explained cheerfully.

"*First* wife?" Mrs. O'Neill cried. "Una is his first wife."

"I'm afraid not," Maeve said. "Mr. Yorke's sister Cecelia was married to Pollock before she disappeared."

"What do you mean, disappeared?" Nicholson asked, his broad face turning a dangerous shade of red.

"I mean Pollock claims she died, but he never notified the family or put it in the newspapers, and he wouldn't say where she's buried either."

"She died in childbirth," Una said. "Randolph told me all about it. But that was years ago. Is this Mr. Yorke the man who came to see Randolph the other day?"

Maeve met her gaze with interest. "Yes. Mr. Yorke called on your husband shortly before he was killed. Could it have been the day he died?" she added, wondering if Una would confirm it was the very same day.

Una furrowed her brow. "Oh my, I do remember he called, but was it that day? Everything is so muddled. But it must have been! This Mr. Yorke must be the person the servants heard Randolph arguing with that morning!"

Was it true? Could Yorke have really been there that morning? And if the servants could confirm it, maybe he really was the one who had killed Pollock.

"Well, now, that's good news," Nicholson said. "We'll have to look into this Mr. Yorke."

"Oh yes," Mrs. O'Neill said with forced enthusiasm. "I'm sure he's the one who killed poor Mr. Pollock."

"Whether he is or not is not my concern," Nicholson said. "But having someone else we can tell the jurors about, somebody who was in the house and who had a reason to hate Pollock, well, that's all we need to get Mrs. Pollock acquitted."

"But I don't want to go to trial at all," Una said.

"Then find out who really killed your husband," Nicholson said.

"I DON'T LIKE THAT MAN," UNA SAID WHEN THEY WERE on the sidewalk outside.

"He isn't very nice," her mother agreed, "but I'm told he's the best attorney in the city."

"If he was, I would be free now."

"At least you're not in jail anymore," Maeve reminded her. "Not many accused killers get out on bond."

Una sighed. "I'd like to go home now."

"Of course you would, dear," her mother said. "I'll be so happy to have you back with me again. It will be just like before."

Una's lovely face crinkled in distaste. "I'm not going home with you. I'm going to my own home."

Even Maeve was surprised at that. "You want to go back to the house where your husband was murdered?"

"It's my *home*. Randolph bought it for me, and he'd want me to be happy there."

From what she knew about Randolph, Maeve doubted that very much, but she said, "I guess it's a good thing we made the servants stay, then."

"What do you mean?"

"I mean they wanted to leave, so we were going to let them go and close up the house."

Now Una really was angry, although she knew how to control it pretty well. Except for the red blotches on her cheeks and the icy sparkle in her eyes, Maeve could hardly tell at all. "Who are you to make decisions about my house and my servants?"

"We just thought it was for the best, with you, uh, gone, and everything," her mother hastily explained. "Who would pay them, after all?"

"I'll pay them," Una said. "I need a cab." She looked around.

"Do you have money to pay for one?" Maeve asked, certain she didn't.

Una frowned. "Give me some money," she told her mother.

"Paying your bail took almost everything I had," her mother said, digging in her purse. "I only have a few dollars left."

"You won't need that. You can walk home from here." Una snatched the bills from her mother's unresisting fingers.

So much for the "good girl" Mrs. O'Neill had described to Maeve that first day.

"Then you probably want to stop and pick up your trunk on the way," Maeve said.

"What do you mean?" Una asked suspiciously.

"I mean we packed up all your belongings, and I took them home with me for safekeeping, because we were planning to close up your house. You and I can share a cab and you can drop me off at my house and pick up your trunk on your way."

Una plainly didn't care for this arrangement at all, but she obviously had no choice. She stepped to the curb and hailed a cab with such ease that Maeve understood instantly what an advantage true beauty really was.

Una was climbing into the cab when her mother hurried over. "Don't forget your things," Mrs. O'Neill called, holding up the bundle of Una's belongings that she had brought over from the jail.

Una took it from her without a word and found her seat in the cab.

"I'll keep you informed of what happens," Maeve told Mrs. O'Neill.

"Thank you for all your help, Miss Smith," she said, her gaze darting nervously to Una in the cab. "I guess I can come to visit you now," she told her daughter.

"Suit yourself," Una replied, not even glancing her way.

Maeve climbed into the cab and gave the driver the address on Bank Street. Then she settled back against the seat and looked over at her companion in the snug confines of the cab.

Una no longer looked like the sweet young thing who had charmed the judge. Her glare was sharp enough to draw blood. "Who *are* you?"

"I told you, your mother hired me to help. I work for a detective agency." Or at least she would when Frank and Sarah Malloy got back from their honeymoon and opened it.

"How did my mother hire a detective agency? She doesn't have any money."

If she knew that, didn't Una wonder how her mother had paid her bail? "We worked it out. Your mother is good friends with the owner's mother."

She gave an unladylike snort. "Charity, then. Well, I don't need your charity, and I don't need a detective agency."

"Not even if we're trying to find out who really killed your husband?"

She gave Maeve a long, considering look as the cab made its weary way through the clogged city streets. At last she said,

"I thought you decided that fellow killed Randolph. What's his name, Cecelia's brother?"

"Mr. Yorke," Maeve supplied. "I think we just suggested that he might have. He admits he was there, which seems odd if he really is the killer, though."

"Why?"

"Because the killer should claim he wasn't there at all."

"But if people know he was, it's foolish to claim he wasn't."

Maeve had to admit, she had a point. Una couldn't claim she wasn't there, of course. She could only claim she didn't remember what happened, which saved her from remembering that she killed her husband. If, of course, she did kill him. Or maybe she didn't want to remember who actually killed him, which was equally interesting. "We were going to close the house because there was no money to pay your servants. How will you keep the place going without your husband?"

Una's expression gave nothing away. "That's really none of your business, but I'll manage."

Which meant that Una probably knew about the money in Pollock's safe. And if she did, was that another reason to kill a husband who regularly beat her?

Of course it was.

Maeve knew from growing up in the tenements that most women stayed with abusive husbands because they needed the man to support them and their children. Even childless, Una probably would have been afraid to leave Pollock. Could she have gone back to her job at the cigar store or even the one at the factory? Probably not. No one wanted married women in those jobs. She would have had to bear the shame of a failed marriage, too. And that's assuming Pollock allowed her to leave him in the first place. A husband could even get the law to bring a runaway wife home, if he wanted to.

Maeve looked at the smug smile on Una's lovely face and

decided she wouldn't mention that the safe in Pollock's office was now empty. That money probably didn't belong to Pollock anyway, so it was just as well for Una to think it had been stolen.

Una didn't have much to say as the cab made its way to Bank Street. She perked up a bit when they stopped at the Malloy house, however. Even though it wasn't a fashionable neighborhood, the house itself was rather impressive. "You live here?"

"Yes," Maeve said, offering no other explanation. She asked the cab driver to fetch Una's trunk from the front hallway, but she didn't invite Una inside to warm up while he did it. Maybe she would have felt kinder if Una hadn't taken her mother's last cent for cab fare. She tipped the driver generously when he'd wrestled the trunk into the cab.

"I trust I'll find *all* of my belongings in the trunk," Una said with what she must have thought was a look of warning.

Maeve smiled, even though Una had just accused her of being a thief. "Don't you remember how I got your things back for you when you were in the Tombs?"

"Oh yes, thank you for that." She didn't sound particularly grateful, but Maeve didn't challenge her. "It's been a pleasure meeting you, Miss Smith. Perhaps we'll encounter one another again sometime."

"Perhaps we will," Maeve said, mocking her, although Una didn't seem to notice.

Maeve stood on the front porch and watched the cab drive away. Now that she thought about it, someone should really be there to see Una's reaction when she discovered the break-in and the missing money, assuming she knew about the money in the first place. Maeve realized she should have offered to deliver the trunk instead of letting Una get it herself, but it was too late now. So who could break the news about the robbery instead?

Gino would go to the house this evening unless he stopped

at the Malloy house first and found out Una had been released. But that would be too late to get her reaction. No, someone should be at the house to greet her when she arrived, and Maeve knew just who that should be.

"IF I HADN'T BEEN AT HOME WHEN MAEVE TELEPHONED, would you have come here alone?" Felix asked as they made their way up the front steps at the Pollock house.

Elizabeth smiled innocently. "Of course not, dear. I would have telephoned you to come home, just as I did when Mr. Truett came to call."

He didn't look like he believed that, but he was too gentlemanly to call her a liar. Instead he gave the brass knocker a resounding thump. The door opened almost instantly, and the maid greeted them with a cautious smile.

"Good afternoon to you both. Please, come in."

"Good afternoon," Elizabeth said. "Hattie, is it?"

"Yes, ma'am. It's nice to see you folks. I recognized your carriage right off. Did you want to speak to all of us?" Her hopeful smile reminded Elizabeth that she had promised to provide them with letters of reference and pay their wages so they could leave.

"Yes, but not for the reason you might think. I do have some good news for you, though." At least she hoped it was good news.

After some discussion about where they should meet, since the servants didn't like going into the parlor anymore and Mr. Pollock's office was still a mess, Hattie showed them to the dining room and went to fetch the rest of the servants.

"Do you really think they'll be happy to hear their mistress is coming home?" Felix asked, strolling around the room to examine the furnishings.

"I think it will be informative to see their reactions, at least. This is a pleasant room."

The table was large enough to seat a dozen people, although the thin layer of dust on its bare surface gave evidence that it hadn't been used in a while. A matching sideboard and glass-fronted cabinet sat against the walls. Dishes and crystal in the cabinet glittered in the light from the electric chandelier. Pale winter sunlight filtered through the lace curtains that lined the dark blue velvet drapes on the tall windows. When she looked out, Elizabeth recognized that the lace was as much to block the view of the small, weedy yard and the alley behind the house as it was to keep curious eyes from looking in.

After a few minutes, the servants filed in. Elizabeth had almost forgotten about the boot boy, Eddie. He looked around as if he expected to see someone else in the room, and frowned when he realized it was only her and Felix.

"Is this everyone?" Elizabeth asked, thinking there should be more.

"All but Jane," Hattie said. "She left. Snuck away this morning. Took all her things with her."

Elizabeth supposed she couldn't blame the poor girl, although she must have been desperate indeed if she left without her pay and a reference.

The remaining servants huddled together uncertainly just inside the door. She and Felix moved closer, but that just seemed to make them more nervous.

Felix cleared his throat. "Mrs. Decker and I just wanted you to know that Mrs. Pollock has been released from jail after paying her bond. She'll be arriving here shortly."

The two women weren't sure if this was good news or not, but the boy obviously thought so. He broke into a huge grin.

"She's coming to stay, then?" Hattie asked.

"That's my understanding," Elizabeth said.

"At least for the time being," Felix added.

"But her clothes is all gone," the cook said. "That girl took them."

"I believe Mrs. Pollock has retrieved her trunk and is bringing it with her," Elizabeth said.

"So she's coming home for good?" the boy asked.

Elizabeth exchanged a glance with Felix. What should they tell them? What was the truth? "She may have to go on trial, but for now, she'll be here."

Only the boy seemed happy. He was probably too young to understand how serious the situation was. Or perhaps he simply admired his mistress so much, he was happy to have her back no matter what the circumstances.

Elizabeth sent the servants back to their duties, and she and Felix waited in the dining room until someone knocked on the front door less than an hour later. They stepped out into the hallway just as Hattie opened the door to a lovely young woman.

"Welcome home, missus," Hattie said.

"Thank you. It's good to be here," she said.

The other servants had followed Hattie to the door, and Una Pollock stopped to greet them.

"Oh, Velvet, could you fix me something to eat? I haven't had a bite all day. Jane . . . Where's Jane?" she asked with a frown.

"She gone, missus," Hattie said. "She left this morning."

"What a bother. Oh well. Hattie, my trunk is in the cab. Would you have the driver carry it upstairs? Eddie, it's so nice to see you." To Elizabeth's surprise, she touched him lightly on the cheek. Elizabeth couldn't see his expression, but she imagined he was thrilled by the attention.

Then Una swept past them, probably intending to head toward the stairs, but she stopped dead when she saw the

Deckers waiting for her. Her lovely face creased into a frown. "Who are you?"

"Felix Decker, at your service, Mrs. Pollock. And this is my wife, Elizabeth."

She looked them up and down, silently evaluating them. Elizabeth knew this because she would have done the same thing had she found two strangers unexpectedly in her home. Elizabeth knew exactly what she saw: two perfectly respectable, expensively dressed, well-mannered people. Una's expression softened from suspicion to caution. "Why are you here?"

"We've been looking after the house while you were gone. Your mother asked for help, you see, and—"

"Are you private detectives?" Her disbelief was obvious.

Elizabeth looked at Felix. Where had she gotten that idea?

"We're friends of your mother's," Felix said, although he hadn't actually met Mrs. O'Neill yet.

"When we heard you'd been released, we wanted to be here to greet you in case you had any concerns," Elizabeth said.

"Because of what happened," Felix added.

"What did happen?" She fluttered her eyes at him in a way Elizabeth recognized. She had used it herself in her younger days when she wanted to charm a man.

"Perhaps we should show her," Elizabeth said to break the spell, in case Una really was casting a spell on him.

"Show me what?"

"This way, my dear," Felix said, confirming Elizabeth's theory about a spell. He gently led her to the office door, which was closed.

She hung back a bit, obviously reluctant to see whatever he was equally reluctant to show her. Then he stepped forward and opened the door and even Elizabeth gasped at the chaos inside.

"Good heavens," Una said, moving past Felix and stepping into the office. "Look at those chairs! They're ruined."

Which struck Elizabeth as an odd thing to say, but Felix was still entranced. "Yes, they are," he said. "We think whoever broke in was looking for something."

"Inside the chairs?" she asked, still oddly obsessed with the ruined chairs and missing the larger implications.

"Yes, but more importantly, in the safe." He gestured toward the safe, which stood empty, with its door wide open.

"Oh." She batted her eyes again. "They robbed his safe, too."

"I'm afraid so, and whatever was inside is gone."

Elizabeth had to admire the way he'd managed to tell the complete truth. Perhaps he wasn't as entranced as he seemed.

"Oh, that's . . . terrible," Una said faintly.

"Do you know what was inside?" Felix asked.

"I . . . Valuables, I'm sure."

"Money?"

"Perhaps. Mr. Pollock never discussed such things with me, you understand. But wouldn't he have kept his money in the bank?"

"That seems likely," Felix said. "We didn't contact the police about the robbery because we didn't know what might have been stolen, if anything, and we didn't know your wishes. We left the room just as we found it, though, so if you'd like to send for them now . . ."

"Oh no," she said. "I've seen quite enough of the police, thank you. And I can't imagine there was much of value here."

Not much of value? Could she really have not known about the money in the safe? Even if she didn't, however, shouldn't she be upset about the robbery itself? Elizabeth tried to imagine coming home to discover someone had broken into her house. She would have been hysterical merely at the violation of it, even if nothing at all had been stolen.

Eddie and the cab driver were bringing the trunk in, so Elizabeth had to step into the office to get out of their way.

As she did, she saw Una look sharply at Eddie but he seemed intent on his task and didn't even glance in her direction.

The other servants had dispersed, except for Hattie, who waited in the hall. When the men had started up the stairs with the trunk, Una stepped out of the office.

"Hattie, you can put that room to rights now." She turned to Elizabeth and Felix. "Thank you so much for taking the time to see me, but I'm sure you'll understand when I tell you that I am exhausted after my ordeal and really unfit for company."

"Of course," Elizabeth said. "Please let us know if you need anything at all. Hattie has my card."

"I'm sure the cabbie will be happy to take you home as soon as he's finished," Una said.

"That won't be necessary," Felix said. "We have our carriage."

"Oh," Una said as something seemed to register with her. "I saw it outside, but I had no idea it belonged to my own visitors. I must thank you again for your concern. You have been very kind."

So, Una had finally decided the Deckers were worth cultivating. "Don't thank us," Elizabeth said. "You should thank your mother for bringing your case to our attention. Come along, Felix. We'll leave Mrs. Pollock to recover from her ordeal."

Hattie followed them to the door to help them into their coats. By the time they reached the sidewalk outside, their coachman had drawn up to receive them. When they were tucked inside, Elizabeth decided to test the waters. "She's a lovely young woman, isn't she?"

Felix smiled. "I liked her much better after she realized we were wealthy."

This made her laugh, as he had intended. "Oh, Felix, I was afraid you were completely besotted."

"I'm sure I wouldn't be the first."

"No, she must have had a lot of admirers when she worked in the cigar store. I think it's interesting that the one she chose mistreated her, though."

"Yes, that was unfortunate, although he seems to have gotten his just deserts."

Elizabeth sighed. "I wonder if that will have any influence on a jury if she does go to trial."

"I'd like to think so. If she was acting in self-defense, they would have to let her go."

"So you would think. But here we are, assuming she's guilty." Elizabeth shook off her dark thoughts. "We need to go see Maeve. She was going to send a message to Gino to stop there after he's finished work today."

"Why don't we invite them to our place for supper instead?"

"What a good idea, although that means I don't get to see the children."

"Tomorrow is another day," he reminded her with a smile.

GINO WASN'T SURPRISED TO SEE THE DECKERS' CARRIAGE outside the Malloy house when he arrived. The coachman tipped his hat and Gino waved. Maeve opened the door before he knocked. The children, she told him over their squeals of delight, had been watching for him.

"Sorry I'm late. I got stuck on a case."

"That's all right." She explained the Deckers' invitation to dinner.

"I thought I was supposed to go see Yorke this evening."

"I guess that can wait. The Deckers have some important things to tell us. They eat dinner late, so you've got time to play with the children for a bit before we leave."

When Gino had paid adequate attention to the children, he

and Maeve finally were able to make their escape in the carriage, heading uptown.

"This is so much nicer than a cab," Maeve said, stroking the fine wool lap robe.

"Much more private, too," he said, remembering his claim that Maeve was his girl and wishing it were true.

He thought she gave him a look, but it was too dark to be sure. "Yes, we don't have to worry about little ears hearing what we say. I think that's why Mrs. Decker suggested we go to their house."

Gino managed not to sigh his disappointment that she didn't get his hint. Or had chosen to ignore it. "Your note said Mrs. Pollock got released today. How did that happen?"

"Nicholson got them to hold a bond hearing, and Mrs. O'Neill posted it."

"How much?"

"Just four hundred, which was good, because that's all she had left of what I gave her. The funny thing was, Una didn't even ask her where she got the money to pay it."

"That is funny. What did she say when she found out Pollock's safe was empty? Or did you tell her you have the money?"

"I didn't tell her any of that. I asked Mrs. Decker to meet her at her house and break the news to her, so she'll tell us what happened this afternoon. Gino, Una isn't as . . . as nice as we thought."

"What do you mean?"

"I mean she was mean to her mother after the poor woman got her bailed out of jail, and she wasn't very nice to me when she found out I had all her belongings."

"Maybe she was out of sorts from being in jail. The Tombs isn't the nicest place to start with, and now there's all that construction noise going on . . ."

"I tried to make excuses for her, too, but . . . Well, even Mrs. Malloy said she was a sly one."

"Mrs. Malloy doesn't like anybody."

"That's not true. She likes me and Mrs. Brandt—"

"She's Mrs. Malloy now."

"Mrs. Frank Malloy," she corrected herself, "and Brian and Catherine, and she adores you."

"She does not!"

"Of course she does. Why do you think she tries to feed you every time you walk in the door?"

Gino had no answer for that. Women were always trying to feed him. He'd never thought of it as a sign of adoration.

"Anyway," Maeve said, "Una wasn't nice to me or her mother today, for whatever reason. She also told me she doesn't need a detective agency, even though Nicholson told her the only way to avoid a trial is to find out who really killed her husband."

"So are we going to quit?"

"Una didn't hire us. Her mother did, so until Mrs. O'Neill fires us, I say we keep on working. Even if she isn't nice, Una shouldn't go to prison if she's innocent. Did you find out anything interesting last night?"

He reached into his pocket and pulled out the list of names he'd copied from the ledger. "I got addresses for all the men who invested in the Panama deal."

"That's wonderful!" she said. "Where did you find them?"

He told her about spending the night in Pollock's bedroom.

"I should've thought to search it when I was there," Maeve said, "but the maid was with me the whole time. Do you know Una warned me that she'd better find all her belongings in the trunk, as if I'd steal something from her?"

"No wonder you don't like her."

She seemed pleased by that, although he couldn't be sure in the dark. "What else did you find out?"

"I found out Yorke really was at Pollock's house the morning he was killed. The maid Hattie told me."

"And Una remembered that, too."

"You mean she remembered what happened? Did she say who killed Pollock?"

"She still claims she doesn't remember what happened to Pollock, but at least we know for sure that Yorke was there that morning."

He told her about his conversation with Broghan and the maids' descriptions of the murder weapon, and by then they were at the Decker house.

The maid took them right up to the Deckers' family parlor. Mr. Decker offered Gino a whiskey, which he accepted, and Maeve a sherry, which she declined.

When they were settled, Mr. Decker handed Gino a section of newspaper. "I happened to see this just now." He pointed to a small headline on page three of the *World*: "Widow Released on Bond."

As Gino scanned it, Maeve leaned over to read it, too. It said little beyond the fact that Una had been charged with murdering her husband, but they all knew what it meant.

"The reporters will be beating down her door tomorrow," Gino said.

"And all the people who invested in Pollock's railroad scheme will know he's dead," Maeve said.

Mrs. Decker said, "Then we need to make plans. Dinner will be ready shortly, so why don't we start sharing the information we have? Perhaps we should share it in the order in which we received it. That means, Gino, you go first, then Maeve, and then us."

Gino didn't like being the center of attention, but he told them about meeting the Pollocks' servants.

"What did you think of the boy, Eddie?" Mrs. Decker asked.

"He's moony over Mrs. Pollock."

Maeve made a disgusted noise, and Gino bit back a grin.

"You're right," Mrs. Decker said. "She encourages it, too."

"Does she?" he asked with interest. "I guess he'll never say a bad thing about her, then."

"Or tell anyone if she killed Pollock," Maeve said.

The Deckers gaped at her in surprise.

"Do you really think she did?" Mrs. Decker asked.

"Maeve doesn't like her," Gino said.

"Neither does Elizabeth," Mr. Decker confided, earning a swat from his wife.

"I can't wait to meet her," Gino confided back, earning a glare from Maeve, which heartened him to no end.

"Tell them about the list," Maeve said, sounding a little testy.

Gino explained how he'd toured the house and then searched the master bedroom. "I wrote down all the addresses for the men on our list. Those were the only names in the book except for Truett, so I wrote down his address, too."

He pulled out the list and handed it to Mr. Decker.

"We already have Mr. Truett's address," Mrs. Decker said. "He tried to get into the Pollock house, so the servants sent him here."

"What did he want?"

The Deckers exchanged a glance. "He said he wanted some important papers from Pollock's house," Mr. Decker said. "But we think he probably wants the money."

"Did you tell him about the robbery?" Maeve asked.

"Yes, and he seemed very surprised to hear about it," Mr. Decker said.

"Surprised and upset," Mrs. Decker added, "so I'm sure he knew about the money."

"Of course he did," Maeve said. "He was Pollock's partner,

after all, which is why I thought he was most likely the one who broke into the house."

"But he just found out Mr. Pollock was dead this morning when the servants told him," Mrs. Decker said.

"That's what he told you," Gino said, "but we don't know if that's the truth."

"He seemed quite upset when I told him about the robbery, though," Mr. Decker said. "I'd wager he didn't know about that until then."

"If he's involved with a phony investment scheme, he knows how to be convincing," Maeve said.

"Do you think he could have been the one who broke into the house?" Mr. Decker asked.

"It could've been anybody, as far as we know right now," Gino said. "We can't rule anybody out yet."

"Could he be the one who killed Mr. Pollock, too?" Mrs. Decker asked.

"If he was the one who broke into the house, then he certainly killed Pollock. How else would he have known Pollock was dead?" Maeve said.

"Maybe," Gino said. "But somebody else might've killed Pollock, and if Truett found out somehow that Pollock was dead, he'd want to get the money out of the house as soon as possible."

"And if he was the one who killed him, he'd still want to get the money," Maeve argued.

"And maybe poor Mr. Truett really did just find out Pollock was dead today and just found out the money is missing," Mrs. Decker said.

"So the truth is that we still don't have any idea who killed Pollock," Mr. Decker said.

"Well, I also found out from the servants that Yorke did visit Pollock on the very morning he died," Gino said.

"And Una said she remembered that when I mentioned it to her today. So he could have done it."

"I can't believe he did," Mrs. Decker said. "You didn't see his face when we told him Mr. Pollock was dead. He was devastated."

"But he hated Pollock," Gino said.

"I'm sure he did," Mr. Decker said, "and I honestly think he might have wanted to murder Pollock himself, but not until he found out what happened to his sister. Oh, I just remembered, you were going to see him tonight, weren't you?"

"Yes, and now that we know he was there that morning, we need to at least ask him if he saw anybody else. But I guess that'll have to wait until tomorrow," Gino said. "Do we have any other ideas about who could be the killer?"

Mr. Decker held up the paper Gino had given him. "It could also be anyone on this list."

"Any of them who found out the scheme was a fraud, at least," Mrs. Decker said.

"I see you found first names, too. That will help," Mr. Decker said, scanning the list. Then he suddenly stiffened and his face went white.

"Felix, what is it?" his wife asked.

"One of these men . . . he's dead."

8

"WHAT DO YOU MEAN, HE'S DEAD?" MRS. DECKER ASKED.

"He killed himself," Mr. Decker said. "Last week. He's a member of my club, and that's all anyone was talking about for days."

Mrs. Decker took the list from him. "Oscar Norwalk?" she guessed. "I thought he had heart failure."

"That's the story his family gave out, but the truth is that he hanged himself."

"Good heavens!"

"His valet found him in his dressing room."

"Why did he do it?"

"No one knows, or at least no one did know. Now I'm wondering if he found out he'd been cheated by Pollock."

"How awful," Maeve said.

"How much had he given Pollock?" Gino asked.

Mrs. Decker looked at the list again. "Five thousand."

"Would that be enough to ruin him?" Gino asked.

"You wouldn't think so, unless it was the last in a long line of bad investments," Mr. Decker said. "I'll have to see what I can find out."

"We should call on his family," Mrs. Decker said.

"That's a good idea," Maeve said.

"Do you know anyone else on the list?" Mrs. Decker asked.

"Lawrence Zimmerman, although I only know him slightly. I think Oscar introduced us, as a matter of fact."

"You should go see him, too," Mrs. Decker said. "At the very least, you can suggest that he might get some of his investment back."

"I would be happy to reassure all of these men of that very thing," Mr. Decker said, gesturing to the list.

"Caroline Norwalk might be very grateful for that news," Mrs. Decker said. She carefully laid the paper down on the table beside her, as if afraid of further damaging the men listed on it. "What else did you learn, Gino?"

Gino was only too happy to talk about something besides suicide. He told them what he'd learned from the servants and from Broghan.

"Do the police have the statue that killed him?" Mrs. Decker asked.

"Probably the district attorney has it by now."

"I'd like to see it. It sounds like an interesting piece," she said.

"Probably Egyptian," Mr. Decker said.

"That's what Broghan said."

"Many people like the Egyptian style, but I've never cared for it," Mrs. Decker said.

"If the maids couldn't tell if it was a frog or a lizard," Gino said, "I don't think I'd care for it either."

"What else did you learn?" Mr. Decker asked.

"I think that's everything. Maeve had an interesting day, though."

Maeve told them about her early-morning visit from Mrs. O'Neill and the bond hearing. "Nicholson was very interested to hear the story about Pollock's first wife disappearing and her brother coming to see Pollock. He thinks he can convince the jury that Mr. Yorke had more reason to kill Pollock than his wife did."

"If the jury doesn't know that he beat her, Nicholson may be right," Mr. Decker said.

"But you said you were sure Yorke didn't kill him," Maeve said. "We couldn't let him be arrested if he didn't do it."

"Just because Nicholson makes a jury think Yorke could have killed Pollock doesn't mean the police will charge him, even if Mrs. Pollock is acquitted," Mr. Decker said.

"That's right," Gino said. "If the police are sure she did it, they won't charge anyone else, no matter what the jury decides."

"I felt so sorry for Una when you told me her husband beat her," Mrs. Decker said. "But now . . ."

"We promised Mrs. O'Neill we'd help," Maeve reminded her. "And if she really didn't kill her husband, she still needs that help."

"I suppose you're right."

"I guess she was pretty upset when she saw her husband's office," Gino said.

"Not nearly as upset as I expected," Mrs. Decker said.

"Yes," her husband said. "She was more concerned about the damaged chairs than she was about the empty safe."

"Really?" Maeve asked. "Do you think she didn't know what was in the safe?"

"She seemed to think her husband would have kept his money in a bank," Mr. Decker said. "So we didn't correct her."

"She didn't even have money for cab fare today," Maeve

remembered, "but when I asked her how she intended to pay the servants, she said she'd manage."

"Maybe Pollock did have money in a bank," Gino said.

"We didn't find any record of that," Mr. Decker said.

"Oh dear," Mrs. Decker said. "I just happened to think that whoever broke in must have known about the money in the safe, even if Una didn't, so they must be wondering where it is, too."

"And they might think Una knows where it is," Gino said.

"And if they saw the article in the newspaper, they know she's at her house alone and unprotected . . . ," Mrs. Decker said.

Gino sighed. "I guess I need to go back over there tonight."

Maeve didn't look happy about that, he was gratified to note. "Is it really our job to protect her? She's not actually alone in the house, after all."

"And you haven't had supper yet," Mrs. Decker said.

"The Pollocks' cook will give me something to eat, and I don't think her servants will be much help if someone comes in looking for the money. I'd better go." He rose.

"I should go with you," Mr. Decker said, rising as well. "To introduce you to Mrs. Pollock."

"Felix, dear, the servants know him," Mrs. Decker said with some amusement. "And Gino is a police officer. He certainly doesn't need help protecting someone."

Gino could see how much Mr. Decker wanted to take some action, but also how foolish his wife thought he was being to rush off to rescue Mrs. Pollock. "Is she really that beautiful?" he said, making it a joke.

Mr. Decker smiled. "Not beautiful enough to make a man forget himself entirely, I guess. I'll get the carriage for you."

"I can get there faster on the El. Mrs. Decker, I'm very sorry to miss having supper with you."

"And we're very sorry to miss your company. We'll make it up to you when this is all over."

He glanced at Maeve and was happy to see her disgruntled frown. "I'll try to get away early in the morning so I can stop by and tell you what happened before I go on duty."

"I'll be very interested to hear your opinion of Mrs. Pollock," she said with just the slightest edge in her voice.

He gave her a wink that brought color to her cheeks and made Mrs. Decker cough to cover a laugh.

"Won't you need some things if you're going to spend the night there again?" Mrs. Decker asked.

"I still have my bag from last night. I left it in the carriage."

"I'll send one of the maids for it. Let me see you out," Mr. Decker said.

Gino caught Maeve's eye one last time and was relieved that she still looked very unhappy to see him go.

"Do you think she's really in danger?" Maeve asked Mrs. Decker when the men were gone.

"I think she well may be. Someone was looking for the money from the investments, and they didn't find it. Whether Una knew it was there or not, she is the most logical person to know where else Pollock might have hidden it, and we're the only ones who know she doesn't."

So many things about Una Pollock didn't make sense. "I really expected her to be upset when she found out the house had been robbed."

"I did, too. Of course, if she didn't know the money was in the safe, she couldn't be upset to think it had been stolen, but the mere thought that someone had broken into my house would terrify me."

"Me, too. And if she did know the money was in the safe, why wasn't she hysterical to find it was gone?"

"These are all very good questions, Maeve. How do you think Frank and Sarah would go about finding the answers if they were here?"

Maeve had been wondering that herself. "I think they would start by asking Una Pollock, but that would mean admitting that we knew about the money, too. I'm afraid to do that, because then she might figure out that you and I could have taken it. Now that I know Una better, she would probably have us arrested for stealing it."

"I think you may be right, and since you actually do have it, that would look very bad. So how can we pretend to find out about the money in some other way?"

Maeve thought about this for a moment. "Mr. Decker seems awfully eager to help. Maybe he should go talk to some of the investors. He can tell them he discovered their names connected to Pollock somehow and wanted to let them know he was dead."

"Felix is very clever. I'm sure he'll figure out a story to tell them."

"Thank you, my dear," he said, coming back into the room. "What story are you sure I'll figure out?"

"A story to tell the investors. We realized that we can't admit we know about the money because Una might figure out that we're the ones who took it."

"How would she figure that out? Isn't she most likely to think whoever broke in stole it?"

"Yes," Maeve said, "but she's acting like she doesn't know about it at all, so how would we unless we'd looked in the safe?"

"You're absolutely right. I hadn't thought of that. I do hate leaving that poor girl penniless, though."

"She didn't seem too worried about it when I asked her how she was going to pay the servants," Maeve said.

"And she did seem very certain that her husband kept his funds in a bank," Mrs. Decker reminded him.

"And we certainly won't let her starve to death," Maeve said.

"But if she figures out that we have Pollock's money, she might accuse poor Maeve of stealing it," Mrs. Decker said.

"We can't have that," Mr. Decker said.

A tap on the door was the maid telling them supper was ready. They spent the majority of the meal rehashing everything they had learned about Pollock's murder and realized they still had learned practically nothing of importance.

ONCE AGAIN, HARLEM HAD SETTLED DOWN FOR THE night by the time Gino arrived at the Pollock house. He'd decided to pretend he didn't know Mrs. Pollock had been released and was just planning to guard the house overnight as he had the night before.

Strangely, no one answered his first knock. He pounded the knocker a second time with much more enthusiasm. This time Hattie opened it just a crack until she saw it was Gino.

"Oh, Officer Donatelli, thank heaven you're here." She threw open the door and ushered him inside.

He'd expected her to be happy to see him, but she looked harried instead. "Is something wrong?"

"That Mr. Truett is here. He's in with Mrs. Pollock, and we heard him shouting at her, but we didn't know what to do."

"Mrs. Pollock is here?" he said with what he hoped sounded like genuine surprise.

"Oh yes, sir, she got released today and come home."

Just then he heard a man's voice raised in anger. He couldn't make out the words, but the tone was enough.

"I'll take care of this." He handed his bag to Hattie and hurried over to the parlor door. He was just about to open it when he noticed Eddie lurking in the hallway. He looked furious, and Gino could imagine his frustration at wanting to help his mistress but knowing he didn't dare.

Gino pushed the parlor door open, startling both occupants into silence. Mrs. Pollock sat on the sofa near the fire, and he saw instantly that Mr. Decker had been wrong. She *was* beautiful enough to make a man forget himself. She also looked as if she wanted to cry, which only made it worse. Truett, however, was a toad of a man, short and stocky and crammed into a checked suit that wouldn't have flattered anyone. His face was beet red, and Gino had surprised him in mid-shout. He closed his mouth with a snap, like a fish latching onto a hook.

Truett turned to her in outrage. "Did you send for the coppers?"

Gino had forgotten he was in uniform.

"Of course not. What are you doing here?" she asked Gino, rising to her feet. She looked even better standing up.

"I'm Officer Donatelli. Mr. Decker sent me to guard the house overnight. I didn't know you'd been released, Mrs. Pollock."

Recognition flickered in her eyes. "Yes, Hattie told me about you." She turned to Truett. "After the robbery, Mr. Decker thought the servants would feel safer if someone was here."

Truett turned his wrath on Gino. "Since when does anybody feel safer with the cops around?"

Gino decided not to respond to that, since Truett was only too right. "Mrs. Pollock, is this gentleman annoying you?"

"Annoying her?" he snapped. "What is that supposed to mean?"

Mrs. Pollock totally ignored his question and rewarded

Gino with a small smile. "Mr. Truett was my husband's business partner. He tells me some . . . important papers are missing, and he won't believe I don't know anything about it."

"Very *valuable* papers," Truett said, glaring at her.

Gino supposed that greenbacks could be called "valuable papers." "Mrs. Pollock was in the Tombs when the house was robbed," Gino said, giving her a pretty good alibi.

Several emotions flickered across Truett's fleshy face, with anger being the most prominent. "I didn't say she did it."

"Thank you for that, at least," she said. Even her voice was beautiful. Most men could probably listen to her all day.

"If you have any ideas about who *did* rob the house, I'd be happy to hear them," Gino told him.

"Why? So you could steal the stuff back for yourself?" Truett asked.

Gino had to admit that the reputation of the police could be embarrassing at times. He also noticed that Truett didn't seem the least bit interested in figuring out who had robbed the house, just as Una Pollock hadn't been. That seemed strange, unless Truett was the one who had done it. If so, he would still be looking for the money, which he apparently was. Very interesting.

Before he could ask Truett a pointed question about all this, someone pounded loudly on the front door.

"Good heavens, who could that be?" Mrs. Pollock asked.

Gino was very much afraid he knew. He went to the front window. About a dozen people had gathered on the sidewalk in front of the Pollock house and more were cruising down the gaslit street toward it on their bicycles. "It's the Wrecking Crew and their friends."

"The what?" Truett said, hurrying over to see for himself.

"Reporters," Gino said.

"You mean from the newspapers?" she asked in alarm.

"Yes," Gino said. "The *World* had a small story about your release in the evening edition. I guess it took a while for them to find out where you live."

Hattie appeared in the still-open parlor doorway, looking frightened. She jumped when someone pounded on the door again.

"Don't open the door," Gino told her.

"Who is it?" Hattie asked.

"Reporters," he said. "They'll probably be out there every day from now on."

"Every day!" Mrs. Pollock cried. "Why on earth would they be here every day?"

"Because," Truett told her with way too much satisfaction for Gino's taste, "they want to know all about the beautiful woman who murdered her husband."

"I didn't murder my husband," she said.

Eddie appeared beside Hattie in the doorway. "Should I run them off, missus?"

She gave him a sad smile. "If only you could, my dear boy."

Gino looked at Truett, suddenly realizing how to get rid of him. "They'll want to know who you are and why you were visiting the widow. I'm guessing they'll have sketch artists out there to capture your likeness, so you can be on the front page."

"I can't have that," Truett said, his eyes wide with panic.

"Then you'd better slip out the back way while you still can," Mrs. Pollock said.

Someone pounded on the door again. Mrs. Pollock sighed wearily, and Truett glared at her again.

Hattie darted away, and for a moment Gino was afraid she was going to open the door, but she quickly reappeared. "Mr. Truett, here's your things." She held his overcoat and hat. "I'll take you out the back."

He turned to Mrs. Pollock. "This isn't finished."

"I can't help you, Gordon. He never told me anything."

Truett made a humphing noise and strode out. Hattie scurried after him, still carrying his coat.

Gino made careful note that Una had called Truett by his first name. That was interesting.

The pounding started again.

"This is going to drive me insane," she said.

"I can't make them go away, but maybe I can make them stop knocking," Gino said.

"I'd be grateful."

When Gino reached the parlor door, Eddie stepped aside, his expression murderous. Gino hoped he was only angry with the reporters.

"Come with me," Gino said, "and hold the door to make sure they don't force their way inside. We don't want them to get to Mrs. Pollock."

The boy's eyes widened in alarm, but he followed Gino and stood by, eager to help.

As soon as the pounding stopped, Gino threw open the door, surprising the half-dozen men clustered on the stoop. Before they could react, he shoved the front two backward so he could step outside and close the door behind him.

"Get off the porch. You're trespassing."

"And who are you?" one of the reporters asked, pad and pencil ready to jot down his name and make him famous. Or infamous.

"I'm a police officer sent to protect Mrs. Pollock. She doesn't want to talk to you bums, so get off the porch and stop banging on her door."

They didn't move except to take notes. Gino thought he saw someone down on the sidewalk with a big pad of paper, working feverishly to sketch his likeness.

"We just want to get her side of the story, Officer," one of them said. "Doesn't she want the world to know she didn't do it?"

"She wants some peace and quiet. Now get off the porch before I have to start throwing you down the steps."

The threat seemed to impress them a little. The reporters farthest from the door started to retreat, and then someone shouted. Like hounds on the scent, every one of them turned toward the sound, which had come from the side of the house.

A young man in a bowler hat came running up from between the houses. "A fellow came out the back door."

The reporters on the sidewalk took off down the side of the house. Gino hoped Truett could outrun them. The ones on the porch turned back to Gino and started shouting all at once.

"Who was it?"

"Is it her lover?"

"Did he kill Pollock?"

"Are they in it together?"

"How much money did he leave her?"

"Did she kill him for the money?"

"We'll pay you for the story."

Gino was sure they would. They wouldn't even care if what he told them was true. And if he didn't tell them anything, they'd make something up. Which was worse? He had no idea.

"Just let us see her for a minute!" one pleaded.

"Is she as pretty as they say?"

"Doesn't she want to see her picture in the newspapers?"

"I don't think she does," Gino said. "Now, I warned you about getting off the porch." He pulled out his nightstick. Luckily, he'd thought to put it back in his belt when he retrieved his bag from the Deckers' carriage earlier.

The sight of the nightstick sent the reporters stumbling back.

"No reason to get mean!"

"We're just doing our job!"

"We just want to tell her story."

Gino took a step forward, raising the locust-wood stick.

The reporters scrambled down the steps, shoving and tripping one another until they were safely on the sidewalk again.

"Who are you, copper?"

"Are you her lover?"

"Did you kill Pollock?"

"What're you doing here?"

"If anybody pounds on the door again, I'll club him," Gino shouted down to them.

They glared up at him, but nobody said a word. Gino noticed the sketch artist had flipped the page and was drawing again.

With a sigh, he turned back and found the front door bolted securely. "You can let me back in now, Eddie," he called, setting off another chorus of questions.

"Who's Eddie?"

"Is that her lover?"

"Did he kill Pollock?"

Fortunately, he heard the bolt being drawn and then the door opened, slamming shut the instant he was back inside.

"Would you really club them?" Eddie asked.

"Nothing would give me more pleasure, but nothing would get me fired faster either, so probably not. Unless they were threatening Mrs. Pollock, that is."

"They're like rabid dogs," Mrs. Pollock said, hovering in the parlor doorway. "Will they leave now?"

"No. I doubt they'll stay all night, though. It's too cold for that, but they'll stay until the house is dark and be back at first light, I'm sure. Did Truett get away?"

"I don't know," she said.

"I think he did," Hattie said, hurrying down the hall. "He started running when they saw him. There was some men hiding out back, too, I guess, and they started shouting when he got to the alley."

"Will you stay until they're gone, at least?" Mrs. Pollock asked.

"I'll stay until morning, if you like."

"You don't have to do that," Eddie said quickly. "I'll look after Mrs. Pollock."

She gave the boy a grateful smile that made him drop his gaze, embarrassed. "Do you really think I need protection?" she asked Gino.

"Somebody did break in the other night." He didn't mention that the crook probably hadn't gotten what he'd come for, which was exactly why Gino was here. But was Truett the burglar? Was that why he'd shown up here this evening? Certainly, he was looking for the money, and Mrs. Pollock was still claiming ignorance, whether that was true or not.

"Yes, and they emptied my husband's safe, so I have nothing left worth stealing."

That much was true, of course. "The question is, do any other possible burglars know that?"

"I can't imagine I have more than one possible burglar interested in robbing me. A few days ago, I would have sworn I had none at all."

Of course the one burglar was probably still interested in robbing her, since he hadn't gotten what he'd come for, but he couldn't say that. "It's no trouble for me to stay."

"You wouldn't have no place to sleep, what with Mrs. Pollock home and all," Hattie said.

He hadn't thought of that. He remembered the empty bedrooms upstairs with a sigh, and glanced into the parlor. The sofas there didn't look very inviting or nearly long enough to accommodate him, and spending the night in the room where Pollock had been murdered wasn't particularly appealing, but he'd slept in far worse circumstances in Cuba during the war. "I can sleep on the floor if necessary."

"We can't ask you to do that," Mrs. Pollock said. "There's no reason for you to stay all night, but I do think it's a good idea for you to wait here until the reporters have gone. I'd hate for you to have to run down St. Nicholas Avenue to escape them."

Gino would hate that, too. "I'll be glad to stay for a while."

"Good. Have you eaten? Mr. Truett's visit delayed my supper, and I'm starving. I'm sure Velvet can manage to feed us both."

"Thank you, ma'am. I'd appreciate that."

Gino thought he caught Eddie giving him a black look. The poor boy really was besotted with Mrs. Pollock if he was jealous of Gino.

Mrs. Pollock sent Gino to wash up while she went to instruct the cook, and he took the opportunity to comb his hair, too. Of course, he'd combed it earlier in preparation for dinner with the Deckers and Maeve, but that was hours ago. He found Mrs. Pollock in the dining room, sitting at the head of the long table. Someone had set a place for him at her right.

"Do you know much about trials, Officer . . . ? I'm sorry, in all the excitement, I didn't catch your name."

"Donatelli."

"That's Italian, isn't it?" Her eyes were an amazing color of blue. He'd never seen anything like it.

"Yes."

"Officer Donatelli," she said as if she were trying out the taste of his name on her tongue. The thought made a little shiver go up his spine. "Do you know much about trials?"

"A little."

"My attorney, Mr. Nicholson, is he really good?"

"He gets a lot of people off."

"Off what?"

Gino was glad to see Hattie come in with a tray to serve their supper. It gave him a minute to think. He should have realized Mrs. Pollock would have no experience with the justice system and its particular jargon. By the time Hattie had served them the fried beefsteak, roasted potatoes, and stewed tomatoes, he'd thought through what he wanted to say.

"I meant to say that a lot of Mr. Nicholson's clients are found not guilty at the end of their trials."

"But not all of them?"

He couldn't help smiling at this. "Some of them are just too guilty for even him to help."

She smiled back, but it didn't quite reach her beautiful eyes. She was worried and rightly so.

"Your mother asked us to help you," he said. "You could help yourself if you could remember what happened that day."

She took a sip from her glass, then turned her attention to cutting her steak. For a minute he thought she wasn't going to reply at all, but at last she said, "I really can't remember what happened, no matter how hard I try. Apparently, my husband had a visitor that morning, the brother of his first wife, or so I'm told."

"Mr. Yorke."

"Is that his name? I didn't meet him, of course. I'm sure his visit wasn't pleasant, and Randolph would have wanted to protect me from that."

"So you don't know what they talked about?"

"Of course not. Randolph may have told me before . . . Well, I can't even say that for sure, because if this Mr. Yorke is the one who killed him, he wouldn't have been able to tell me anything at all about the visit."

"Do you remember finding your husband?"

She stopped with her fork halfway to her mouth, then

slowly lowered it again. "Thankfully, I do not. I vaguely remember the police arriving and taking me away in this horrible wagon, and of course I remember being at the jail." She shuddered delicately. "What an awful place. I think I'll die if I have to go back there."

Gino didn't tell her that if she was found guilty of killing her husband, she'd go to a place far worse than the Tombs. "The best way to keep from going back to jail is to figure out who really did kill your husband."

She smiled sadly, which made him want to help her somehow. "You are not the first person who has suggested this to me. Believe me, I would tell you what happened if I knew. In the meantime, please eat your supper, Officer Donatelli."

To his surprise, he realized he hadn't taken so much as a bite, even though he'd been more than hungry when he'd arrived at her door. He obediently began to eat, conscious of her gaze resting on him now and then.

After a few minutes of silence, she asked, "How did you come to know Mr. Decker?"

He looked up in surprise. Knowing a man like Felix Decker as well as he did—he'd been invited to eat at his house this very night, in fact—was certainly a marvel. He was the son of Italian immigrants. He was an immigrant himself, in fact, although he'd been too young to even remember making the trip, while Felix Decker's ancestors had settled New York generations ago. Gino was also a cop, a far-from-respectable profession, while Felix Decker's name was on the Social Register. Still . . .

"I used to work with his son-in-law," he said, which was the simplest explanation.

"Mr. Decker's daughter is married to a *policeman*?"

She had a right to be surprised. Frank Malloy was pretty surprised himself. "He's not with the police anymore. He . . . he's done pretty well for himself."

She thought that over for a minute. "Does he live on Bank Street?"

"Yes." For a minute, he couldn't imagine how she knew.

"And that girl, Maeve, she works for him?"

So that was it. Mrs. Pollock had been to Malloy's house to pick up her trunk. "Yes."

She nodded as if he'd confirmed something important. "The son-in-law is a private investigator, then."

"Where did you get that idea?"

"The girl told me she works for a private investigator."

Of course Maeve had said that. "I guess she does. Mr. Malloy, he helps people out when they need it."

Her beautiful blue eyes went cold. "People like my mother."

"Yes," he said, uneasily.

"Well, you can tell this Mr. Malloy that I don't need help from him or anyone else, and I want all of you to leave me alone."

9

THE HOUSE HAD BEEN DARK FOR HALF AN HOUR NOW. Gino had argued his case with Mrs. Pollock again, but she had been adamant that she didn't need a bodyguard. He could have forced her to accept his protection, but he didn't want to upset her any more, so he was just waiting for the right time to leave. He'd sent her and the female servants upstairs to their beds, with instructions to extinguish all the lights in hopes of discouraging the reporters. He and Eddie had waited downstairs, also in the dark. For understandable reasons, Eddie had refused to wait in the parlor, so he sat in a chair in the front hall while Gino positioned himself near a crack in the lace curtains on the parlor's front window, watching the people milling on the sidewalk.

Earlier, the crowd had contained a few women, the ones who typically reported on social events and fashion, but they had left at some point while Gino and Mrs. Pollock were eating supper. As the night grew colder, the crowd grew smaller, and finally, the last of them pedaled off on their bicycles. He waited awhile, just to make sure nobody was planning to sneak back in hopes of scooping the other newspapers, but no one did.

"I think they're gone," he called to Eddie, who appeared instantly in the doorway.

"Are you leaving now?"

He seemed awfully anxious for Gino to go. Gino figured Eddie was jealous of the attention he was getting from Mrs. Pollock, and he couldn't blame him. He felt sorry for the boy, knowing that when everything got sorted out, he and the other servants would most likely be moving on and he'd probably never see Una Pollock again. "Yeah, I guess it's time." Gino went out into the hall, where Hattie had left his bag, and as he left the parlor, he remembered something.

"What happened to the rug?" The bloodstained rug had been rolled up in front of the door last night.

"Mrs. Pollock had me take it to the basement."

That made sense. She wouldn't want it around to remind her. "Lock up behind me."

"Don't you worry. I'll look after Mrs. Pollock," the boy said.

Gino was sure of that. "Don't forget, if anything happens, send for Mr. Decker."

"Missus won't like that."

Gino had no answer for him. He stepped out onto the porch, bracing himself for the blast of cold, then waited to hear Eddie throw the bolt. Satisfied that he'd done all he could, Gino set off down the steps and down the street. No one accosted him or even seemed to be around. The only sound was his own shoes slapping against the pavement as he hurried to the El station. Too bad it was so late. He desperately needed to tell Maeve and the Deckers about Truett's visit, but it would have to wait until morning. He only hoped Truett was spooked enough to stay away from the Pollock house until they'd had a chance to figure out what to do about him, because he didn't think for one second that Eddie would be able to handle him.

BECAUSE IT WAS SATURDAY, MAEVE, MRS. MALLOY, AND the children were still at breakfast when someone knocked on the door the next morning.

"That will be Gino," Maeve told Mrs. Malloy, signing for Brian's benefit.

Both children wanted to jump up and run to the door, but Mrs. Malloy told them sternly to finish eating, and she went to answer it.

Maeve had wanted to jump up and run herself, so she was actually glad Mrs. Malloy had gone. No sense in giving Gino the impression she was anxious to see him, even if she was. She could hear his voice as he chatted with Mrs. Malloy on their way to the kitchen, and even though she couldn't understand the words, she knew he was charming her the way he always did.

"Good morning, Officer Donatelli," Catherine sang out politely, just the way Maeve was teaching her to do.

"Good morning, Miss Catherine," he replied, charming her as well. Really, it was disgusting.

"And good morning to you, Mr. Brian." He ruffled the boy's hair, earning a grin and a flurry of signs that Mrs. Malloy interpreted as his greeting.

"Sit down," Mrs. Malloy said. "I'll get you some breakfast."

Maeve was certain Mrs. Pollock's cook wouldn't have sent him off without feeding him first, but she didn't say a word.

"Thank you, Mrs. Malloy," he said, just like he was starving, and pulled out the chair at the end of the table, which just happened to be at a right angle to Maeve's. "Good morning to you, Miss Smith," he said with a twinkle in his dark eyes that almost softened her resolve not to completely melt.

"And how is Mrs. Pollock this fine morning?" Maeve asked.

"You wouldn't be jealous, would you?" he asked with a wicked grin.

Mrs. Malloy set a cup of coffee down in front of him and gave him a little pinch on the arm.

"Ow!"

"Don't tease the girl," she said.

The children giggled until Mrs. Malloy shushed them, and Maeve didn't bother to hide her grin.

Effectively chastened, a more sober Gino turned back to Maeve and said, "I have no idea how she is because she shooed me off last night after the reporters gave up and went home."

"Reporters?" Maeve said, gladly changing the subject.

"Oh yes. They showed up shortly after I got there last night. There was probably twenty of them, banging on the door and wanting to interview Mrs. Pollock."

"That's disgraceful the way they bother people," Mrs. Malloy murmured from where she was cooking Gino some eggs.

Maeve couldn't seem to work up any sympathy for Una Pollock this morning, though. "I'm guessing you protected her from them." She didn't sound like she approved.

"I got them to stop pounding on the door," he admitted with fake reluctance. "They almost caught Truett, though."

"Truett was there?" she almost yelped.

"Oh yes. We were right. I think Truett was the one—"

"Here's your eggs," Mrs. Malloy said, plopping a plate down in front of him. Maeve saw Mrs. Malloy had scrambled at least three eggs for him. Maeve hoped he was hungry. "Come along, children. Maeve and Officer Donatelli have business to discuss."

Brian was protesting with flying fingers and Catherine

dragged her feet and pulled a miserable face to let them know how sad she was to leave. Neither tactic moved Mrs. Malloy, and soon Maeve and Gino were alone in the kitchen.

He was shoveling in the eggs as if he hadn't eaten in a week. "Didn't Mrs. Pollock feed you last night?"

He stopped long enough to give her a smirk. "I had supper with her in the dining room."

Maeve could've kicked herself for even asking. "So what is it you think about Truett?"

He swallowed and took a sip of his coffee. "He was pretty mad when I got there. The maid said he'd been shouting at Mrs. Pollock. He claimed there were 'valuable papers' missing, and he thought she knew where they were."

"And you think the valuable papers are really the missing money."

"What else could he mean? So Truett could be the one who broke into the Pollock house and that's how he knows the money is missing."

"Except that the Deckers told him about the robbery, and that could be how he knows," Maeve reminded him. "And I suppose poor Una had no idea the money was even there."

"Truett didn't mention money when I was there, just 'papers,' but she did say she didn't know anything about Pollock's business."

"I guess she was crying and all hysterical."

Gino started to smirk again but stopped when he saw her expression. "She was holding up pretty well when I got there."

"I can't believe she's still pretending she didn't know about the money," Maeve said in disgust.

"Don't forget, I don't know what she might've said to Truett before I got there. For all I know they started out with Truett telling her the money is missing and what did she do with it, and her saying she had no idea because she was in jail when it all happened. But when I got there, Truett was very careful not to say exactly what the missing papers were, and he actually accused me of wanting to steal them myself."

"Poor Gino," she said, only half sarcastically.

"I don't think it was personal," he said cheerfully. "He just hates all cops."

"So I guess we need to talk to Mr. Truett."

"I don't think it would be a good idea for me to question him. After last night, he'll be suspicious. But Mr. Decker could, I think."

"He'll have a busy day. He and Mrs. Decker were going to visit the widow of the man who killed himself, and he was going to see that other fellow whose name he recognized, too."

"That doesn't leave much for you to do today," he said.

"Which will make Catherine happy. We haven't spent much time together lately. Oh, I know. I can take the children to see the Deckers this morning and tell them what you found out about Truett. Catherine and Brian love playing in the nursery there, and Mrs. Decker will be happy to see them. She doesn't have much to do today either."

"What about Mrs. Malloy?"

"She deserves some time to herself. I think she's secretly making some Christmas gifts, so she'll be glad to be able to work on them without the children around."

"Just don't go see Mrs. Pollock."

"Why would I do that?" she asked in amazement.

"I don't know, but she told me last night that she doesn't need our help and she doesn't want us to bother her anymore."

"That's pretty ungrateful."

"I thought so, too."

He was trying to look all innocent as he shoveled in the last of his eggs, but Maeve wasn't fooled. "What are you thinking?"

"About Mrs. Pollock? Are you sure you want to know?"

"Oh yes."

He grinned at that. "Well, if I were a woman who was falsely accused of killing my husband and had been locked up in the Tombs and was going on trial for my life, I'd be grateful for all the help anybody wanted to give me."

"And if I were a woman who really had killed her husband and people were trying to prove me innocent, I'd be grateful for that help, too," she said.

"So why doesn't Mrs. Pollock want our help?"

"That's a very good question, Officer Donatelli. I think when we figure out the answer, we'll know a lot more about Pollock's murder than we do now."

"But if Mrs. Pollock doesn't want us to help, why would we continue to work on her case?"

Maeve smiled sweetly. "Because we might find out that she's guilty."

Gino pretended to be shocked. "Now I know just how much you don't like her."

"Yes, you do. I know you have to go to work, so Catherine and Brian and I will go visit the Deckers and give Mr. Decker his additional assignment for the day."

"He'll be happy, I'm sure. He really wanted to go to the Pollock house last night."

"I doubt he'll be as happy to visit Truett as he would have been to visit Una, but at least he won't be sitting at home all day, wondering what's happening, like Mrs. Decker and me."

"Poor Maeve," he said. "You also don't have to arrest drunks all day, so count your blessings."

ELIZABETH WAS THRILLED TO SEE MAEVE AND THE CHILdren. Because Maeve had telephoned to let her know they were coming, she had already enlisted a maid to entertain the little ones in the nursery for a while so she and Felix could get Maeve's report from Gino.

"So Gino thinks this Truett is the one who broke into the house," Felix said when Maeve had finished.

"Yes, because he knew the money was missing," Maeve said.

"But we told Mr. Truett about the robbery when he came here yesterday," Elizabeth said. "Remember, he said he'd gone to see Mr. Pollock that morning and the servants told him Pollock was dead. He claimed that was the first he knew."

"I do remember, and remember I thought he might've just been pretending to be surprised about the murder and the robbery so we wouldn't suspect him of anything." Maeve was always so suspicious of people. Elizabeth wished the girl could be more trusting. "He's Pollock's partner, after all. He would've known the money was in the safe and not invested in Peru or wherever the railroad was supposed to be."

"But how could he have known Mr. Pollock was dead before yesterday?" Elizabeth argued. "It wasn't in the newspaper until last night, and there still hasn't been a death notice."

"He'd know if he was the one who killed Pollock," her husband said.

"Or maybe he found out some other way," Maeve said. "Mr. Malloy would tell us we need to talk to him and find out." Elizabeth thought she was probably right.

Felix gave Maeve a small smile. "I'm sure he would. I think I can manage that after I call on Lawrence Zimmerman this morning."

"Oh, Felix, do you really think you should?" Elizabeth said in alarm. "You were furious with me for meeting with Mr. Truett alone because he might be a murderer."

"And you pointed out to me that whoever killed Pollock has no reason to harm you, so I will point out that he has no reason to harm me either."

"But if he thinks that you suspect him—"

"He won't. I'm just going to ask him about the Panamanian project and see what he has to say. He seemed eager to explain it to me when he was here yesterday. He probably thinks he can get me to invest, too."

"How will that help you figure out if he killed Pollock?" Maeve asked.

"If I'm considering investing in his project, I'll be concerned over Pollock's murder. I'm going to ask him who he thinks did it and why anyone would want to and see what he says. I'm also going to mention Oscar Norwalk's suicide and see if he's aware of it. That should give me the man's measure, at least."

"Ask him why he thinks Una Pollock knows where the money is, too," Maeve said, making Felix smile again. The girl had really taken a dislike to the widow Pollock.

"I'd better get started then," he said. "I'll be back for luncheon, and we'll call on Caroline Norwalk this afternoon."

When he had taken his leave, Maeve said, "Do you suppose he intends to include me in the visit with Mrs. Norwalk?"

"No, dear, I don't."

Maeve sighed.

"Maybe you and the children could go shopping this afternoon," Elizabeth said to cheer her. "I saw some lovely things at Macy's, and Santa Claus was wandering the aisles, thrilling the little ones."

"Or scaring them to death. I've seen children screaming in terror when they saw him."

"I suppose he is rather frightening if you have no idea who he is. I wonder if Brian knows about Santa."

"If not, we'll make sure he finds out."

"I have a feeling Sarah and Frank will be bringing back some wonderful gifts from their honeymoon."

"Yes. She sent me a cable telling me to expect some crates soon."

"Then maybe you shouldn't shop very much," Elizabeth said with a grin. "Let's go upstairs and visit the children, shall we?"

Felix decided to call on Lawrence Zimmerman first. Before confronting Truett he wanted to get an idea of how much the investors really knew about the project. Zimmerman lived in what was probably the family home, a tidy town house in Lenox Hill. A maid took Decker's card and, after a short wait, escorted him upstairs to a book-lined room that was obviously Zimmerman's masculine lair.

"Mr. Decker, what a surprise," he said, obviously pleased to be visited by someone of Felix's social position. Zimmerman was in his thirties with a shrinking hairline and a growing paunch. His fair hair and light eyes gave him a rather nondescript air, as if he might be fading away. He was still adjusting his suit jacket when Felix came in. "Have a seat. Can I get you something? Coffee or something stronger? It's early but . . ."

"No, thanks. I just came to get your advice about something."

Nothing could have ingratiated him any more with Zimmerman. "My advice? What could you possibly want my advice about?" he asked when they'd seated themselves in the leather chairs beside the fire.

"It's an investment opportunity in Panama. I've been invited to participate, and I understand you are involved."

Zimmerman's pleasure at Felix's visit vanished instantly. His expression hardened. "Yes, I . . . What would you like to know?"

"Is something wrong?"

"I don't know what you mean." Zimmerman wasn't a very good liar. Something was very wrong.

"Let me explain myself. You see, I was considering participating in this project after Oscar Norwalk had introduced me to Randolph Pollock." Zimmerman stiffened at the mention of Norwalk, but Felix pretended not to notice. "And now Pollock has been murdered."

"Has he?" Zimmerman pretended to be surprised. "That's terrible."

Felix continued to play along, although he noticed Zimmerman didn't ask him any questions about how Pollock was killed or who might have done it. "Yes, I saw a small article in the *World* last night. It said his wife murdered him."

This time he truly was surprised. "His wife? But that's impossible. She's so . . . I can't imagine such a thing."

"Nevertheless, Pollock is dead, and she was arrested for killing him. She's been released on bail, I understand."

Zimmerman just stared, completely overwhelmed by the thought.

Felix gave him a few moments to absorb all this. Then he said, "So you can see my concern. Pollock's death combined with Norwalk's . . ."

He stiffened again. "Norwalk? But . . . that was his heart."

"That's what the family said, of course."

Zimmerman sighed. "I didn't think it was common knowledge."

"It's not, but there was talk at our club. And of course he had also invested in this Panama project."

"Yes, he introduced me to Pollock, as well. He thought . . . Well, my mother had some funds—I manage her affairs, you see—and I thought it would be a good opportunity for her."

In other words, Zimmerman didn't have any money of his own, at least not yet. So if he'd made a bad investment, he'd have the added burden of knowing he'd lost his mother's money.

"Do you have any idea if . . . ? Well, this is difficult to put delicately, but naturally, I was concerned after Norwalk's unfortunate circumstances and now Pollock's violent demise."

"You're wondering if everything is on the up-and-up, I suppose." Zimmerman's face had gone chalk white. "Well, it's not. Pollock is a thief and a scoundrel. No one is building a railroad in Panama because there's already a railroad there."

"When did you discover this?"

"I didn't. Norwalk did. A couple weeks ago, I guess. He confronted Pollock and demanded his money back, but of course Pollock refused. He'd known all along. It was all a swindle."

"And Norwalk told you?"

"Yes, he felt honor-bound, since he was the one who'd suggested it to me in the first place."

"Was that why he . . . ?"

Zimmerman's eyes filled, and he rubbed them angrily. "I don't know, not for certain, but . . . Norwalk was a proud man. He was ashamed that he'd been taken in by Pollock's scheme, of course, but he was devastated that he'd brought his friends in, too."

"You weren't the only one, then? There were others?"

"Yes, although he never said who. He'd never embarrass them, of course."

"Of course." Felix could understand completely. Being tricked would make a man feel like a fool, but making fools of his friends as well would be impossible to bear. So maybe the financial loss had been serious, but the blow to Norwalk's pride would have been even worse. How could he face anyone after that? But he wasn't here about Norwalk. "How did you find out Pollock was dead?"

Zimmerman blinked several times, his gaze darting

around the room as if he were looking for a satisfactory answer. "Uh, you just told me."

"Yes, but you already knew it."

He didn't deny it, Felix noted. "I, uh, I saw it in the newspaper last night, just as you did." He really was a terrible liar. "In any case, what does it matter?"

"Only a few people knew he was dead, including his killer."

"But you said his wife killed him." And he had been surprised to hear it, which meant he really hadn't seen the newspaper article.

"I said she'd been arrested for killing him, but she denies it."

"Of course she denies it. Wouldn't you?"

"Do you think she could have done it? A few minutes ago, you said you couldn't imagine it."

"And I can't! Have you met her?"

"Yes, I have."

"Then you know what I mean. She's so . . ." He gestured helplessly.

"Lovely?" Felix offered.

"Not just that," Zimmerman said, the color rising in his face. "She's so feminine and . . . and refined."

"Too refined to bash her husband's head in, you mean?"

"Exactly!"

Felix studied him for a long moment. "How did you know Pollock had his head bashed in?"

Zimmerman started blinking again. "What?"

"I asked how you knew his head was bashed in. It wasn't in the newspapers."

"I don't . . . that is, you said it."

"And you weren't surprised. You knew. How did you know?"

"I suppose someone told me."

"Someone who knew Pollock was dead before it was in the newspapers. And who would that be?"

His expression hardened again. He wasn't going to betray his friends either. "I don't remember."

"Except for his wife and servants, only Pollock's killer knew how he died. Are you going to protect his killer and let his wife take the blame?"

"The person who told me didn't kill him. I promise you that."

"Then why won't you tell me who he is?"

He smiled at this, a stiff rictus of a grin. "Because you'll accuse him of murder."

"It's not my place to accuse him of anything. I'm just trying to protect an innocent woman. I would expect you to do the same."

"I will, if it comes to it, but they won't charge a woman with a crime like that."

"They already have," Felix reminded him, exasperated.

He had no answer for that.

"You have my card," he said finally. "When you're ready to do the right thing, let me know."

Felix didn't wait for the maid. He showed himself out.

Gino usually enjoyed this time of the day. He'd finished rousting all the drunks from the doorways and alleys where they'd crawled to sleep off their carousing from the night before and it was too early yet for any serious crime. He strolled along his beat, tipping his cap to ladies he passed and scowling at boys who looked like they might be up to no good. Shopkeepers would usually nod respectfully when he passed, but this morning, they weren't nodding. They were just staring. Then he passed a group of ladies huddled around a newspaper one of them held, and they all turned to look at him as he walked by and giggled when he tipped his cap.

He shrugged it off the first time, but in the next block,

a shopkeeper grinned at him knowingly and then two attractive young women saw him and started whispering behind their hands and pointing. Automatically, he checked to make sure his pants were properly buttoned up, but everything seemed to be in order. Why was everyone staring at him?

He'd gone another block with more staring shopkeepers and giggling females when he saw two detectives coming toward him. They weren't smiling, though. They looked a little mad, truth to tell, and one of them was Broghan. He'd probably heard about Gino asking questions of his cousin about the Pollock murder. This might be bad.

The detectives waited for him on the corner, and by the time he reached them, Gino was starting to feel more than a little nervous.

"Good morning, gentlemen," he tried. "Did something big happen on my beat?"

They didn't return his greeting. Instead, Broghan took a newspaper from where he'd been carrying it under his arm and snapped it open to the front page. It was the *Journal*, and there was a remarkably accurate sketch of him standing on the Pollocks' front stoop, brandishing his nightstick at a group of reporters. The headline read, "Handsome Italian Police Officer Protects Beautiful Murderess."

"Hey, that looks like me," he tried, hoping to brazen it out.

The two men exchanged a glance. "Yeah," O'Brien said, "that's what the chief thought, too."

"So did my cousin," said Broghan. "He said he saw you coming out of the Pollock house yesterday, too. And how many handsome Italians we got on the force, after all?"

Gino had no answer for that, and he could see they weren't here just to tease him. "What does the chief want?"

"He wants to see your handsome face," O'Brien said with a mirthless grin. "Right now."

"But my beat . . . ," he tried.

"We'll send somebody to replace you."

Gino looked at the men again. "Why did he send two of you?"

"In case you resisted," Broghan said. "Are you going to?"

"Uh, no."

"Too bad," O'Brien said.

Gino decided not to press his luck any further, and he took off for Headquarters. If the detectives were following, they weren't trying to keep up. On the way, he stopped a newsboy and bought a copy of the *World*, which also had a sketch of him. He didn't think this one was as good a likeness, but the headline again identified him as both handsome and Italian. The *World* had a second sketch, though, and no one had to guess who it might be. Gino would have known her immediately, but it was also clearly identified as the beautiful murderess, Una Pollock.

Where had they gotten her likeness? She'd been careful not to show herself last night for just that reason. Then Gino read the article beneath the picture, an interview with her mother. Some enterprising reporter had taken advantage of Mrs. O'Neill's innocence and convinced her to talk about Una. The unfortunate woman had probably even provided a photograph of her daughter for the newspaper sketch artist. Una wouldn't be happy at all when she saw this. Poor Mrs. O'Neill, she was only trying to help her daughter. Too bad Una wouldn't see it that way.

Meanwhile, however, Gino needed to worry about himself. How was he going to explain what he was doing up in Harlem in the house of an accused murderess that wasn't even in his precinct? Oh, how he wished Frank Malloy were in town. He'd know just what to do.

Or would he? Frank Malloy no longer worked for the New

York City Police because he'd displeased them. Of course, Mr. Malloy had displeased them by becoming a millionaire, and Gino certainly had not done that. Was this bad enough to lose his job over? Gino didn't even want to think about that.

When he reached Police Headquarters on Mulberry Street, Tom the doorman gave him a pitying look as he held the door for him. "Better hurry upstairs, son," he said. "The chief is expecting you."

That's when he knew. They were sending him to Goatsville. Goatsville wasn't a town exactly. It was a general term of derision for the country, where nothing happened and where cops who shook down the wrong businessman or the wrong madam or who accidentally shot the wrong person got sent to die . . . of boredom. Getting fired, he thought, would actually be better.

Felix RECOGNIZED THE BUILDING ON EAST FORTY-EIGHT Street where Truett lived as a hotel with bachelor apartments. These residences had flourished in the past few years and provided small apartments for single men or childless couples. The building would have a restaurant that could send meals up to residents who didn't want to cook for themselves and would provide a staff to clean and do laundry. Residents would have all the comforts and amenities without the expense of maintaining a house and servants.

Felix paid the cab driver, and a doorman in uniform admitted him. The lobby was small but tastefully decorated and well maintained. A man in a suit with a fresh flower in his lapel greeted him from behind a desk. "May I help you, sir?"

"Yes, I'm here to see Mr. Truett, if he's in."

The man checked the rows of boxes on the wall behind him, where each tenant's key would be placed if he was out.

Then he smiled his professional smile. "Is Mr. Truett expecting you?"

"No, but if he's out, I can come back later."

His smile wavered a bit. "He is usually out at this time of day, but I see his key isn't here, so you're in luck. Let me telephone to make sure this is a convenient time." Felix saw a small switchboard beside the boxes, and the man moved to it, inserted a plug into one of the holes, and turned the crank on the side. He picked up the earpiece and waited for the call to go through.

Felix was trying to be patient, but after a long few minutes, the clerk put down the earpiece and removed the plug from its hole. "I'm sorry, Mr. Truett isn't answering."

"But you said he was in."

"His key hasn't been returned, that's true."

"Did you see him go out this morning?"

"No, I did not, but he might have slipped by me. Perhaps if you made an appointment for your next visit, you will find him at home."

Felix didn't like the sound of this. Two people involved with the Panama deal were dead, and Truett was more involved than most. Another possibility was that he had fled, although Felix doubted he'd leave without the money. "Would you mind going upstairs and checking Mr. Truett's rooms? I'm concerned about his well-being."

"Why would you be concerned?" the clerk asked with a frown.

"Because, well, his business partner was murdered a few days ago. I was calling on him today to ask him what he knows about it. If he's simply not home, then we can all rest easy, but if something has happened to him . . ."

"This is a respectable hotel, sir. Things like that simply do not happen here."

Felix smiled. "I'm sure they don't. In which case, you should have no objection to checking Mr. Truett's rooms."

He thought the clerk might have argued some more, but just then the elevator doors opened and a maid came running out, her eyes wide with terror. The elevator operator came running behind her, and they were both heading straight for the desk where Felix was standing.

The woman was making incoherent noises, half screaming and half panting. The clerk rushed out to meet her and grabbed her arm when he reached her. "What on earth is the matter?"

"He's dead!" she gasped.

Felix's heart dropped.

"Who? Who's dead?" the clerk demanded.

"Mr. Truett," the elevator operator said.

10

Maeve and Mrs. Decker were in the nursery, having a tea party with the children, when the maid tapped on the door.

"I guess luncheon is ready," Mrs. Decker said, getting up out of the child-sized chair to answer the door.

"Mr. Decker said he'd be back in time to eat with us," Maeve said.

"I know, and I'm sure he would have let us know if he'd returned. I'll have them hold our meal for us until he gets back."

She opened the door and had a brief conversation with the maid, but instead of returning to the tea party, she said, "Children, I'm sorry, but Maeve and I need to go downstairs for a while. The girls will bring your luncheon up to you in just a few minutes."

Catherine frowned in disappointment and signed the bad news to Brian, who also pouted.

Maeve said, "We'll be back in a little while, and then I'll take you to Macy's to see Santa Claus." Neither she nor Catherine knew how to sign "Santa Claus," but Catherine signed something that made Brian smile again. Maeve left them deep in conversation, their fingers flying.

"Is Mr. Decker back?" Maeve asked when she and Mrs. Decker were out in the hall.

"No, but Gino is here."

"Gino? In the middle of the day?" Something must be wrong.

Mrs. Decker was already hurrying to the stairs. Maeve followed on her heels. They found him waiting in the family parlor, where the maid had left him. He jumped to his feet when they entered, and Maeve instantly knew she'd been right about something being very wrong.

"Where's your uniform?" He looked very nice in his suit, but he shouldn't be wearing it now.

He gave them a smile but there was no joy in it. "I'm not a police officer anymore."

"Good heavens," Mrs. Decker said. "Please, sit down and tell us what happened."

"I guess you haven't seen a newspaper this morning," he said, still maintaining that awful smile that didn't do a thing to cover the sadness in his dark eyes.

He picked up a newspaper that lay folded on the table and opened it for them to see.

Maeve felt the jolt of recognition clear to her toes. The sketch artist had really captured Gino's likeness and the drama of the scene. She could easily imagine how angry he must have been at the reporters threatening Una Pollock.

"It's very flattering," Mrs. Decker said with feigned enthusiasm.

He winced at that. "So I'm told."

"They fired you over this?" Maeve said, not certain exactly

why she was so angry. Probably it was because they'd fired him, but it might have also been because she didn't like the idea of him defending Una Pollock.

"They didn't fire me. I quit."

"Why would you do a thing like that?" Mrs. Decker said.

"Because they were going to send me to Goatsville. Because of this." He tapped the picture in the newspaper.

"Where on earth is Goatsville?" Maeve asked, certain now that she was angry at the New York City Police Department.

"It's where they send cops who get in trouble. It's not really a place. It's just out in the country. They call it Goatsville because nothing ever happens there, so the beat cops have time to help herd the goats."

"Really?" Mrs. Decker asked in amazement.

"No, not really," he said. "At least I don't think so. But I didn't want to find out for sure. Besides, I can't leave the city now, not while we're working on this case. So I quit."

Maeve couldn't think of a single thing to say to that, and apparently, Mrs. Decker couldn't either.

"They called you handsome," Mrs. Decker noticed, glancing at the newspaper again.

He reached out to snatch up the paper, but Maeve slapped her hand over it. "Wait. Where did they get this picture of Una?"

"If you read the article, you'll see they interviewed her mother."

"Mrs. O'Neill?" Mrs. Decker said. "Oh dear. I guess no one warned her about the newspapers."

"Una's attorney tried, but they can be awfully persistent. They probably even paid her for the story," Maeve said. "At least I hope they did. I'd hate to think they got all this for nothing."

"Those rats probably convinced her she'd be helping her daughter," Gino said.

"That's a very good likeness of Una, too," Mrs. Decker said. "Do you suppose she posed for it?"

"Did she?" Maeve asked, outraged.

This made Gino smile for real, she was sorry to see. "I think her mother might've shown them a photograph of her."

Maeve discovered she didn't want to be placated. She wanted to be angry about something. Anything. "What are you going to do for a living?"

Gino raised his eyebrows. "I don't know. Maybe I'll go to work for Mr. Malloy's detective agency."

"Does Frank have a detective agency?" Mrs. Decker asked in surprise.

"No, he doesn't," Maeve said.

"Maeve told Una Pollock that he does," Gino told Mrs. Decker with a wink.

"I see. I suppose he does then, if we count as detectives."

"I don't think we do," Maeve said.

"Speak for yourself," Gino said. "I'm a detective."

"But nobody's paying us, don't forget."

"I thought we were using Mr. Pollock's money," Mrs. Decker said.

"To pay for Una's bail and attorney," Maeve said, "but I don't think we can pay ourselves with it."

"Besides, it's not Pollock's money in the first place," Gino said. "And I don't need to be paid."

"Oh, did you suddenly become a millionaire like Mr. Malloy?" Maeve asked, hating the acid in her voice but unable to hold it back.

To her annoyance, this only made Gino grin again. "No, but I've got some money saved, so I can work for free for a while."

"And what will you do after that?" Mrs. Decker asked in genuine concern.

Gino shrugged. "I can probably get a job with a real detective agency. And maybe Mr. Malloy will really open one when we tell him how much fun we've been having."

"You think this is fun?" Maeve asked, outraged again.

"Yes, and so do you, when you're not being jealous of Una Pollock," he replied.

"I'm not jealous of anyone!"

Gino's grin never wavered, which made her even madder. "Maybe if you bash my head in, they'll put *your* picture in the newspapers."

"Children, please don't fight," Mrs. Decker said, and even though she was trying not to, Maeve could see she wanted to laugh at them.

Maeve supposed they were pretty funny. "Lucky for you, I don't really want my picture in the newspapers."

"And it will be nice to have your help full-time, Gino," Mrs. Decker said. "I'm sure Mr. Decker will agree."

"Where is he, anyway?" Maeve asked to change the subject, which was becoming very uncomfortable.

"I don't know. I thought he'd be back by now. Maybe I should be concerned. He was going to see a possible murderer, after all."

"Mr. Decker can take care of himself," Gino said with more confidence than Maeve thought he should have on the subject.

Even Mrs. Decker looked skeptical.

The maid tapped on the door and stepped in. "Telephone for you, Mrs. Decker. It's Mr. Decker."

"Well, at least he wasn't murdered," she said, rising from her seat. "And he'd better have a good excuse for being late for lunch."

Maeve and Gino stared after her, wide-eyed.

"Do you think she was serious?" Gino asked when she was gone.

"I hope not."

That made him grin yet again.

"You're much too happy for someone with no job."

"I'm not too worried. My mother would let me live with them forever, and Mrs. Malloy will always feed me. You said so yourself."

She wanted to be mad at him, but she found herself melting just a bit. "And maybe Mr. Malloy really will open a detective agency."

"What do you mean, *maybe*? All that's left is to tell him about it."

"I wonder what he'll say when he finds out Mrs. Decker works for him."

That made them both laugh.

"Who did Mr. Decker go see this morning?" Gino asked when they'd sobered again.

"Truett and that investor he knows. Zimmerman, I think his name is. This afternoon he and Mrs. Decker are going to visit the widow of the fellow who killed himself."

Maeve told him about the discussion she and the Deckers had earlier about whether or not Truett could be the killer. "Mrs. Decker still thinks he didn't know about the robbery until she told him."

"I guess that's possible, even if he killed Pollock. He might've figured he could just walk right into the house and get the money, so why go to all the trouble of waiting until the middle of the night and breaking in?"

"Then who did break in? Who else even knew the money was there?"

Before he could answer, Mrs. Decker returned. They both jumped to their feet when they saw her expression.

She gave them a small, sad smile. "Mr. Truett is dead."

* * *

TRUETT'S HOTEL WASN'T TOO FAR FROM THE DECKERS' house. Gino didn't bother with a cab, so he was there in short order. The building was fairly new and very nice. He'd have to consider a place like this for himself when he got another job.

He saw two uniformed police officers he didn't know in the lobby and stopped, not wanting to get on their wrong side. If only he'd been wearing a uniform—but he'd have to get used to being a civilian now. He noticed a harried-looking man with a carnation in his lapel standing by the desk.

"I'm looking for Mr. Decker," Gino told him, wishing he'd gone home and changed into his good suit. He probably looked presentable enough in his old suit to be one of Mr. Decker's employees, but he knew people judged you on how you dressed. "He sent for me."

"Oh yes," the man said. "He asked me to send you right up. It's the fourth floor, right rear. He's all right," he added to the cops who probably would've stopped him.

They didn't look happy, but they let him pass. At least they weren't likely to recognize him from his picture in the paper. They wouldn't know he was a cop, or at least had been a cop until a few hours ago, so they probably wouldn't make the connection.

The elevator operator was a white man who was even whiter than usual. Gino was used to seeing colored men operating elevators, but in nicer hotels where the tips were better, white men got the job.

"Did you know Truett?" Gino asked when he'd closed the door and the gate and cranked the handle to set the car in motion.

"Of course I knew him. I know everyone who lives here."

"Did he get many visitors?"

"Are you with the police?" he asked suspiciously.

Gino managed not to wince. "I'm a detective."

"You're kinda young, ain't you?"

To be a police detective, he was, of course. "I'm very good."

The man snorted, but he said, "He didn't get many visitors. He was gone a lot, so I expect he saw his friends outside."

"No visitors at all?"

"Well, a colored boy came by from time to time, but he was just delivering things."

That was probably Eddie. Gino wondered what Eddie was delivering, but probably even Eddie didn't know that. "No lady friends?"

"We don't allow the gentlemen to have lady visitors."

Gino nodded. "And it's your job to make sure they don't sneak in, I guess."

The man shrugged, and Gino knew that Truett could've had a female visitor if he'd tipped the elevator operator well enough. But that information wasn't helping him figure out who killed Truett. "Did anybody visit him recently?"

"You mean since I took him up to his apartment last evening?"

Which would have been just after he left Una Pollock's house. "Yes."

"No, I didn't see a soul."

"Were you here all night?"

"No, that would be Fred."

So the first order of business was to figure out when Truett was killed, and then if this Fred had seen anyone. "When does Fred come in?"

"He'll be here at six tonight. Here you are," he said as the elevator lurched to a stop, and he flung open the gate and then the outside door.

Gino thanked him and stepped out into the hallway. He didn't need the instructions the clerk had given him downstairs. The gathering outside Truett's door would've tipped him off as to which apartment it was. He strode up to the group mingling in the hallway. A young woman was comforting an older couple who seemed quite distressed. The young woman was assuring them it must have been an accident. Gino, of course, was sure it wasn't.

Gino excused himself, sidled past them, and made it to the door, where a uniformed cop stood guard. "Is Mr. Decker here? He's expecting me."

"Ah, Mr. Donatelli," Mr. Decker's voice called from inside. He had been talking with another man in the entryway. "I'm so glad you were available."

"So am I. Do we know what happened?"

The other man had come over, and he looked Gino up and down with no sign of approval. Gino did the same to him, noting his cheap suit, worn shoes, and the fact that his bowler hat sat firmly on his head even though he was indoors. Gino pegged him instantly as a police detective but, fortunately, not one with whom he'd worked before. He was probably one of the precinct detectives who wouldn't have spent much time at Headquarters.

"Gino, this is Detective Sergeant Kilroy. Detective, Mr. Donatelli."

"You said he was a detective," Kilroy said. "He don't look old enough to shave."

"He fought in Cuba with Governor Roosevelt."

"He ain't the governor yet," Kilroy said with a disgruntled frown.

Mr. Decker just smiled. They all knew Roosevelt had been elected and would be sworn in the first of the year, which was just a few weeks away. "Would you mind telling Mr. Donatelli what you told me?"

Kilroy looked Gino over again. "Maybe you'd like to see for yourself where it happened."

He didn't make it sound like an invitation, but Gino said, "Yes, I would, thanks."

"It's pretty bloody," he said with a mean grin.

"So was Cuba, Detective Sergeant."

Kilroy snorted and started into the next room. Gino followed, although he noticed Mr. Decker did not. Mr. Decker had not gone to Cuba. The first room was a parlor with a small dining room table squeezed into one corner. What stopped Gino, however, was the condition of the room.

The place was sparsely furnished, but the desk on one wall and a cabinet on another had been turned out, all the drawers dumped and the contents scattered on the floor. The sofa cushions had been tossed on the floor and cut open. It looked, in fact, exactly like Pollock's office had looked.

"Was it like this when you got here?"

"You think this is how cops search a place?" Kilroy asked with disdain.

Gino knew it wasn't, but Kilroy seemed like somebody who might not follow the rules too closely. Kilroy had already moved on, and Gino hurried to catch up. The next room was the bedroom, and Gino saw at once this was where Truett had been killed.

The body was still there, sprawled facedown on the rug and clad only in a nightshirt, his pudgy bare legs splayed. The head was a bloody mess and blood had soaked into the rug around it. Blood had also splashed onto the ceiling and wall, which meant Truett had been struck several times.

"What did the killer hit him with?" Gino asked, glancing around.

"A lamp." Kilroy jutted his chin in the direction of the

far corner where a lamp base lay. It appeared to be made of brass or some other metal and was clotted with blood.

Gino glanced around the room again. It contained a double bed, a nightstand, a chest of drawers, and a wardrobe. No need for a washstand, because the apartment included a real bathroom, which he could see through an open doorway. Yes, this was a very nice place. All the drawers in here had been dumped out as well, and the contents of the wardrobe lay on the floor. The bedclothes had been stripped off and the mattress was askew, which probably meant the killer had checked underneath it. Whoever had done the search was thorough.

One thing that hadn't been disturbed was the lamp on the bedside table. Gino pointed at the murder weapon. "Where did it come from?"

"What do you mean? It came from here."

"I mean, was it in this room?" Gino looked around again. "Where's the shade?"

Kilroy looked around, too. Neither of them saw it.

Gino went back into the parlor, and he found it there, on the floor in front of the sofa. It was dented, as if it had been torn off in haste and tossed aside. The table beside the sofa was the logical place for it, and no lamp sat there. Then he did what Frank Malloy had taught him. He pictured what had most likely happened.

"The killer got the lamp from in here, ripped off the shade, and went in there to kill Truett with it, or at least to hit Truett with it."

"So?" Kilroy said.

Gino realized he was being tested, but he didn't mind, because he knew he was right. "So that means he went into the bedroom with the intention of hitting Truett. This was probably his main purpose in coming here."

"How can you know that?" Kilroy asked. "This is obviously a robbery. See?" He snatched something off the table where the lamp should have been and tossed it to Gino, who caught it clumsily against his chest. It was a wallet. Gino instinctively opened it to check its contents.

"You're wasting your time," Kilroy said with a grin. "It was empty when we got here."

"Are you sure?" Gino asked, knowing full well that the first officer on the scene had the privilege of taking whatever ready cash remained on the victim, if any.

"I'm sure. The first officer was whining about it when I got here. So it looks like Truett woke up during the robbery and the burglar defended himself."

"First of all, why would somebody break into the hotel and choose Truett's room in particular? This doesn't look like a place where somebody rich lives."

This was true. The furniture, while new, was cheap.

"And how much do you think Truett had in his wallet? Enough to make it worth all this trouble? Also," Gino continued, "why rob the place while Truett was here?"

Kilroy wasn't convinced. "But why go to all the trouble of tearing the place apart?"

"I think he was looking for something besides what was in his wallet." Something he didn't find, Gino would bet, judging from the way every last corner of the place had been ransacked. "After he killed Truett, though. This searching took some time and it wasn't quiet. Truett would've woken up, and a real burglar would've just run out."

Gino saw that Mr. Decker had stepped into the parlor to listen to Gino's theories. When Gino glanced back at Kilroy, the man was staring at him with dawning recognition.

"You're that dago cop that was in the newspapers this morning."

Gino simply stared back at him.

Kilroy was still thinking. "Wait, that was the Pollock murder you was involved with. His wife killed him, and you was at her place last night." Kilroy frowned as he considered this information. "What does this Truett have to do with that?"

"Mr. Truett was Pollock's partner," Mr. Decker explained.

Even Kilroy could understand that. "And you think Truett's murder and Pollock's are connected?"

Mr. Decker nodded to Gino, silently telling him to answer.

"They were business partners. Both of them were killed by blows to the head. Someone broke into Pollock's house a couple days after he died, and his office looked just like this afterward."

"What kind of business were they in?" Kilroy asked, still skeptical.

"Cheating people," Mr. Decker said. "They were getting people to invest in a bogus railroad project in Panama."

"Where's Panama?"

"Central America," Mr. Decker said. "At any rate, it seems likely that their deaths are connected."

"I thought Pollock's wife killed him," Kilroy said.

"It's possible, I guess," Mr. Decker said. "But she was in jail when her house was broken into, and I'm afraid I just don't see her sneaking into this building, breaking into Truett's apartment, overpowering him, and bashing his head in, and then searching this entire place and sneaking out again, all in the middle of the night. Can you?"

"It's possible, I guess," Kilroy mocked, tired of their theories. "Donatelli, is it? What are you doing here if your precinct is in Harlem?"

This was the question Gino had been dreading, because he no longer had a precinct anywhere. "I'm not with the police department anymore."

"Since when?"

"Since this morning."

"He's working for me in a private capacity," Mr. Decker said. "On behalf of Mrs. Pollock."

"I could see that from the newspapers," Kilroy said with a leer. "She's quite a looker, that Mrs. Pollock. Which one of you is screwing her?"

Gino should have been outraged to hear a lady's name besmirched like that, which was probably what Kilroy was hoping for, but he couldn't seem to summon much anger.

For his part, Mr. Decker could only manage a disgruntled scowl. "Really, Kilroy, is that any way to talk about a lady you've never even met?"

Kilroy just frowned his disappointment that he'd failed to get a rise out of them.

Gino decided they should change the subject. "By the way, how did the killer get into the apartment?" He walked over to the entry hall to examine the entry door, which still stood open. The uniformed officer glowered at him, having overheard the entire conversation with Kilroy. Gino ignored him and concentrated on the door. "I don't see any pry marks. Do you think he picked the lock?"

Kilroy cleared his throat. "Uh, no. The other tenants tell us they don't usually lock their doors because nobody can get into the building unless they live here."

Gino stared at him in amazement. "Really? Do you think one of the other tenants killed Truett?"

"Considering who else lives here and what you told me about Pollock, then no, I don't."

"Then how would somebody who didn't live here get in?" Gino remembered his theory about bribing the elevator operator, but that didn't seem like something a killer or even an ordinary burglar would do.

"Probably through the restaurant kitchen downstairs, then up the back steps."

"And nobody would see them?"

"Not if they came in after the restaurant was closed; and in the middle of the night, most of the staff is gone. They told me they don't lock the alley door because the staff goes out there to smoke."

"Who would know that?" Gino asked.

"Probably anybody who's ever been in that alley," Kilroy said.

So, half the population of New York. "Mind if I take another look around before I leave?"

Kilroy shrugged. "Suit yourself."

"Thank you for your help, Detective Kilroy," Mr. Decker said. "Tell me, who is your supervisor? I'd like to commend you to him."

While Decker kept Kilroy occupied, Gino dug through the piles of papers that had been dumped out of Truett's desk. He found nothing of interest, but under one of the sofa cushions, he found a package that had been ripped open. The brown wrapping paper was still mostly in place and the string that had tied it had only been pushed half off to reveal the contents—a stack of official-looking documents printed on heavy vellum. A quick scan showed them to be contracts for the investors in the Panamanian Railroad project, the ones they'd never found at Pollock's house.

Gino knew better than to ask if he could take the contracts. He left them where they were and finished his cursory search of the rest of the room. Then he returned to where Mr. Decker and Kilroy stood watching him. "Thank you, Detective Sergeant Kilroy."

"Aren't you going to tell me who the killer is? Isn't that what Sherlock Holmes always does? He looks at all the evidence and sees what all the other idiots missed."

Gino smiled at the jibe. "I'm not Sherlock Holmes, but if we find out who killed Pollock, we'll certainly let you know."

Kilroy didn't look particularly happy with this promise. Or grateful either. Mr. Decker thanked him again for his help and then quickly ushered Gino out of the apartment.

They didn't exchange a word until they were outside and safely ensconced in a cab.

"You did a very nice job in there, Gino," Mr. Decker said. "I think Kilroy was impressed."

"Do you?" Gino wasn't so sure.

"Yes, indeed. You told him some things he hadn't noticed before. A man like that would never admit such a thing, but I could see it. I'm sure you did, too."

He had, of course, but he didn't want Mr. Decker to think he was a bragger. "What I told him was true. It looked like somebody had gone there to kill Truett and to find something important."

"Do you think they found it?"

"No, I don't."

Mr. Decker seemed impressed by his certainty. "And why not?"

"Because the entire place had been ransacked. Think about it. If you're looking for something, and you find it, do you keep looking?"

"No, of course not. I see what you mean. If he'd found what he was looking for, he would have stopped searching at that point."

"So part of the place would be a mess and part would be untouched."

"You don't think it was a simple burglary then, do you?"

"No self-respecting burglar would touch Truett's place . . . unless he knew Truett had broken into Pollock's house and taken the money."

"And who would know that?"

"I have no idea. I don't think Pollock and Truett had any other partners who might've known."

"What about the investors?"

"How would they know the money was still in Pollock's safe? Wouldn't they think it was invested?"

Mr. Decker sighed. "I don't know, but I had a disturbing conversation with one of them this morning."

ELIZABETH HAD HELD LUNCH UNTIL GINO AND FELIX came back, even though she and Maeve were famished. She was pleased to see them return only a little over an hour after Gino had left, and insisted that they discuss the latest events while they ate.

"I don't want anyone to miss any more meals because of this situation," she told them as they filed into the dining room.

Gino and Maeve looked askance at the first course of baked oysters, but Elizabeth very ostentatiously began to eat hers, demonstrating the technique for them so they quickly figured out which utensils to use.

"So, Felix, dear, can you tell us what happened to poor Mr. Truett?" she asked.

"Not while we're eating, my dear, but suffice it to say he was killed the same way Pollock was, and his apartment was thoroughly searched, although we have no idea for what."

"How did the killer get in?" Maeve asked.

Felix explained about the hotel where Truett lived and how it was always staffed by a desk clerk and an elevator operator but that the kitchen door was left unlocked and unwatched for the most part overnight.

"And people just leave their doors unlocked?" Elizabeth said, horrified.

"Apparently. They were under the impression no one could get in."

"Well, at least Truett didn't really have the money," Maeve said.

"And now it looks like he might not even have been the one who broke into Pollock's house in the first place," Mr. Decker said. "Say, Gino, I forgot to ask if you found anything interesting among Truett's papers."

Gino looked up from prying an oyster loose. "The only interesting thing I found was a package that had been ripped open. It looked like it was contracts or something to do with the railroad. All very official and important-looking."

"A package, you say?" Elizabeth asked.

"Yes, it had been wrapped with brown paper and tied with string, like someone had sent it to him, except it didn't look like it had been mailed or anything."

"That's odd," Felix said. "When he was here yesterday, he said he needed to get into Pollock's house to get the contracts."

"But you thought he was lying about that," Elizabeth reminded him.

"Yes, and now it looks like I was right. He must have had them all along."

"Or maybe he did break into Mr. Pollock's house and took them then," she said.

"He couldn't have, because they weren't there," Maeve said. "Remember, I searched the office the day before the break-in, and I didn't see anything like that."

"And he wouldn't have wrapped it up like that if he was stealing it," Gino said. "Now that I think of it, the elevator operator told me the only visitor Truett got was a colored boy who delivered things to him. I thought he must have meant Eddie."

"So maybe Eddie delivered the package with the contracts," Maeve said, "but that would've been before Pollock died, so I can't see how it would matter."

"Neither can I," Gino said. "Except that I asked Pollock's servants if they knew where Truett lived, and Eddie never said a word."

"I'm sure he was just frightened, poor boy," Elizabeth said, remembering the young man and how upset he had been that first day. "I understand the police can be quite intimidating to the servant class."

"Not as intimidating as they'd like to be," Gino said, remembering how often people had refused to help him in investigations.

Then the maid came in and cleared away the oysters. Next she served chicken croquettes and baked potatoes with some lovely peas. The cook had done well.

When they were alone again, Maeve said, "Do we still think Truett killed Pollock?"

"I don't," Gino said. "They were killed in almost exactly the same way, so it was probably the same person who killed both men."

"Was Mr. Truett beaten with an Egyptian statue?" Elizabeth asked.

"No, a lamp," Gino said.

"Which is hardly a topic for polite conversation with ladies, particularly at the table," Felix reminded them.

"So if Truett didn't kill Pollock, who killed both of them?" Maeve said.

"We think it's someone who was trying to get the money back," Gino said.

"Who is this 'we'?" Elizabeth asked, looking at Felix, who smiled smugly back.

"Gino and I. I had an interesting conversation with that

Zimmerman fellow this morning. He already knew that Pollock was dead."

"That's not surprising. It's been in the newspapers. It's all over them now, in fact," Elizabeth said.

"He knew it before that, though. He says someone told him, but he won't say who it was."

"Mr. Decker and I think this person must be the killer, if he even exists," Gino said, "and if Zimmerman made him up, then Zimmerman himself is the killer."

"But why would he want to kill these men?" Maeve asked.

"Oh, because he found out the Panama scheme was a swindle," Felix said. "I forgot to mention that part. Apparently, poor Norwalk is the one who discovered the fraud. He'd been introducing people to Pollock and recommending the project."

"Oh dear, and when he found out they were being cheated, he killed himself," Elizabeth said.

"After warning Zimmerman and maybe some of the others as well," Felix said.

"So it could have been Zimmerman or one of the others who killed Pollock," Gino said. "Remember, the servants said Pollock was arguing with somebody. They thought he was just yelling at his wife, as usual, but it could have been someone else."

"And it could certainly have been Mr. Yorke," Maeve reminded them.

"So," Elizabeth said with a smile, "all we have to do is find out who Mr. Pollock was arguing with."

11

"I FEEL SO SORRY FOR GINO," ELIZABETH SAID AS THEIR carriage took them to the Norwalk house.

Felix smiled and patted her hand. He loved how soft-hearted she was, but he didn't want her to waste her sympathy. "Don't be sorry. He never really wanted to go back to the police department when he got back from Cuba anyway."

"He didn't? Then why did he?"

"He needed a job and Frank Malloy was leaving the country for several months, so going back to the police was the easy thing to do."

"And you think he was just waiting for Frank and Sarah to come back from their honeymoon?"

"I think he expects Frank will open his own detective agency when he gets home."

Elizabeth smiled at that. "Maeve is sure of it. According to her, we're already part of it."

"We? You mean you and I?"

"You and I and Maeve and Gino."

"But that's . . ." He'd intended to say *ridiculous*, but plainly it wasn't ridiculous because here they were, going to visit the widow of a man who was connected to the murder they were investigating.

"That's what, dear?" she asked with a knowing smile.

"I guess that's *correct*. Although it won't be a recurring situation, of course."

"Of course."

He didn't like the way she'd immediately agreed. That meant she was humoring him. She should have argued instead, but he knew there was nothing to argue about. She'd been helping Frank and Sarah with investigations for years. She thought he didn't know, but he'd always known. He should have forbidden her to participate in such potentially dangerous situations, but forbidding Elizabeth to do something would only ensure that she would do it.

Felix decided not to discuss Frank Malloy's detective agency anymore. "How are we going to find out who Norwalk told about the Panama scheme? I doubt that Caroline knows anything about his business interests."

"You might be surprised. Most women know what's going on, even if their husbands don't discuss it with them. And I'm sure Oscar was troubled when he found out the investment scheme was a fraud. She would have been concerned and probably would have tried to find out what was bothering him. Even if Oscar didn't tell her anything, she may have spoken to her attorney by now about the estate, so she may know about the missing money, especially if it means she's penniless."

"Let's hope that's not the case, but at least we can tell her she'll receive a portion of the money back."

"People hate talking about money," Elizabeth reminded him.

"Only if they have it."

The mourning wreath still hung on the front door, and the maid informed them that the mistress wasn't receiving visitors.

"Would you take her my card and tell her we need to speak with her about something very important?" Elizabeth asked.

To Felix's surprise, the girl did as she asked, allowing them to wait inside while she delivered the message.

"How do you do that?" he asked.

"Do what?"

"Get people to do whatever you want."

She smiled sweetly. "I have no idea what you're talking about."

Felix knew better than to argue, so they waited in silence until the maid returned and escorted them upstairs to the formal parlor, where Caroline Norwalk awaited them.

"**W**HAT ARE YOUR PARENTS GOING TO SAY WHEN THEY find out you quit your job?" Maeve asked Gino as they waited in the family parlor for the Deckers' carriage to return and take them and the children back home.

Gino nearly smiled at the knowledge that Maeve was concerned about him. "Ma'll be worried, because she worries about everything, but they'll both be glad because they never liked me working there in the first place."

"They didn't? Why not?"

"Because in Italy, the police . . . Well, I guess not just the police, but the whole government is crooked. Nobody trusts them, and for good reason."

"That's true here, too."

"Yeah, but it's not as bad. Not everybody is out for themselves. Mr. Malloy, for one, and Colonel Roosevelt for another."

"He's Governor Roosevelt now," she said with a grin.

"He's not the governor yet," he said, remembering Kilroy. "Just a few more weeks."

Yes, things were changing in New York, but how much they'd change, no one knew. "When are the Malloys coming home?"

"By Christmas, for sure. I guess it depends on what ship they get and the weather, of course. They'll send us a cable to let us know."

"Soon, though."

"Yes, soon." She studied him for a long moment. "So you *are* worried about not having a job."

He grinned, unwilling to admit such a thing. "I'm just having so much fun being a private investigator that I don't want to give it up."

She gave a humph of disbelief.

"Aren't you having fun?" he asked.

"Of course, but when the Malloys get back, I'll just be a nursemaid again."

"Oh." He hadn't thought about that.

"Yes. Oh."

"Maybe when they find out how good you are, they'll hire somebody else to take care of Catherine."

"That's just it. I don't want anybody else to take care of Catherine."

Now that *was* a problem. "Oh."

"Yes. Oh."

The maid came to tell them that the carriage had returned, and then another maid brought Brian and Catherine down, so they had no other opportunity to talk, but Gino now realized that there were worse problems than not having a job.

*   *   *

"I'M SURPRISED SHE AGREED TO SEE US," FELIX WHISPERED as the maid led them up the staircase.

Elizabeth smiled. "She's probably bored senseless by now. You can only cry so much."

Caroline Norwalk had aged ten years since the funeral, Elizabeth noted. At that time, she'd merely been in shock, stunned by the suddenness of her loss and numbed by her mind's unwillingness to accept it. By now, however, she'd faced her reality and felt the real pain of the blow life had dealt her.

"Elizabeth, Felix, what a surprise. How good of you to come," Caroline said, holding out her hands in welcome.

Elizabeth took both of them in hers and kissed her cheek. "How are you faring?"

Caroline smiled sadly. "I hardly know. I still don't think I have my feet under me properly yet."

Elizabeth stepped aside while Felix greeted her, and then they sat down by the hearth, which had been converted to gas. The fire had obviously just been lit and had not begun to touch the chill in the room.

"I've sent for some tea. You must be frozen," Caroline said, her ingrained good manners compelling her to consider the comfort of her guests first.

"You're probably wondering why we've intruded on your grief," Felix said.

She was too well mannered to agree, of course. "I'm always glad to see you both."

"Please know that we're sorry to have to bother you at this time," Elizabeth hastily explained, "but we've come across information that might provide you with some relief."

"Unless you're going to tell me Oscar isn't really dead, I

can't imagine what you could say that would give me relief," she said with the most heartbreaking sadness.

Elizabeth blinked at the sting of tears. "Oh, my dear friend, I wish we could."

"Caroline," Felix said, commanding her attention and staving off a collapse into tears by the firmness of his voice. "I'm afraid I have become aware of the unfortunate circumstances of Oscar's death." She gasped, but he hurried on before she could succumb to her grief again. "It isn't common knowledge, I'm glad to say, and the only reason I would mention it to you is because Oscar's name came up in another matter. You see, we have been assisting a young woman whose husband was murdered."

Elizabeth was relieved to see this information intrigued Caroline enough to make her forget her own problems for a moment. "Murdered?"

"Yes," he said. "Do you by any chance know a man named Randolph Pollock?"

"Pollock? I don't think so. Should I?"

"Probably not, but Oscar knew him. In fact, he invested some money with him."

Her eyes widened as understanding dawned. "Dear heavens, is he the one . . . ?"

"The one who cheated Oscar? Yes, he was."

"Was? Does that mean . . . ? You said *murdered*." Color had bloomed in Caroline's pale cheeks.

"Someone murdered Randolph Pollock a few days ago," Felix said baldly, but he did not need to spare Caroline's feelings. This was exactly what she wanted to hear.

She closed her eyes, as if she wanted to absorb the full implications of this in private. Elizabeth reached over and squeezed Felix's hand.

After what seemed a long time, Caroline opened her eyes

again. "Thank you for telling me this. It won't bring Oscar back, of course, and I would never wish that anyone be murdered, but . . ." Her voice broke, and she pulled a black-bordered handkerchief from her sleeve and pressed it to her lips.

"There's more," Elizabeth said when Caroline had regained her composure a bit. "A little good news, I think."

"What could possibly be good about any of this?" she asked.

"I understand that Oscar had invested five thousand dollars in Pollock's scheme," Felix said, not stopping when Caroline winced. "I believe we will be able to return most of it to you."

Now they had her full attention. "Return? How is that possible? Oscar went to see this man when he found out it was all a fraud. I didn't know his name, but Oscar told me he'd confronted him and demanded his investment be returned. He felt so awful because he'd convinced others to participate as well. But this Pollock person laughed at him. *Laughed* at him! Can you imagine how humiliated Oscar was? And he had to tell his friends the truth, how he'd been swindled and had led them like lambs to be slaughtered as well. That's what he said, *slaughtered*. I've never seen him so distraught."

"I'm sure Pollock had no intention of returning any of the money," Felix said, "but we have located what's left of it. He'd spent some, but we recovered most of it, and we'll see that the investors each receive their fair share."

Caroline simply stared at them. Elizabeth had begun to worry for her sanity when a single tear rolled down her face. "You have no idea what this means to me," she said at last. "How can I ever thank you?"

"That's not necessary," Elizabeth said. "We're just glad that we can do this small thing."

"It's no small thing, Elizabeth," Caroline said fiercely. "Oscar had made a bad decision that cost us a lot of money, but he could have lived with that. He could not bear the shame of having misled his friends, though. One had lost the bulk of his mother's savings."

"Young Zimmerman," Felix guessed.

"How did you know?" she asked in amazement.

"I've spoken to him. Do you know who else was involved? Who else he told about the fraud?"

"He only mentioned Lawrence's name to me. Because the money was his mother's, I think. I knew there were others, but not who."

"Show her the list, Felix," Elizabeth said.

"Oh, of course." He pulled it out of his pocket and offered it to her. "Do you recognize any of these names?"

"Are these the men who were cheated?" she asked as she looked at the list.

"Yes."

"I recognize Lawrence, of course. And Paul Reed, although I don't think Oscar mentioned his name to me. But not the other names. Are they all Oscar's friends?"

"Probably not all of them," Felix said, taking the list back. "I'm sure Pollock had others he lured into his scheme."

Caroline shivered. "What a horrible man. I wouldn't wish death on anyone, but I can't say I'm sorry to hear of his. Did you say he was married?"

"Yes, which is why Felix and I are involved," Elizabeth said. "His wife has been accused of his murder, and her mother asked us to help prove her innocence. When we started looking into his business dealings, we discovered what he had done, and that led us here. I'm so very sorry, Caroline."

"And I'm sorry for this poor woman. Is there anything I can do to help?"

Elizabeth and Felix exchanged a glance. Obviously, he couldn't think of anything either.

"Just let us know if you think of anything you feel would be helpful," she said.

"Or if anyone contacts you about Pollock's project," Felix said.

"Why would they do that?" she asked in alarm.

"They probably wouldn't, but we don't think all of the investors know about the fraud yet," he said. "We know Oscar told Lawrence and perhaps Reed as well, but we don't know about the others. So if anyone asks about it, just send them to me."

"Thank you for taking care of this, Felix," Caroline said. "You have saved me."

"You give me too much credit, Caroline," he said gently.

"Oh no, not at all! You couldn't possibly understand. I spoke with an attorney the other day. He explained to me that there's hardly any money left. Oscar's business dealings had been disastrous recently, and with the loss to Pollock . . . Well, I'm going to have to sell the house and everything in it and move in with one of my daughters. I would have gone to them with practically nothing, as a charity case, but with the money you've found, I can have a small income of my own. I don't know how to thank you, Felix."

She was crying again, and this time Elizabeth got up to comfort her while Felix looked on helplessly. He was, Elizabeth realized, not used to being considered a hero.

"Granny, we saw Santa Claus!" Catherine reported to Mrs. Malloy when they arrived back home after their visit to Macy's department store.

"Did you now?" Mrs. Malloy said with a knowing smile, signing for Brian's benefit. "What did he look like?"

Brian replied to that. He didn't know the sign for *beard*,

but he improvised, leaving no doubt that Santa's beard was very long.

"He gave us candy," Catherine added.

"Where is it?" Mrs. Malloy asked.

"We ate it."

Maeve smiled. "It was just penny candy. Santa was handing it out to all the children in the store."

"A cheap enough way to get them to come back to the store again," Mrs. Malloy remarked with a wink. "And who's this carrying all your packages?"

Maeve realized Gino had lifted the pile of boxes he carried to cover his face, as if she'd loaded him down so much he couldn't even see. She snatched the top box off the pile to reveal his wicked grin.

"Gino," Mrs. Malloy said. "What are you doing here this time of day?"

"It's a long story, Mrs. Malloy," Maeve said. "We'll tell you when the children are in bed."

"Officer Donatelli isn't a policeman anymore," Catherine said. "That's why he's not wearing his uniform."

"Is that so?" Mrs. Malloy said, raising her eyebrows at Gino. His grin faded, but she didn't scold him. That would come later, when the children weren't around, Maeve knew. "What did you buy?"

This was enough to distract the children, who had Gino carry the packages into Mrs. Malloy's private parlor. Some of them they couldn't show her, of course, but the children were thrilled to unwrap and display the tin and glass Christmas tree ornaments they'd chosen.

"What's wrong with stringing popcorn?" Mrs. Malloy wanted to know.

"It's fine," Maeve said, "but we've got to have more than

that. Mr. Malloy's a millionaire now, and we have to keep up appearances."

Mrs. Malloy snorted her opinion of that, making Maeve and Gino laugh.

"And this is really going to shock you," Gino said, opening the last box.

"What on earth is all that?" she asked, eyeing the lights and wires with grave suspicion.

"They're electric lights for the Christmas tree," Maeve said.

"I never heard of such a thing! All those wires! Why, if you turned on all those lights, the tree would go up in flames!"

"That's just it," Maeve explained, managing to bite back her smile at the reaction she'd expected from the old woman. "It's much safer than candles."

"Mama and Papa will be so surprised," Catherine said.

"They will be that," Mrs. Malloy said. "And how much did all this cost?"

"I charged it to their account," Maeve said, knowing the amount would shock Mrs. Malloy but that Frank Malloy could easily afford it. "Now let's help Mrs. Malloy with dinner."

The children scampered off to the kitchen with Gino on their heels, but Mrs. Malloy held Maeve back. "Mrs. Decker telephoned while you were out this afternoon."

"And you answered it?" Maeve asked in amazement. Mrs. Malloy feared the telephone even more than she feared electric lights.

She managed to look offended. "Of course I answered it. People don't make telephone calls unless it's important."

"What did she say?"

"She asked if you and Gino could come back to her house after supper."

"Did she say why?"

Mrs. Malloy frowned, a terrifying sight if she was frowning at something you'd done, but Maeve knew she wasn't upset with her. "She got a note from that Una girl, asking for help."

FELIX WAS STARTING TO AGREE WITH GINO ABOUT USING his carriage. He could have walked to Paul Reed's house faster than his carriage was taking him. One simply didn't arrive at someone's door on foot, however, at least if one wanted to make an impression.

He'd never met Reed, but he thought he knew some members of the man's family. The question was if Reed would see him, a total stranger. Felix was planning to mention Oscar Norwalk's name if he needed to. That would probably get him in the door, but nothing would guarantee Reed would give him any information.

The maid gave a start when she saw him, making him wonder what it was about him that had shocked her. Did her master receive so few visitors?

He had to admit the house did have a neglected air to it. The wallpaper in the entry was dark but faded in spots, probably where the sun shone through the glass in the door. Elizabeth would never have let their front hall get into that condition, he realized. The chairs placed against the wall for visitors to sit in while they waited sagged a little in the seat and dust coated the umbrellas hanging from the coatrack.

The maid returned after a few minutes, her eyes downcast this time, as if she were afraid to meet his gaze. "Mr. Reed will see you. Please follow me."

She led him up the stairs. This floor looked no better than the one below. The carpets were worn and the furniture unpolished. She took him to the rear parlor, which would be the room the family used, not the usual place visitors were received. She opened the door and announced him, then stepped out again and scurried off, still not looking up.

Felix shrugged off the feeling that he should understand her odd behavior and schooled his expression to pleasant politeness to greet Paul Reed.

Reed was a man of middle age, thin and a bit stooped, although he boasted a thick mane of gray hair. It looked like he'd been running his fingers through it instead of a comb, however, and he wore a dressing gown over his shirt and trousers. Not the normal attire for receiving visitors. Like his house, he had a neglected air. "Decker, to what do I owe this honor?"

Plainly, he didn't consider Felix's visit an honor, but Felix ignored his tone and stretched out his hand. "It's a pleasure to meet you, Reed."

Left with no choice, Reed shook his hand and invited him to sit, but he still hadn't smiled.

"I'm also a friend of Oscar Norwalk's," Felix explained. "That's why I'm here."

"If you've come to tell me about the Panama project, you're too late. Oscar was here already. Two days before he . . . died. If you're hoping to get your money back, I can't help you. Pollock is dead, or have you already heard?"

"Yes, I knew about Pollock's murder. That's how I got involved in all this, as a matter of fact. I'm not an investor."

"You were lucky, then. Or maybe you're the one who told Oscar he'd been swindled."

"I'm afraid not. If I were, I hope I could have prevented his . . . what happened."

"I would hope that, too," Reed said sadly.

"Did he say who had told him? Not by name, obviously, but . . ."

"Someone from his club, he said. Oscar had been looking for more investors, apparently, and found someone who knew Panama."

"Do you know how he met Pollock in the first place?"

"A chance encounter. Buying cigars, I think he said."

Good heavens, had Pollock actually met prospective investors at the store where he'd also met his wife? "How did *you* find out Pollock was dead?"

He must have sensed that this was the most important question Felix had asked him so far. Instead of replying, he studied Felix for a long moment. "If you're not an investor, what is your interest in all this?"

"You may also know that Pollock's wife has been accused of killing him. Her mother asked me to help."

"To help figure out who did kill him?" Reed asked in amazement. "Isn't that the job of the police?"

"The police think *she* killed him, but she says she didn't."

"Of course she does, but surely they have a good reason for thinking she did."

Felix wasn't going to go into that with Reed. "Did Lawrence Zimmerman tell you Pollock was dead?"

Reed's face settled into a scowl. "I don't remember."

Felix smiled at that. Reed probably thought he was protecting Zimmerman, but his answer only made Felix more suspicious. "I'm not your enemy, Reed. In fact, I came to tell you that we may be able to return most of the money you invested with Pollock."

Now he had Reed's full attention. "What do you mean? How could you do that?"

"We have located the money, which obviously wasn't invested in Panama or anywhere else. Pollock spent some of it, but I plan to see that the investors get a fair share returned to them."

Reed's eyes grew suspiciously moist, and he remembered Caroline's tearful relief. "Why would you do this?"

"Because it's the right thing to do. I only wish I had been able to help before Oscar died, but at least his widow will benefit."

Reed pulled a handkerchief from his pocket and blew his nose without bothering to make the excuse of a nonexistent cold. "I'm sorry, Decker," he said when he'd tucked the handkerchief away again. "I misjudged you."

"That happens frequently, I'm afraid. Now would you mind telling me how you found out Pollock was dead?"

"HE SAID ZIMMERMAN TOLD HIM," MR. DECKER SAID.

Maeve and Gino had arrived at their house a few minutes ago, and they were all sitting in the family parlor. Mr. and Mrs. Decker had just finished telling them about their afternoon visits.

"We could have guessed that," Gino said. "What we need to find out is how Zimmerman knew."

"Probably because he's the killer," Maeve said, knowing they were all thinking it.

"But nobody saw him at the house," Mrs. Decker reminded them.

"The servants said that sometimes Pollock answered the door himself if he was expecting someone," Mr. Decker said. "And we know he argued with someone right before he was killed."

"Oh my goodness, with all the business with Truett's death, we've completely forgotten Mr. Yorke. At least we know he was actually at the house that day," Maeve said.

They all stared at her in surprise.

"You're right, dear," Mrs. Decker said after a moment. "We'd completely forgotten him."

"Not completely," Gino said. "I did think to stop at his hotel on my way over here after I, uh, parted ways with the police department, but he wasn't in."

"So at least we know he's still in town," Mrs. Decker said. "I still can't believe he's a murderer. He seemed like such a nice young man, not like Mr. Truett, who didn't seem nice at all."

"Lawrence Zimmerman is probably a nice young man, too," Mr. Decker said, "but I'm thinking that in the heat of anger over the swindle and Oscar Norwalk's suicide, he might have done anything."

"The same is true for Yorke," Gino said. "More so, in fact, because Yorke thinks Pollock killed his sister."

"And he might have," Maeve said.

"But," Gino said, "why would Yorke have killed Truett?"

Maeve had no answer for that, but Mr. Decker did. "We're assuming the same person who killed Pollock also killed Truett. It seems likely, but maybe that's not true. Maybe Yorke killed Pollock in the heat of anger over his sister. Then someone found out Pollock was dead and broke into the house to steal the Panama money. It wasn't there, so this person assumed Truett had it, and he went to Truett's hotel to get it."

"But it wasn't there, so he killed Truett?" Gino scoffed.

"No, he killed Truett because he was *sure* it was there."

That made a strange kind of sense, Maeve realized. "Except it wasn't there, because we have it."

"And I'm beginning to think we should return it to the investors as soon as possible," Mr. Decker said.

"Do you think that's wise, dear?" Mrs. Decker asked. "Won't they need it for evidence or something?"

"I can't imagine why. Can you, Gino?"

Gino shook his head. "In fact, if the police get their hands on it, it might disappear completely. That's a lot of money, and a lot of temptation."

"Would the police actually steal it?" Mrs. Decker asked.

Maeve and Gino gave her a pitying look, but Mr. Decker said, "I'm afraid it's a possibility we must consider, my dear, and even if it isn't stolen, it might never be returned to the investors. So the sooner we return it, the better."

"I took five dollars out to bribe the matron at the jail," Maeve said. "I think we should count that as an expense."

"Why did you need to bribe her?" Mrs. Decker asked.

"To look after Una," Maeve said, grinning at the memory. "That was before I got to know her, though."

"So, Felix, you should figure out how much each investor should get, based on how much is left. Then you can deliver it to them. That will also give you an excuse to visit the ones you haven't seen yet."

"Yes," he said with a faint smile, "and I can also ask them if they killed Pollock while I'm there."

She ignored that. "Oh dear, should we give Una some money to pay the servants, too? We did promise them."

"Estimate how much you think they're owed, and I'll subtract that from the total," Mr. Decker said.

"But where will we tell her it came from?" Maeve asked. "Are you going to pretend it's from you, Mrs. Decker?"

"Maeve's right," Gino said. "We can't let Una know we have her husband's money, because she'll want it all."

"And think she's entitled to it, if I've judged her correctly," Maeve said.

Gino suddenly sat up straighter and grinned. "I just thought of something. If we prove she didn't kill her husband, she'll get the bail money back."

"That should be enough to pay the servants and give her some spending money besides," Mrs. Decker said. "And if not, I'll happily take care of them, poor things."

"So it's settled. I'll start returning the investors' money as soon as I figure out how much each of them should receive."

"What if one of them killed Pollock and Truett?" Gino asked.

"It's still their money. They can use it to pay for an attorney," he added with an ironic smile.

"And what about Mr. Yorke?" Mrs. Decker asked.

"I can definitely go see him tomorrow," Gino said.

"I'm glad we got all that settled," Mr. Decker said, "but that's not the reason we asked you to come here this evening, of course."

"What did Una's note say?" Maeve asked. She'd been dying of curiosity ever since Mrs. Malloy had given her the message, but the Deckers had distracted her.

"It was a telegram, actually, although I can't imagine how she got away to send it with the reporters on her doorstep." Mrs. Decker handed it to Maeve.

"It's to *Mr.* Decker," she noticed.

"I'm sure she felt he would be the most sympathetic to her plight," Mrs. Decker said with just a hint of sarcasm.

"I can't help it. I was trained from birth to protect helpless females," Mr. Decker replied with a glint in his eye.

"It's too bad you don't know any helpless females," Maeve said, earning a grin from Mrs. Decker.

Gino had leaned over to read the message, too. "She wants you to come to the house, but she doesn't say why."

"I think we can assume she thinks he can assist her in some way," Mrs. Decker said. "She must be going crazy with her house surrounded by reporters all day."

"But she told me she didn't want our help," Gino said. "She didn't even want me in the house."

"She doesn't need help from a poor Italian police officer," Maeve said gently. "She does need help from a rich, middle-aged society gent."

Gino's dark eyes widened with understanding. "I see!"

"We see as well," Mrs. Decker said. "Which is why we're sending you to help her, Gino."

12

"IT'LL BE MIDNIGHT BEFORE WE GET THERE," MAEVE SAID. "I don't know why we had to take their carriage."

Gino grinned in the darkness of the comfortable vehicle. When he was alone with Maeve, he didn't care how long it took to get there. "Are you in a hurry to see Mrs. Pollock?"

He couldn't see her expression, but he could imagine her adorable scowl. "No, but I thought you would be."

"I can wait. Besides, Mr. Decker was right. Una Pollock is much more likely to open the door to us if we arrive in his carriage."

"The newspapers will love it, too."

"Yeah, they might put your picture on the front page this time. 'Beautiful Irish Girl Rescues Widow.'"

"They'd never say that."

"They said I was handsome," he reminded her.

"Yes, but you really are handsome."

Gino silently cursed the darkness that hid her expression. Did she really mean that or was she teasing him? When he was in Cuba, the men had spent a lot of time talking about the mysteries of women, and he'd thought he'd learned a lot. He couldn't remember anything that would help him now, though, so he had to rely on honesty. "And you really are beautiful."

Had he stunned her speechless? She didn't reply for a full minute, and then she said, "More beautiful than Una Pollock?"

Gino didn't need anyone's advice to know the right answer to this question. "No."

He waited for Maeve's gasp, then added, "She's just pretty. You're beautiful."

If he'd expected Maeve to melt into his arms, he would have been disappointed. Luckily, he hadn't expected any such thing. "And you, Officer Donatelli, are full of malarkey."

"I'm not an officer anymore," he reminded her, happy to realize it no longer hurt to say so.

"But you aren't denying the malarkey?"

"I don't even know what that is."

"Ask Mrs. Malloy."

"Which one?" he teased.

"The old one. She'll be only too happy to explain," she teased right back.

Gino settled back into the seat, glad Maeve couldn't see his expression, because he was grinning with satisfaction. For once he'd said exactly the right thing to her. She'd scoffed at his compliments, but she wasn't mad at him. This was definitely progress.

"What do you suppose she wants?" Maeve asked after a minute.

"Mrs. Pollock? Money, probably."

"You think that's all?"

Gino considered. "What else could it be?"

"Pretty girls like Una Pollock are used to having men look after them."

"Who looked after her before Pollock?" he asked.

"The man who owned the cigar store, for one. He rescued her from a factory, where she probably got the easiest jobs because the foreman there thought she was pretty. Before that, she probably got special treatment at school, and before that—"

"And how could you know all this?"

"Because I've seen it before."

"Is this what happened to you? You got special treatment because you're so pretty?"

"I thought I was beautiful," she said a little sharply.

"Beautiful, then. You got special treatment because you're beautiful?"

"No, I didn't, because I'm not pretty or beautiful. I'm just an ordinary girl with ugly red hair who got teased all the time. The teacher never picked me to pass out papers or clap the erasers."

"Who wants to clap erasers? And your hair isn't ugly. Whoever said that is an idiot."

"Anyway, Una is probably looking for a new man to take care of her, and Mr. Decker must seem like a good prospect."

"But he's married."

"Rich men can take care of more than one woman."

Gino needed a minute to think about this. "You mean she wants to be his mistress?"

"I mean she'd probably do anything for a man who'd get her out of trouble. Why do you think Mrs. Decker sent us instead of him?"

"He didn't want to go either," he reminded her.

"I know. I never liked Mr. Decker very much before, but now . . . Well, I think he really loves Mrs. Decker."

"Just like Mr. Malloy loves Mrs. Brandt. And my father loves my mother."

"What are you talking about?"

"I'm talking about how there are lots of men in this world who love their wives . . . In case you were wondering."

Maeve would, of course, never admit if she'd given this matter any thought. "You're crazy."

"Probably. I still think Una wants money."

"Or a man who has it."

"It's the same thing. So do you think she knew about the money in the safe?"

Maeve thought this over for a minute. "I can't believe she did."

"Why not?"

"Because she wasn't upset at all when she found out she'd been robbed. If that was me, I would've been screaming bloody murder. Nobody acts calm if they've lost thirty-seven thousand dollars."

"Yeah, Mr. Decker said she was mostly worried about the damaged chairs."

"Which is why she couldn't possibly have known about it. And because she didn't know about the money, she's not wondering where it went or looking for it. Instead she decided she'd ask the richest man she knows for help."

That made sense, except she wasn't getting the richest man she knew. She was getting Gino. "Why did you decide to come with me tonight?" he asked.

"What do you mean?"

Ah, so Maeve didn't want to answer that question, which made Gino think he'd like her answer very much. "You know what I mean. Mrs. Decker said I should go and find out what she wants. You didn't need to come."

"I just wanted to hear for myself what she has to say."

"I would've told you tomorrow."

She sighed in the darkness. "I thought you might need a chaperone."

"You think I'm in danger from the lovely widow?" he asked in feigned amazement. "She can't be interested in me. I don't even have a job."

"She doesn't know that. For all she knows, you're still working for the police."

"Oh, and she'll think maybe I can do something for her."

"I don't know what she thinks, but I told you, girls like that use people. Even Mrs. Malloy told me she's a sly one."

"Mrs. Malloy thinks everybody is a sly one."

"In Una's case, she's right."

Gino thought this over and decided he liked her reasoning just fine. "Thank you for coming along to protect me, Miss Smith."

This earned him a swat on the arm, which made him grin much more broadly than he would have dared if it hadn't been so dark in the carriage.

MAEVE COULDN'T BELIEVE HOW MANY REPORTERS WERE standing on the sidewalk outside the Pollock house. "Don't they get cold?" she asked as the carriage pulled to a stop across the street.

"They're used to it, I guess. It's what they do."

"But it's so late. I thought they'd be gone by now."

"They're hoping something will happen, like one of the richest men in town driving up in his fancy carriage to pay the widow a visit."

"Oh, that would make a good story for the front page. No wonder Mr. Decker didn't want to come."

"They'll probably find out this is his carriage, so I guess I need to make sure they see my face and know I'm not him."

"How would they find out it's his carriage?"

Gino sighed. "You don't have much experience with newspaper reporters, do you? As soon as they realize we're here to see Mrs. Pollock, they'll be climbing up to bribe the coachman, and if that fails, they'll probably follow us home."

"I don't want them coming to the Malloy house!"

"Then we need to tell the coachman to let himself be bribed." Gino reached up and knocked on the roof to let the driver know they were ready to get out.

"Don't forget your hat," Maeve said, shoving the top hat into his hands.

He settled it on his head. "This is a really nice coat. I think I'll get one like it."

Maeve snorted at the thought. They both knew the coat cost a small fortune. The Deckers had given them Mr. Decker's overcoat and hat and one of Mrs. Decker's coats and a fur muff to wear. They didn't care about fooling the reporters, but they were afraid Una wouldn't open the door if she knew who her visitors really were.

The carriage sagged as the coachman climbed down from his perch, then bounced back before the door swung open.

"You've had a busy day today, John," Gino said to him as he adjusted his hat as low over his eyes as he could, and pulled his scarf up over his chin.

"These past few days is the most excitement I've had in a long time," the driver replied, reaching up to help Gino out.

"They're going to offer you money to tell them who the coach belongs to, so go ahead and take it. Just don't tell them the truth. Tell them who I really am so Mr. Decker's name doesn't end up in the newspapers."

"I'll do that," he replied with a grin.

"Wait until I signal you," Gino said over his shoulder, making Maeve groan. Did he think she'd forget?

Gino hesitated a moment, probably gathering his courage, then started across the street toward the mob of reporters who had been watching their arrival with great interest to see if they would turn into a possible story.

As soon as they realized Gino was heading toward them—and consequently toward the Pollock house—they all started shouting at once and surging at him. He ducked his head and barreled forward, shouldering the bolder ones aside when necessary. Maeve hoped she didn't have to fight her way through like that. She wasn't nearly as big as Gino.

The driver still stood holding the door open and ready to hand her out when the time came. "I'll come get you if they get too rough," he whispered.

"Thanks."

The gaslight from the streetlamps cast too many shadows to see exactly what was happening, but someone in a top hat had reached the top of the front steps and pounded on the front door. It opened immediately, so Una had obviously been watching.

"Now," the driver said, taking her arm.

Maeve hopped out, snatched up her skirts, and ran across the street before the reporters realized she had even been in the coach. They were all looking up to where the man in the expensive overcoat and top hat stood before the open front door. He'd turned to look down at them, or so they thought. He was really looking to see where she was.

She managed to worm her way through to the bottom of the steps, earning some grunts of displeasure but no real notice until she started up the steps.

"Hey, who's that?" someone yelled.

Maeve didn't look back. Someone tried to grab her arm, but she shook them off, and then she was clear and Gino reached out his hand. She took it and he pulled her inside.

Hattie slammed the door on the surge of outraged reporters determined to find out who had just outsmarted them. Their furious roar made Maeve wince.

"Are you all right?" Gino asked.

"I'm fine." She shook out her skirts and looked up to see Una Pollock standing in the parlor doorway. If the reporters had been furious, Una was enraged.

"What are you doing here, and where is Mr. Decker?" she demanded.

Gino swept off his tall hat and sketched her a little bow. "He couldn't come, so he sent us."

Una gave a howl of rage, turned on her heel, and disappeared back into the parlor, slamming the door behind her.

"She's been upset," Hattie said by way of apology. The poor woman looked like she hadn't slept much since Maeve had last seen her.

"I'm sure," Maeve said. "It must be hard with those reporters out there all the time."

"We can't even go out to get food," Hattie said.

"I'll tell Mrs. Decker. She'll make sure you get some provisions," Maeve said, removing Mrs. Decker's coat and handing it to Hattie.

Gino handed her his coat and hat, too, then eyed the parlor door warily. "Should we try to talk to her?"

"I don't think we have much choice if we want to find out why she needs help. Or is it just the food?" she asked Hattie.

"I don't know, miss. She got real upset this morning. She was screaming at poor Eddie something awful. Then she made me go out to send Mr. Decker the telegram. I had to walk for blocks, but they were still following me. I finally got on the El. They got on behind me, so I waited until it was starting to leave and then I jumped out. I could hear them shouting when the train pulled out, but I got away."

"Oh, Hattie, that was very clever," Maeve said.

"I don't know about that," she said with a sigh. "I was thinking how easy it would be to just keep going and never come back here, like Jane did."

"Jane? Did she leave?"

"Oh yes, miss. She left yesterday morning. Even before Mrs. Pollock come home. She must've packed up all her things and hid them out back somewhere when nobody was looking. I sent her out to the market that morning, and she never come back. We checked her room and it's cleaned out. But I couldn't leave Velvet and Eddie here alone, so after I sent the telegram, I come back. I was starting to think nobody got the message, though."

"The Deckers were out all afternoon, so they didn't see it until late," Maeve said, stretching the truth a bit. She looked at the parlor door again. "Do we dare go in there?"

"Oh, for pity's sake." Gino strode over to the door like he was going to throw it open, but to Maeve's amusement, he stopped and knocked softly instead. "Mrs. Pollock? We're here to help you."

Apparently, she didn't reply. He looked back to Maeve, shrugged, and opened the door. Maeve didn't think she would've been that brave. He did hesitate a moment, in case a vase came crashing, but when nothing happened, he pushed the door wider and stepped in.

Emboldened, Maeve followed. He stopped a few steps in, and Maeve came up beside him. Una Pollock sat in a chair on the other end of the room, by the gas fire, glaring at them. She wore a dark blue skirt and bodice that Maeve remembered from packing up her clothes. It fit her perfectly and made her eyes look even bluer than they usually did. She was giving them a look that could have drawn blood.

Gino didn't seem to notice. "Mr. Decker asked us to call

on you to see what you needed, Mrs. Pollock. He told us to help you with whatever it is."

She looked them over as if she were examining something she'd stepped in on the street. "And exactly what can you do to help me?"

"Anything Mr. Decker can."

She sniffed in derision. "And what about your little doxy? Why is she here?"

Maeve saw a little twitch in his cheek, as if he wanted to smile at that, but he said, "She's here in case you need a woman to confide in."

Una stared at them for another moment, then to Maeve's surprise, she covered her face with both hands and began to sob. Gino glanced down at Maeve, horrified and obviously helpless. Muttering an imprecation on the Deckers for sending her here, she called out, "Hattie, bring Mrs. Pollock some tea, please." Then she glanced around for a cabinet that looked like it might contain liquor. She had to open a few doors before she located the proper one. The selection was modest, but she settled on brandy and poured some into a glass she found there.

Una was really working herself into a state by the time Maeve reached her. "Here, drink this."

Una either ignored her or was simply too upset to care. Maeve grabbed one of Una's wrists with her free hand and yanked it away. Shocked into momentary silence, Una stared up at her stupidly.

"Drink this," Maeve repeated, pressing it to her lips. Una obeyed, taking a sip that promptly started her choking. When she was finished, Maeve made her drink some more. After a couple small sips, she pushed the glass away and glared up at Maeve with renewed hatred.

Maeve returned the favor, furious that Una Pollock even

looked pretty when she cried. Her long eyelashes were spiked and the color in her cheeks was rosy. Maeve wanted to dash what was left of the brandy in her face. Instead, she said, "Now tell us what all the fuss is about."

"I don't know what you're talking about," she said, still glaring.

"Hattie told us you were screaming at Eddie, and you've been upset all day."

"Wouldn't you be? Do you know what's going on outside my house?"

"Of course we do. We just fought our way through because you asked for help."

"We can't go outside. We can't have visitors. No one wants to be interrogated by those jackals outside."

"You might as well get used to it, because they'll be there every day until the trial."

Una's dismay heartened Maeve a little, but then she looked like she might start crying again, so Maeve got angry all over again.

"Just tell us what you wanted Mr. Decker to do for you."

Una's gaze darted over to where Gino had been standing, and when Maeve looked, she saw he'd slipped out, the sniveling coward. If Una had thought to use her wiles on him, she'd missed her chance, at least for the moment.

Maeve watched Una's face as she considered her options. Whatever she'd intended to ask Felix Decker must have depended on using her feminine charms because she obviously had no intention of asking it of Maeve. After a minute or two of deliberation, Una stuck out her chin and said, "I want to see my mother."

"Your mother?" This was the last thing Maeve had expected to hear.

"Yes, I . . . I miss her. She was so kind to me when I was

arrested. She got me an attorney and paid my bond so I could get out of that horrible jail. I need to see her to . . . to thank her. And I just need her support right now. She's the only family I have left."

She managed to end this little speech on a sob, and she pulled a lacy handkerchief from her sleeve to dab her now-dry eyes.

"And this is why you sent for Mr. Decker?"

"Of course."

There was no "of course" about it, in Maeve's mind. If she just wanted her mother, why didn't she send the telegram to Mrs. O'Neill instead of Felix Decker?

GINO TOOK ONE LOOK AT UNA POLLOCK SOBBING AND decided he needed to check on poor Eddie. Eddie might also be sobbing if Una had yelled at him, but Gino was pretty sure he could deal with that. He knew very well where the kitchen was, so he found the stairs and hurried down them. Maeve, he was sure, could handle Una all by herself.

He found the three remaining servants in the kitchen. Velvet was preparing a tea tray while Hattie waited impatiently. Eddie sat at the kitchen table looking like his best friend had just shot his dog. His eyes were swollen from crying, but he didn't seem to be crying now, thank heaven.

"How are you folks doing?" he asked with as much cheer as he could muster.

"Oh, Officer, I don't know what's going to become of us," Hattie said. "Those reporters is going to hound us from now on. That's what they said when they was following me today. They said I might as well tell them what they want to know because they'll find it out some other way if I didn't. They said they'd pay me, too. Can you imagine? They'd pay me money to talk about Mr. and Mrs. Pollock!"

"I'm glad somebody's willing to pay us money," Velvet said to no one in particular, reminding Gino that Mrs. Decker had promised them their wages. He knew only too well that Una Pollock had no way to pay them. Maybe she'd already figured that out and that's why she'd sent for Mr. Decker.

"As soon as we find out who killed Mr. Pollock, this will all be over," he said.

Eddie groaned as if he were in pain. Hattie scurried over to comfort him. "There now, chile. Don't you be fretting yourself."

He obviously didn't take any comfort from these words, because he put his head down on his arms and started sobbing.

"He's been like this all day," Velvet said. "The missus lit into him something fierce this morning, and his poor heart is broke. He thinks the world of her, you see."

Hattie was patting him on the back, but that only seemed to make it worse. Gino figured talking about it wasn't the right thing to do, what with Eddie sitting right there and everything. "What's this about Jane leaving?" he tried by way of changing the subject.

"Oh, she just up and left. Hattie sent her to the market but she never come back," Velvet said.

"I guess she wanted to get away from the reporters."

"Oh, she left before they got here. She left before the missus come home, even."

"Where would she go without a reference?" Gino asked. He didn't mention the part about her back pay since he didn't want to remind them of it.

"That girl was up to something," Hattie said. "I caught her writing a letter."

"A letter?" Velvet scoffed. "She don't got no family that I know of. Who'd she be writing a letter to?"

"That's what I was wondering, but she got real uppity when I asked and wouldn't say."

"When was this?" Gino asked.

"When she was writing the letter, you mean?" Hattie asked.

"Yes. When did she write it? Before or after Mr. Pollock died?"

"After, for sure. She wouldn't write no letters if Mrs. Pollock was in the house. The next day, I think."

"Oh, I remember now," Velvet said. "She was acting all funny. Said she had to go out to get something, but I put a stop to that. I bet she wanted to mail her letter."

Gino noticed Eddie had stopped sobbing to listen. He'd raised his head and was scrubbing at his face with his sleeve. "She give it to me."

"Give what to you, honey?" Hattie asked.

"The letter. She give it to me to mail."

"What'd she do for a stamp?" Gino asked.

"You don't need no stamp. The person what gets it will pay, if they want the letter," Eddie said. "That's what she told me."

"Who was it addressed to?" Gino asked, wondering if he'd found the answer to one of their many questions.

Eddie looked away and shrugged. "Didn't notice."

Velvet touched Gino's sleeve to get his attention and mouthed, "He can't read much."

Gino nodded. "Do you have any idea where Jane might've gone? You said she didn't have any family, but did she have friends?"

"Nobody that would take her in, I don't think," Hattie said. "Maybe she heard about another job and went to try for it."

"Where would she hear about another job?" Velvet asked. No one had an answer.

The water had started boiling, so Velvet poured it into the teapot. Everything else on the tray was ready. "You can take this up now," she said to Hattie.

Left with no more excuses, Gino followed her up the stairs and back to the parlor, where he hoped Una Pollock was no longer weeping.

"I'LL BE GLAD TO TELL YOUR MOTHER THAT YOU WANT TO see her," Maeve said, still puzzled by the request. "I'm sure she'll be happy to see you."

Una said nothing. She was more interested in dabbing at what was left of her tears and patting her hair back into place. Maybe she thought Mr. Decker was still coming.

"Your mother said she hasn't been invited to your house since you got married," Maeve tried.

Una looked up sharply but took her time responding. "Randolph wasn't very sociable. He didn't like company."

"I thought you regularly entertained his business associates. Didn't they come for dinner?"

Una frowned, obviously not enjoying being contradicted. "Why are you so interested in my social life?"

"I'm just making conversation, trying to keep your mind off your troubles."

"I wish you could."

They heard the clatter of the tea tray in the hallway. Maeve stood up, ready to help, although she noticed Una did not. She was used to being waited on. Maeve wondered how long it took for that to happen. Maybe it came more naturally for pretty girls.

Hattie glanced warily at her mistress, as if she were prepared to bolt, tea tray and all, if Una's mood wasn't just right.
Una had run out of steam, however, and didn't even turn her
head in Hattie's direction.

Hattie set the tea tray down on the side cabinet where Maeve
had found the liquor. "Should I pour?" she asked Maeve softly.

"I'll do it."

Hattie nodded gratefully and made her escape. Only then
did Maeve notice Gino lurking just outside the still-open
doorway.

"Welcome back," she said as she crossed to pour the tea.

He stepped into the room as if he'd intended to all along.
"How are you feeling, Mrs. Pollock?"

"Better, thank you." She even used a different tone of voice
when she was talking to a man she wanted to manipulate,
Maeve noticed.

Instead of going to her, as Maeve had expected, Gino
came to where Maeve was pouring tea into three cups. "Do
you think she knows about Truett?" he whispered.

Maeve looked up in surprise. They hadn't even considered
this. "How could she?" she whispered back.

"What are you plotting over there?" Una snapped.

Maeve plastered a polite smile on her lips and carried one
of the teacups over to her. "We were just wondering if you've
seen any newspapers."

"Of course not. My staff can't even get out to buy food, and
I wouldn't want to read them anyway."

Maeve handed Una the cup, for which she did not thank her,
and then glanced at Gino with a silent question. He shrugged,
which was not at all helpful, so Maeve decided to plunge ahead.

"Did you know that Mr. Truett is dead?"

Una had just taken a sip of tea, and she spit it out in a
most unladylike fashion and began to choke.

Gino started over, ready to slap her on the back or whatever, but Maeve stopped him with a gesture. She took the cup and saucer from Una while she coughed and got her breath back, letting her struggle without assistance. When she was breathing again, she looked up at Maeve with pure hatred.

"Are you all right?" Maeve asked without much genuine concern.

"I'm fine."

"I guess you hadn't heard about him. I'm sorry to break it to you, but I suppose that's better than reading about it in the newspaper. You must've known him pretty well, since he was your husband's business partner."

Una was still seething, although Maeve couldn't be sure if she was mad because Maeve had made her choke or because Truett was dead or both. Maeve offered her the tea again, and she took it without much grace.

After a sip or two, she looked up at where Maeve still loomed over her. "How did he . . . die?"

"He was murdered," Maeve said. "The same way your husband was."

Una closed her eyes, and the cup rattled in the saucer as her hands shook. This was obviously a shock to her. Maybe she did know Truett well. Maeve felt a niggle of regret that she'd broken the news so baldly. But only a niggle.

Gino came over and pushed a cup of tea into Maeve's hands. "Sit down," he said softly, and she understood that he wanted her to ease up on Una. Maybe he was right, so she sat in the chair opposite and took a polite sip of the tea.

Gino went over to the sofa and sat down, too. Without his tea, Maeve noticed. By then Una had regained her composure. She looked almost angelic sitting there.

"Mrs. Pollock wants to see her mother," Maeve said to Gino.

This surprised him as much as it had her, but he said, "She'll be happy to hear that. She's been worried about you."

Una didn't seem to care if her mother was worried or not. "Do they know . . . ? Do they have any idea who might have killed Gor— Mr. Truett?"

"No," Gino said. "Whoever did it searched his rooms the same way your husband's office was searched, though."

"It was a robbery, then."

Maeve saw Gino hesitate. He wasn't sure exactly how much to tell her, but he evidently decided to go ahead. Maeve was glad, because she wanted to see Una's reactions.

"I went there to see for myself, and it looked to me like whoever broke in killed Truett first and searched the place after."

Una flinched a little at that. "Maybe the burglar didn't know he was home, and Gordon woke up and surprised him."

"That's possible, I guess," Gino said. "The good news is that both Truett and your husband were killed the same way, as if the same person killed them, which could help your case."

"Or they could decide I killed Truett, too," Una said bitterly. "I wasn't in jail, after all, just shut up here."

"It's hard to believe a female alone could have broken into Truett's hotel, beat his head in, searched the entire place, and then gotten out again," Gino said.

As much as Maeve disliked Una Pollock, even she couldn't believe all that. There was no telling what a jury of twelve men would think, though.

"I hope you're right, Officer Donatelli," Una said with a trace of her dazzling smile.

"Did you know that one of the men who invested in your husband's Panama project killed himself a couple weeks ago?" Maeve asked, feeling an urge to torment Una some more.

She didn't look very tormented, though. She just said, "I

don't know anything about his business, and I don't know anything about the investors either."

"Except that you entertained them when they came to dinner," Maeve reminded her.

"I met them, yes, and I made polite conversation when they were Randolph's guests. It was my duty as his wife."

Yes, Maeve thought, and he would beat her senseless if she didn't.

"Now," Una said, all trace of charm gone from her voice, "are you going to bring my mother here or not?"

13

Since the next day was Sunday, the unofficial members of the Malloy Detective Agency couldn't gather until afternoon. Mrs. Malloy and Brian went to mass in the morning, while Maeve took Catherine to church. Maeve's upbringing had not included much in the way of religious instruction, so attending worship services was a new experience for her since she'd come to work for Mrs. Brandt. She did enjoy the music, and the minister sometimes had interesting things to say, even though she often found him to be hopelessly naïve about human nature. This morning the service seemed to drag, however, as she counted the minutes until the Deckers' planned visit after lunch.

Gino showed up before lunch, as she had expected, because he knew Mrs. Malloy was only too happy to feed him. He brought a stack of newspapers, too. The *World*, the *Herald*, and the *Journal*, along with several of the less important rags, like the *Times*, all carried stories about Mrs. Pollock's mysterious visitors.

He spread them on the kitchen table for them to see. The sketches of Gino and Maeve supposedly emerging from the Pollock house in the dead of night had the children giggling.

"Is that really you?" Catherine asked, peering at one particularly inaccurate drawing.

"It's supposed to be," Maeve said. "I wasn't wearing a fancy hat, though."

"And you're not that fat either," Gino said.

"What do you mean, *that* fat?" she demanded with feigned outrage.

"I mean you're not fat at all!" he quickly corrected himself, not sure if she was really outraged or not.

"I've never heard of such a thing," Mrs. Malloy insisted, looking at each of the newspapers in turn. "Can't a person visit another person without it being in the newspapers?"

"Not if you're visiting an accused murderess," Maeve said. "I love the way they lied about who we are, though. I thought John told them our real names."

"Who's John?" Catherine asked.

"Mr. and Mrs. Decker's carriage driver," Gino said. "They gave him a month's pay to tell them, too," he added to Mrs. Malloy.

"They paid him? That's horrible!"

"Not for John," Gino said. "And we wanted them to know who we were so they wouldn't keep looking and find out it was Mr. Decker's carriage and put his name in the stories."

Brian signed something to Catherine that made her giggle. "Brian says Gino looks like an old man in this one."

Gino responded by grabbing Brian and tickling him until he squealed with laughter.

"Who do they say you are?" Mrs. Malloy asked, picking up another of the papers to scan.

"One says we're influential friends," Maeve said. "Another says we're working for her attorney."

"My favorite one says that I'm her lover and Maeve is her mother," Gino said.

"Nobody said that!" Maeve protested.

"Oh, I'm sure they did." He picked up one of the papers and pretended to read it. Maeve gave him a swat that sent the children into new gales of laughter.

"But nobody said we were working for a detective agency," Maeve said when everyone had settled down again. "That's what John told them."

"Well, you aren't," Mrs. Malloy reminded them.

No one had an answer for that.

Because it was Sunday, Mrs. Malloy served their noon meal in the dining room. The long table sported a lace tablecloth and a silver candelabra, and the children were cautioned to use their best manners. Mrs. Malloy allowed no discussion of murders or murderesses at the table. If the food had been good, Maeve might not have minded, but it was the typical Irish fare that Mrs. Malloy always served, boiled and flavorless.

Gino gobbled it up like he hadn't eaten in a week and praised it to the skies, but Maeve decided the first servant they would hire when the Malloys got home was a cook. Mrs. Malloy might be offended, but Maeve was more than prepared to placate her.

After they ate, Mrs. Malloy told Maeve and Gino to take the children upstairs to play while she cleaned up. Maeve thought Gino enjoyed playing with Brian's toys as much as the boy did, and they had a wonderful time until the chiming of the doorbell told them the Deckers had arrived.

The children ran down the staircase as fast as they could, completely ignoring Maeve's admonitions, and Mrs. Malloy emerged from the kitchen to greet the visitors. She and the children had welcomed them before Maeve and Gino even reached the bottom of the stairs.

When the children had calmed down enough to allow the Deckers to remove their coats, Mrs. Malloy tried to usher them into the formal parlor.

"But our cook sent these lovely cookies," Mrs. Decker said, holding up the box she had brought. "Shouldn't we eat them at the kitchen table?"

Catherine signed the word *cookies* to Brian so that both children immediately chose the kitchen, leaving the adults no choice but to follow. Mrs. Malloy was plainly scandalized at the prospect of entertaining the Deckers in the kitchen, but Mrs. Decker linked arms with her like they were old friends and said, "We're family, after all."

Maeve made Mrs. Malloy sit down while she prepared coffee for the grown-ups and poured milk for the children. Then they all sampled the cookies. While they ate, Catherine said, "Maeve and Gino had their pictures in the newspaper."

"Did they really?" Mrs. Decker asked, her eyes shining because of course she would have seen the newspapers herself.

"Yes, Maeve looks fat."

"And Gino looks old," Maeve added, earning a grin from him.

"I'm certainly glad my picture wasn't in the newspaper then," Mrs. Decker said.

"So am I," her husband said. "I look old enough as it is."

When the cookies had vanished, Mrs. Malloy said, "I'm going to take the children upstairs so you folks can talk, but before I do, I thought you'd want to know we got a telegram yesterday from Francis and Sarah."

She signed something to Brian so he started jumping up

and down and clapping, too, the way Catherine was. Maeve felt like joining them, but she settled for grinning ear to ear and jumping up to read the telegram Mrs. Malloy had handed Mrs. Decker, leaning over Mrs. Decker's shoulder to do so.

"They'll be home in a week, if they have a good crossing," Mrs. Decker said. "Well in time for Christmas."

But not, Maeve realized, in time to be of much help to them on this case. Luckily, she was pretty sure they could do it without them.

When all the adults had read the telegram and expressed their happiness that the newlyweds were coming home, Catherine claimed the yellow paper, clutching it to her heart as Mrs. Malloy escorted them out.

As soon as the children were out of earshot, Mrs. Decker said, "I suppose we need to get back to work now. Was Mrs. Pollock happy to see you last night?"

Maeve glanced at Gino, and they both burst out laughing.

Mr. Decker turned to his wife. "I'd guess that she wasn't."

"She couldn't have been less happy," Maeve said when she had recovered herself. "She was furious. Luckily, she still hoped to charm Gino, or heaven knows what she might've done."

"I can't convince Maeve that Mrs. Pollock doesn't have any interest in me," Gino said.

"I'm sure she's interested in everyone who can help her," Mrs. Decker said. "She probably figures Maeve has nothing to offer, but a police officer . . ."

"You didn't tell her you're no longer with the police, did you?" Mr. Decker asked.

"No. The subject didn't really come up."

"That's good," Mr. Decker said. "Did she tell you why she sent for me?"

"She gave us a reason," Gino said with another glance at Maeve, "but Maeve doesn't believe it."

"What did she say?" Mrs. Decker asked.

"She said she wants to see her mother," Maeve said. "If that's true, I couldn't help but wonder why she didn't just send the telegram to Mrs. O'Neill directly."

"That is a good question," Mrs. Decker said with a knowing smile.

"Did you learn anything else?" her husband asked.

"Oh, one of the maids left," Gino said.

"Oh yes, Jane," Mrs. Decker added. "Hattie told us. I guess I forgot to mention it."

"I don't remember her," Mr. Decker said.

"She's very quiet," Maeve said. "She always looked frightened. I'm not surprised she left. It's more surprising that any of them stayed at all, in fact. Gino said the other servants don't know where she went either."

"That's odd," Mrs. Decker said. "Servants gossip a lot, and they usually know everything about each other's business."

"They knew Jane had written a letter to someone right after Pollock died," Gino said. "The next day, in fact. She got Eddie to mail it for her."

"That's odd. Who was it to?" Mrs. Decker asked.

"That's just it. Eddie can't read very well, so he doesn't know."

"Maybe she wrote to her family," Mrs. Decker said.

"According to the others, she doesn't have any family," Maeve said.

"Which made me wonder if she was writing to somebody who knew Pollock," Gino said. "To tell them he'd been murdered."

"Who would need to know that?" Mr. Decker asked.

"I know it's far-fetched, but what if she recognized one of the investors as somebody she knew," Gino said. "Maeve and I were talking about this on our way home last night, and it makes sense if you think about it."

"How would she even know who the investors are, though?" Mr. Decker asked with a frown.

"They had dinner with Pollock and Una," Maeve reminded him. "Some of them, anyway. We don't know which ones, but maybe Jane already knew one of them."

"I see," Mrs. Decker said. "She might have worked for one of them in the past or had seen them visiting someone she did work for. Maids do come and go with alarming regularity. Sometimes it seems that all I do is hire new maids."

"And investigate murders," Mr. Decker added gravely.

She ignored him. "I don't suppose we know which one of the investors she might have recognized."

"No, nor why it would matter if she did, even if she wrote that person a letter telling him Pollock was murdered," Maeve said.

"Except that one of the investors—I think it was Zimmerman—knew Pollock had been murdered long before it was in the newspaper, didn't he, Mr. Decker?" Gino said.

"That's right, he did. I couldn't get him to tell me how he knew, and when I suggested that the person who told him might be the killer, he scoffed."

"That makes sense if Jane is the one who told him, but why would she go to all that trouble?" Maeve asked.

"I know she was worried about getting paid and getting a reference," Mrs. Decker said. "All the servants were, so maybe she took a chance and tried to ingratiate herself with a former employer in hopes of going back to work for him."

"Do you think it worked?" Maeve asked.

"It could have," Mrs. Decker said. "Did you see her at Mr. Zimmerman's house, dear?"

"I didn't notice the servants at Zimmerman's house at all, but even if I had, I'm not sure I'd remember what this Jane looks like. I can certainly see him first when I start my visits to return the investors' money tomorrow, and I can ask him about her, but I'm not sure why it even matters."

"Maybe it doesn't," Gino said, "but we have to wonder why she left the way she did. They told me she sneaked away when they thought she was going to the market, and this was before the reporters showed up. It was even before Mrs. Pollock got out of jail."

"That is odd," Mrs. Decker said. "I know all the servants were upset, but leaving without a word to anyone sounds almost desperate."

"Maybe she knows something about what happened to Pollock," Maeve said. "Maybe she even saw who killed him. That would explain why she was frightened enough to leave."

"Then I'll definitely ask Zimmerman if he knows where she is. If she did see who killed Pollock, she might be in danger," Mr. Decker said.

"Which is probably why Zimmerman wouldn't even admit that he knew her or that she's the one who told him about Pollock's death," Gino said.

"We're getting ahead of ourselves," Maeve said. "We don't even know why she left, but it's a good idea to talk to her anyway, just in case. I didn't realize you'd be returning the money so soon."

"I think I should, don't you? I spent last evening doing the calculations, and the sooner it's out of our hands, the sooner it will be safe."

That made perfect sense, but it went against everything she had been taught growing up. Maeve couldn't help thinking her grandfather must be turning over in his grave at the prospect of letting so much money go back to its rightful owners.

"And I still need to see Adam Yorke," Gino said. "You said he planned to stay in town for a few more days, on the chance he might find out something more about his sister, but he probably won't stay much longer."

"Let's hope he hasn't already left," Mrs. Decker said, "although the poor man must be at his wit's end. Mr. Pollock was the only one who knew what happened to Cecelia."

"Unless he told Una," Maeve said.

They all looked at her in surprise. "Do you think he might have?" Mrs. Decker asked.

Maeve shrugged. "I don't know for sure, of course, but it seems like something a man like Pollock would talk about if he was trying to frighten his current wife, doesn't it? He could tell her to be careful or she'd end up buried in the rose garden like his first wife or something like that."

Mrs. Decker shuddered. "What a horrible thing to do."

"Bury someone in the rose garden?" Mr. Decker asked.

"No!" she said, exasperated. "Well, yes, I mean burying someone in the rose garden is awful, but threatening your wife like that is awful, too."

"I'll try to remember that," he said quite solemnly, which made her realize he was teasing her.

"Felix, you're liable to end up in the rose garden if you're not careful."

"I'll try to remember that, too."

Maeve had to cover her smile by jumping up to get the coffeepot. She refilled everyone's cup.

When she sat down again, Mrs. Decker said, "I suppose I should be the one to take Mrs. O'Neill to visit Una."

"Oh no," Maeve said. "You can't let the reporters see you. They'll find out who you are and your picture will be in the newspapers, too."

"And you'll probably look fat," Gino said with a perfectly straight face.

"And old, too," Mr. Decker added.

Mrs. Decker was glaring at them, so Maeve hurried to their rescue. "Besides, they'd want to know why a society matron is involved with a murder. They'd probably make up some scandal about Mr. Decker."

"No one who knows Felix would believe that for a second," she said with a twinkle, her good humor restored by the thought of her husband involved in a scandal, "but I am concerned about myself. A lady should only have her name in the newspapers three times during her life."

"And what are those three times?" Gino asked with genuine curiosity.

"When she's born, when she marries, and when she dies," Mrs. Decker said. "I've already used up two of my three, so I suppose I shouldn't expose myself at the Pollock house."

"And you certainly shouldn't die," Mr. Decker said. "I don't think I should escort Mrs. O'Neill either, for all the same reasons, so that leaves Gino and Maeve."

"I'll do it," Maeve said. "I feel sorry for the poor woman, and I don't think for a minute that Una wants to see her because she misses her. She's got something up her sleeve, I'm sure, and she wants to take advantage of her mother somehow."

"That's not very charitable, Maeve," Mrs. Decker said. "But I'm afraid you're right. So please let me know if you need any assistance."

"I know Mr. Decker isn't going to start returning the money until tomorrow," Gino said, "but I think I should try to find Yorke today."

"I agree," Mr. Decker said. "The sooner the better."

"I think I should go see Mrs. O'Neill today, too, to tell her Una wants to see her," Maeve said. "And she'll probably want to visit her daughter right away."

"I would, I know," Mrs. Decker said. "There may be fewer reporters at the house because it's Sunday, too."

Maeve wasn't counting on that, but it would certainly be nice.

"Do you want to take our carriage?" Mr. Decker asked her.

"I think Mrs. O'Neill would be happier if we just took the El, and there's no sense in attracting the attention of the reporters with the carriage again. Besides, it's faster."

Mrs. Decker sighed. "That leaves me with nothing to do except play with the children this afternoon while Felix counts out the money." She rose from her chair, smiling broadly. "I think I'll get started."

GINO WAS GLAD HE'D WORN HIS BEST SUIT TODAY. HIS mother hadn't been happy when he left the house this morning. She was worried about him quitting the police and not having a real job, but he suspected she was even more worried about him getting dressed up and going to see some Irish girl she'd never met. Gino only wished she had something to worry about. He had, as yet, no reason to believe Maeve was the least bit interested in him that way.

But a man could hope.

Adam Yorke was staying in a modest hotel near Washington Square. The desk clerk told him, after receiving a small tip, that Mr. Yorke was in the lounge. Gino found him sitting in an armchair with a pile of newspapers beside him, reading his way through the latest Pollock stories.

"Mr. Yorke?"

He looked up in surprise, then glanced around as if to make sure Gino was alone. "Who are you?"

"Mr. Decker sent me to see you."

Yorke practically jumped to his feet. "Do you have word about Cecelia?"

Gino hated to disappoint him. "No, but I do have some information that might help. Can I sit down?"

"Oh yes, certainly," he said, motioning to the empty chair near his. "May I get you something? A drink?"

Gino had learned from Frank Malloy that he shouldn't drink alcohol when he was working on a case. "No, thanks. By the way, I'm Gino Donatelli. I'm a private investigator working on the Pollock case."

"Why is there a private investigation going on? I thought his wife killed him, and I certainly don't blame her at all."

"His wife's mother hired us. She doesn't believe her daughter is guilty."

"I'm sure she doesn't. I wouldn't blame her if she'd killed him, of course, but I wish she hadn't. Randolph Pollock was an evil son of a bitch, but he was also the only person who knows what happened to Cecelia."

"Mr. Decker told me that Pollock claimed she died."

"Yes, in childbirth, but we could find no record of it anywhere. We also checked every cemetery in Chicago and the surrounding counties. None of them had buried her. But you said you had some information for me."

The man looked like he'd been to hell and back, except for the spark of hope now lighting his brown eyes. Gino hated to extinguish it.

"We've learned some things about Pollock that you might not know. One thing we learned is that he made a habit of hitting his wife."

"Hitting? You mean he beat this woman . . ." He snatched up one of the newspapers and found the picture he wanted. "This Una?"

"Yes. When she was arrested, she was covered with

bruises, and the servants told me that he hit her whenever he got mad at her."

"No wonder she killed him," Yorke said.

Gino didn't want to argue with him, so he just ignored that. "If Pollock was the kind of man who beat one wife, he probably would beat another."

Yorke needed a minute to digest this. "Do you think he beat Cecelia, too?"

"We think it's possible. Maybe even probable. You said Pollock wouldn't let you see your sister after they married. The same thing happened when he married Una O'Neill. Her mother wasn't allowed to visit her or even contact her."

"I knew there was something," Yorke said. "She'd send us a note from time to time. She kept insisting she was fine, but I knew something was wrong, because if she were fine, she would have come to see us."

"We don't know what happened with your sister, but we thought you should know what we found out about Pollock."

"That's why she didn't come back to us when she left him," Yorke said. "She would've been too ashamed. Now she's out there all alone."

Gino had seen it before, the family who refused to even consider the possibility that their loved one might be dead. "I guess she could be."

Yorke stared at him, his eyes registering the silent message but refusing to accept it. Now was the time to move on to an even more sensitive topic. "You visited Pollock the day he was murdered, Mr. Yorke."

"Yes, I guess I did, although I didn't know it was the same day until later. He was surprised I'd found him. He thought he'd escaped us."

"What happened that morning?"

"What do you mean?"

"I mean, what did you talk about? How did you leave things between you?"

Yorke stared at Gino again, and this time his eyes were angry. "What are you asking me?"

"Just what I said."

"No, you're not. You want to know if I killed Pollock, don't you?"

"You had a good reason to."

Color surged into Yorke's face. "No, I did not! I wanted Pollock alive. I wanted him to tell me what happened to Cecelia."

"But what if he told you that she was dead? What if he said he'd only meant to teach her a lesson and accidentally killed her? You would have been enraged. You might have wanted to bash his head in and beat him until he died, just like he'd done to Cecelia."

"*No!*" he cried, surging to his feet, fists clenched and eyes wide with fury.

Gino jumped up, too, ready to defend himself if necessary. But Yorke made no move to strike him or anything else. He just stood there, chest heaving with his silent anger. Then his anger died, leaving him trembling. He lifted a hand to his head. "Dear God, she's dead, isn't she? He killed her." He met Gino's gaze again, and this time Gino saw only despair. "That's what you came here to tell me, isn't it?"

It wasn't, of course. He'd come here to accuse Yorke of murder and see how he reacted. "I don't know what happened to her, not for certain," he said. "Sit down, Mr. Yorke."

He obeyed. He was shaking now and weak as a kitten. His eyes filled with tears. "I guess I knew it already, but . . ."

"Nobody knows for sure except Pollock," Gino insisted. "And it's too late to ask him. But if your sister needed help, she'd come to you, wouldn't she? No matter how embarrassed she was?"

"Yes, I think she would. She knew we loved her no matter what," he said, tears running down his face.

"She'd come to you if she could," Gino said.

Yorke nodded, pulling out a handkerchief to wipe his tears. Gino saw the bartender watching them and signaled for a whiskey for Yorke. By the time he brought it, Yorke was calmer and drank it gratefully.

Gino waited patiently, knowing Yorke would eventually come to terms with his grief and be able to answer questions again. Finally, Yorke turned to him. "Is that why you came here, to make me accept that my sister is dead?"

"No, it isn't. I'm sorry that was part of it. I wish I could tell you something different, but Pollock was an evil man, like you said."

"Why did you come, then?"

"I wanted to ask about your meeting with Pollock the day he died."

"You want to know if I killed him," he said bitterly. "Now I wish I had, but no, I didn't. If I had, do you think I would have stayed in New York? Would I have gone back to his house a second time? Would I have met with the Deckers so they knew my name and how to find me?"

Gino didn't think that was likely. Yorke seemed far too intelligent to do something so foolish, but it wasn't impossible. "Tell me exactly what happened when you saw Pollock that day."

Yorke sighed. "I told you, he was surprised to see me. I told him I wanted to know where Cecelia was, and he told me the same story about how she died in childbirth. I asked him where she was buried and he said he didn't remember. Same old lies he'd told us before."

"Were you shouting?"

"I don't know. I suppose I was, at the end. I wanted to

choke him, but I couldn't, not until he told us the truth about my sister, so I left."

"And Pollock was alive when you left."

"Of course." He gave another weary sigh.

Gino needed to think of a question that would prove Yorke's innocence . . . or guilt. Una Pollock might have seen him leave and know her husband was still alive then, but that wouldn't help her case any, so she wouldn't vouch for him. "Is there any way you can prove Pollock was alive when you left him?"

Yorke frowned, wrinkling his forehead as he tried to recall that day. "Oh, wait! I just remembered. Someone did see me leaving! A colored boy. He was just going in the basement door when I left."

MAEVE WALKED ACROSS TOWN TO THE EAST SIDE BECAUSE the elevated train only ran north and south. She found Mrs. O'Neill's tenement easily, since she lived in the same building the Malloys had once occupied. The children playing outside were happy to tell her which flat belonged to the "murderess's poor, widowed mother," as the newspapers called her.

"Who is it?" Mrs. O'Neill called when Maeve knocked.

Maeve identified herself, and she heard a bolt being thrown. The door opened just a crack at first, as Mrs. O'Neill peered out. When she was satisfied Maeve was alone, she opened the door and pulled her guest into her kitchen before slamming and locking the door behind her.

"Those awful reporters," she explained. "They bother me day and night. I thought if I told my story to that nice lady reporter, the rest of them would leave me alone."

"That was a lovely drawing of Una. How did they know what she looked like?"

"Oh, she had this photograph taken right after she started working for Mr. Winter at the cigar shop." She moved into the front room and picked up a framed picture from a table. "One of the gentlemen who came into the shop had a photography studio, and he offered to make her photograph for free. He put a copy of it in the window of his studio for advertising, and he gave her one for me."

"It's very nice," Maeve said, thinking this was another example of how pretty girls got things no one else did. She set it back on the table. "How are you keeping, Mrs. O'Neill?"

"Oh, I'm doing all right. I miss my girl, though. Have you seen her? Is she well?"

"I saw her just last night, as a matter of fact."

Mrs. O'Neill's eyes lit up. "How is she? Is she all right?"

"She's doing as well as you can expect. She has reporters camped outside her house day and night."

"Oh dear!"

"Yes, but she misses you, too," Maeve said, hoping she wasn't lying too much. "She told me she would like to see you."

"She would?" To Maeve's dismay, the old woman teared up. "Do you think it would be all right if I went to her place now? I've never gone to visit her before, but with Mr. Pollock dead, that is, would anybody else mind?"

"No one would mind at all, but I have to warn you about the reporters."

"Oh yes, you said they were there day and night. But surely, they wouldn't stop me from going in my own daughter's house."

"They wouldn't dare stop you, but they'll be shouting and asking you questions and trying to get you to talk to them. It will be frightening, but you won't be in any real danger."

She looked like she was going to cry again. "Would I have to go all alone?"

"Of course not! I'll go with you," Maeve said, having planned all along to accompany her. She was more than anxious to find out why Una really wanted to see her mother.

"Would you? I'd be that grateful," she said. "How soon can we go? I've missed her so much. I just want to sit down with her and have a long visit."

"Well, I know she was eager to see you, too, so I don't see any reason we can't go right now, if that's all right with you."

"Yes, indeed!" she cried, then touched her hair. "I'd have to fix myself up a bit first. I wouldn't want to shame Una in front of those reporters."

She was still wearing her Sunday best dress, and her hair looked fine, but Maeve said, "I can wait while you get ready."

"Just have a seat, then, won't you? I won't be a minute."

She was a little longer than a minute, and when Mrs. O'Neill emerged from the back bedroom, she had a shopping basket over her arm. Seeing Maeve's questioning look, she said, "It's going to be suppertime and almost dark when we get to Una's, which won't give us much time for a visit if I have to come home this evening, so I packed a few things to spend the night. That way Una and I can talk as long as we want."

"I'm sure Una will be glad you thought of that," Maeve lied. Whatever Una wanted from her mother, Maeve doubted it was her company.

As they left, Mrs. O'Neill carefully locked her door, then told her neighbor she was going to stay with her daughter for a while. The woman promised to keep an eye on her place while she was gone. Maeve suspected she'd also be glad to tell any reporters where she had gone, for a small fee.

The elevated train carried them up to Harlem with remarkable speed. In spite of the cold, the streets were filled with people making Sunday calls or taking Sunday outings, and when they turned down St. Nicholas Avenue, Maeve was relieved to see the crowd of reporters was much smaller than it had been last night. Maybe they were getting tired of the Pollock story and had moved on to more interesting things. Or maybe a lot of them had taken Sunday off.

Even still, the crowd of reporters made Mrs. O'Neill freeze in her tracks. "Will they let us pass?" she asked in alarm.

"Of course they will. Just take my arm and don't say a word."

Maeve set a leisurely pace, as if they were just two women out for a Sunday stroll, and they walked down the opposite side of the street until they were right across from the Pollock house.

"Now we're going to walk across the street and just go straight up the front steps. Don't let go of my arm, and don't look at any of them. All right?" Mrs. O'Neill nodded, her eyes so wide, Maeve thought they might pop out. "Let's go, then."

Maeve set a brisk pace, and Mrs. O'Neill scrambled to keep up, her basket bumping against her hip as they nearly ran across the street. When they were about halfway across, the reporters noticed them and sprang to attention.

"It's that detective girl from last night," one of them said, making Maeve smile. They might not have put that in the newspaper, but they remembered.

"What are you doing back here?"

"Who's that with you?"

"Are you a detective, too, lady?"

Dozens more questions rang through the winter air, but Maeve didn't answer a single one. To her credit, Mrs. O'Neill didn't either, but that was probably more because she was terrified and breathless from running than because she was discreet.

Maeve glared at them and kept barreling forward, and at the last possible second, the ones in her way stepped back, closing ranks behind them immediately so that for a few moments they were surrounded. But Maeve kept shoving forward, and then they reached the steps and started up.

Mrs. O'Neill stumbled, but Maeve righted her and kept going. At the top at last, Maeve reached out and pounded the knocker just the way Mrs. Decker would have. The door opened almost at once and the two women scurried inside.

"My goodness, Miss Smith, is that you?" Hattie asked as she bolted the door against the clamoring reporters.

"Yes, Hattie, and I've brought Mrs. Pollock's mother with me."

"Mother," Una said from the parlor doorway.

"There's my girl!" Mrs. O'Neill cried, hurrying over to embrace her child.

Maeve noticed Una didn't seem nearly as happy to see her mother as her mother did to see her, but that's what she'd expected.

"It took you long enough," Una said to Maeve when her mother released her.

Maeve simply shrugged, since she didn't feel she owed Una any explanations.

"Come inside, Mother. What's that you've brought?" Una asked, noticing the market basket.

"I thought . . . That is, Miss Smith said I should pack some things to spend the night," she said, earning Maeve a black look from Una. Maeve managed not to roll her eyes. "It's already so late, we won't have any time to visit if I go home this evening."

Una ushered her mother into the parlor and closed the door in Maeve's face. So much for hospitality.

"Will you be staying for supper, miss?" Hattie asked.

Maeve honestly didn't know if Una would be willing to feed her or not. Given the difficulty of shopping, maybe she should graciously excuse herself and offer to return to take Mrs. O'Neill back home tomorrow. As much as Maeve wanted to hear what Una had to say to her mother, her hostess obviously wasn't going to include her in the conversation. On the other hand, she wasn't ready to face the reporters again quite so soon.

"Maybe I'll go down to the kitchen for a cup of coffee before I leave," she said.

But before Hattie could reply, the parlor door opened, and Una said, "Miss Smith, would you come in, please?"

Now wasn't this interesting? Maeve happily accepted the invitation, no matter that it had been offered without the slightest trace of welcome. In fact, Una looked a bit angry. When she'd closed the door, she proved it.

"Miss Smith," she hissed, "what have you done with my money?"

14

Gino found Mr. Decker sitting at the Malloy kitchen table, surrounded by stacks of money. He stopped dead in his tracks. Mr. Decker looked up with some amusement.

"Impressive, isn't it?"

"Uh, yeah." Gino approached cautiously, feeling that he should show some respect for so much cash.

"I didn't expect to see you again until tomorrow. You must have found out something interesting."

"I found out something *very* interesting." Gino cautiously pulled out a chair and sat down, being careful to keep some distance between himself and the table.

"It won't bite," Mr. Decker said, still smiling at Gino's expression.

"I just don't want to knock over your piles."

"Thank you. I'm just about finished, as a matter of fact. I'm thinking I'll just take enough for Zimmerman and Reed with me tonight and leave the rest in the safe. I hate carrying around so much money."

Of course he did. "No one will know you have it."

"Yes, that's an advantage. I'll be in my own carriage, too, which is always safer than taking a cab. So what did you find out from Yorke?"

"I don't think he killed Pollock. As he pointed out, if he'd done it, why would he stay in the city, go back to Pollock's house a second time, and then come to see you so you'd know his name and where he lives? He could've just left the city, and it's likely no one would have even known who he was or how to find him."

"That's true. So I guess we can scratch him off our list."

"But I did find out something very interesting from him. I asked if there was anybody who could vouch that Pollock was still alive when he left the house. He said yes, that a colored boy had seen him leave."

"Someone on the street, you mean?"

"No, someone going into the basement door of Pollock's house as he was going down the front steps. It must've been Eddie."

"But Eddie wasn't there when Pollock was killed."

"That's what Hattie told me. She said Pollock had sent him on an errand, and he didn't get back until after they found Pollock dead."

"Why would Yorke lie, then?"

"You mean why would he make up an alibi like that if it wasn't true? I don't think he did. I think he really did see Eddie coming back to the house."

"So you think the other servants lied when they said he wasn't there?"

"No, I think they just didn't see him come in. He probably went upstairs to report back to Pollock or something.

According to the women, Pollock was shouting and carrying on the way he did when he beat Una up. This was probably after Yorke left. When that happened, they'd all gather together in the kitchen to stay out of his way until the storm blew over, and that's what they did."

"Except for Eddie."

"Right, because he was still out on his errand, or so they thought. But now we know he wasn't. He'd come back to the house."

"So he would've heard Pollock beating Una, and we know he adores her."

"He would've wanted to protect her," Gino said, picturing it easily. "He might've even run into the room, and when he saw Pollock hit her, he went a little crazy."

"Then he picked up the statue or whatever it was and hit Pollock with it."

"Maybe he only wanted to stop Pollock, but hitting him once didn't stop him, so he hit him again . . ." Gino could see it clearly now, a young man in love with a woman he could never have. All he could do was save her from her husband's fury.

"And when Pollock was dead, then what?" Mr. Decker asked.

Gino realized he had no idea. Or at least no idea that made sense. "Then Eddie runs away and Una starts weeping over her dead husband until Hattie walks in and finds them."

"If that's what happened, why did Eddie ever come back? Why didn't he run away and disappear? He must have known Una would tell the police who killed her husband."

"Except she didn't," Gino said in wonder. "She claims she doesn't remember who killed Pollock. Maeve thought she was lying because she'd killed him herself."

"Which makes perfect sense if you don't know Eddie was there."

"But if she does remember that Eddie killed him, why did she let them take her to jail?"

Gino shook his head. "I can't think of anything that makes sense. Could they be lovers?"

"Could who be lovers?" Mrs. Decker asked. She walked into the kitchen with Mrs. Malloy on her heels. Both women stopped dead at the sight of the money.

Mrs. Malloy blessed herself and murmured something that might've been a prayer. "Has that been in the house all this time?"

"Just since Maeve brought it from the Pollock house a few days ago," Mrs. Decker said. "Felix is going to return it to the rightful owners."

"I hope he's going to do it soon," Mrs. Malloy said. "I won't be able to sleep a wink knowing how much money is here."

"He's going to start tomorrow, but I'm sure Gino would be glad to spend the night here to guard you if it would make you sleep better," Mrs. Decker said.

Gino didn't think that was really necessary, but he would certainly be glad to spend the night just the same.

Before he could say so, though, Mrs. Decker added, "And you never answered my question. Could who be lovers?"

"Mrs. Pollock and Eddie," her husband said.

"Good heavens, where would you get an idea like that?"

Gino told the women what he'd learned from Yorke and what he and Mr. Decker had concluded. "So none of it makes sense unless Una is in love with Eddie and is trying to protect him."

"That girl never loved anybody but herself," Mrs. Malloy said. The women had by now taken a seat at the money-covered table, too. "And she'd sure never go to jail for a man."

"And certainly not a boy like Eddie," Mrs. Decker added. "He's no more than sixteen and a servant, not the kind of man a woman develops an undying passion for. I could understand it if she'd killed her husband and Eddie went to jail for her, but not the other way around."

"Maybe she did kill him and Eddie saw her," Gino said. "He wouldn't tell anyone because he loves her, and she'd be nice to him so he'd keep protecting her."

"Now that makes a little more sense," Mrs. Malloy said, "but not enough. Una O'Neill isn't going to prison at all, I promise you. She'd betray her own mother before she'd do that. If she did kill her husband, she's going to blame it on somebody else, and who better than a poor servant boy?"

"Then why hasn't she done that already?" Mrs. Decker asked. "And if Eddie killed him, why not just tell the police and be done with it?"

"So we're right back to where we were when you ladies came in," Mr. Decker said.

They sat for a long moment in silence as they each considered the questions they'd raised. Finally, Gino said, "I can't help thinking this Jane must know something. Why else would she run away like that?"

"Because there was a murder in the house," Mrs. Malloy said quite logically.

"But the other servants didn't leave," Mrs. Decker said. "They're too afraid of not finding another position and not getting their back salary. Jane was more afraid of something or someone else than that, or she wouldn't have left."

"And if she just wanted to get away, why not just resign and walk out the door?" Mr. Decker said. "Instead, she makes this elaborate plan to escape so no one would realize she was leaving until it was too late to stop her."

"And no one could ask where she's going or follow her," Gino said. "We need to at least ask her why she was so scared."

Mr. Decker sighed. "I was going to start delivering the

money tomorrow, but now I'm thinking I have time to at least visit Zimmerman this evening. If he was the one Jane wrote to, then he's the one most likely to know where she is now."

"It's getting late for a social call," Mrs. Decker said.

"I'm sure Zimmerman would welcome me in the middle of the night if I'm bringing him four thousand dollars." Mr. Decker consulted his pocket watch. "John should be returning with the coach soon. He'll take me."

"And it's dangerous to be riding around the city with a lot of money in your pocket," Mrs. Malloy said.

"Gino can go with me as a bodyguard."

Gino grinned at that, grateful that Mr. Decker was including him.

"And what about me?" Mrs. Decker asked.

"I think you should wait here for Maeve. She'll want to know what we're doing. Gino and I will come back here when we're finished so we can share what we found out and hear what happened with Una and her mother from Maeve. I guess the children are safely in bed."

"Yes." Mrs. Decker exchanged a smile with Mrs. Malloy. "It was so much fun reading them stories and tucking them in."

"Can you read to Brian?"

"Catherine signs for him while you read. She's so clever."

"She learns the signs as fast as he does," Mrs. Malloy said. "He comes home every day and teaches her what he learned."

"They're both very clever," Mrs. Decker said. "And so much energy! I'm worn out."

"When the men are gone, we'll make some hot chocolate and sit in my parlor with our feet up," Mrs. Malloy said.

"That sounds like heaven," Mrs. Decker said.

"Yes, it does," Mr. Decker said, "but unfortunately, Gino and I have work to do. Gino, I've set aside Zimmerman's share of the money. Help me carry the rest of it back to the safe. I've got each stack labeled, so don't mix them up."

Maeve stood in the Pollocks' parlor and stared back at Una in feigned surprise. "What money are you talking about?"

Maeve was very interested to hear how Una would reply to this. Did she actually know about Pollock's scheme and how he kept the investors' money in his safe? And if so, was she going to admit it after claiming ignorance for days?

Plainly, Una was furious, but she was trying very hard not to lose her temper. She pressed her lips together for a few moments before answering Maeve's question. "My mother tells me you took some money from this house after I was arrested."

"Oh, that," Maeve said with perfect innocence. "Yes. Mrs. O'Neill had come to ask us for help in getting you out of jail. I advised her to hire an attorney, but she couldn't afford to do that. I know from experience that people like you and Mr. Pollock will keep some money in the house for expenses, and I thought I might find some that she could use to pay the attorney."

"And you did find some," Una said.

"Yes."

"How much?"

"I found five hundred dollars." Which was true, as far as it went. Grandfather always said to tell the truth if it would serve your purpose and save the lies for emergencies.

Something glittered in Una's lovely blue eyes, like sun on ice. "And what did you do with it?"

"I gave it to your mother."

"I told you, dear," Mrs. O'Neill said with what sounded like desperation. "That's exactly how much she gave me."

"And what did you do with it?" Una demanded sharply.

Mrs. O'Neill blinked in surprise at her vehemence. "I already told you. I paid Mr. Nicholson and the rest went for your bond money."

"Did you expect there to be more than that?" Maeve asked, knowing her expression betrayed not the slightest hint of guilt. She wasn't guilty of anything, after all.

Una was pressing her lips together again, and probably grinding her teeth, too. She couldn't very well admit she was missing thousands of dollars she'd claimed to know nothing about, but Maeve would have bet twice that amount that she knew perfectly well how much money had been in Pollock's safe. Maeve's only question was why she was only now inquiring after it. And even more important, if she knew it was there, why hadn't she been upset when she discovered the burglary and the empty safe?

"I . . . uh . . . Let's just say I was hoping. You see, I haven't found any information about my husband's bank account, and I'm running short of funds. I thought perhaps you might have found more than that and just . . ."

"Just what?" Maeve asked sweetly. "Stolen it?"

Una's cheeks turned fiery red, and her eyes narrowed in fury.

"I'm sure she didn't mean to suggest that, Miss Smith," Mrs. O'Neill said quickly. "You've been so kind to us, after all."

"And after I took money out of my own pocket to bribe the matron to look after you at the Tombs," Maeve said. The money *had* come out of her own pocket. She wasn't going to discuss where it had come from before that, of course. "And Mrs. Decker offered to pay your servants their back wages and write them references when you were in jail."

"That's so generous, isn't it, Una?" Mrs. O'Neill said pleadingly.

Una didn't so much as glance in her mother's direction.

"I was hoping I would be able to pay my servants myself with my own money."

"I'm sure you were," Maeve said, still being completely honest, since she was now certain Una at least knew there should have been more than five hundred dollars in Pollock's office. "I suppose there might have been more money in the safe. Before it was robbed, I mean."

This seemed to confuse her. "Didn't you look in the safe?"

"It was locked," Maeve said, not really answering the question. "And of course I don't know how to open a safe without the combination." Also perfectly true.

Una pinched the bridge of her nose, as if she might be fighting off a headache.

"Are you all right?" Maeve asked, trying to sound concerned.

"Of course I'm not all right," she snapped. "My husband is dead, I'm accused of killing him, and I don't have a penny to my name."

"Well, if you could just remember who killed him, you'd no longer be charged with murder, and you'd at least get your bond money back," Maeve pointed out.

Una glared daggers at her again. "I've told you, I don't remember."

"And you could also sell the house and the furniture and move back in with your mother," Maeve continued, knowing full well that was the last thing Una would want to do. "You could probably be very comfortable."

Of course, Una really wanted to continue to live in this house and have thirty-seven thousand dollars to live on until she found another rich man to marry her and buy her an even nicer house. Maeve was certain of it, although she knew Una would never admit it. Doing so would reveal that she knew about Pollock's money—and probably his scheme—in the first place. And that would give her yet another motive for killing him.

"Thank you for bringing my mother to see me, Miss Smith. I'm very tired now, and would like to rest. Would you mind seeing that she gets home all right?"

"Home? I just got here, Una," Mrs. O'Neill protested. "I thought we could have a nice visit and I could even spend the night. We haven't really seen each other in months."

Una got up, went to the parlor door, and called for Hattie. "Would you see my guests out? I'm going to bed," she said to the maid when she appeared. Una walked out without another word and headed up the stairs in the hallway.

The expression on Mrs. O'Neill's face nearly broke Maeve's heart. She had half a notion to tell Mrs. O'Neill that Una couldn't possibly have meant to send her away and convince her to spend the night anyway, but then she remembered what Gino had said about the extra bedrooms having no furniture. Mrs. O'Neill would have to sleep on the floor, when she wasn't even welcome in the first place. Maeve couldn't put her through that.

Hattie frowned in confusion, knowing they'd only just arrived. "You're leaving?" They hadn't even taken their coats off.

"Yes, we are," Maeve said with more enthusiasm than she felt. "Come along, Mrs. O'Neill. I'll take you home."

Maeve kept thinking Una would realize how cruel she was being and change her mind about sending her mother back out into the cold night, but she didn't. Even Hattie looked pained as she opened the door for them. Luckily, most of the reporters were gone. They must have decided it wouldn't be worthwhile to wait for hours on a wintry Sunday night to accost the two visitors when they came out again. Maeve could almost smile at the irony. The ones who remained shouted questions, but only halfheartedly, and no one followed them past the corner.

As they stood in the station, waiting for the El to arrive, Maeve said, "Do you know why Una sent for you?" She didn't add what she was thinking: when she was just going to send you away five minutes later.

"I don't know. As soon as I got there, she just started asking me where I got the money to pay for her bail, to get her out of jail."

"And what did you tell her?"

"I told her the truth, that we found it at the house."

"You told her that I found it?"

Mrs. O'Neill winced a little. "Not at first. I . . . I wanted her to think I was the one who helped her. I said I found it in Mr. Pollock's office."

"And that didn't satisfy her?"

"No, she wanted to know where the rest of it was. I told her that was all I found, but she didn't believe me. She just kept asking where I found it and what I did with the rest. That's when I had to tell her you were really the one who found it."

So Una did know Pollock had more than five hundred dollars in his safe. She was awfully angry that it had gone missing, which was understandable, but why was she blaming her mother when she knew the house had been robbed days ago and the safe opened? In fact, she hadn't been upset about the robbery at all, certainly not the way she was upset now.

And why, when the house was robbed days ago, was she just now wondering where the money went?

EVEN THOUGH FELIX KNEW NO ONE COULD POSSIBLY guess what he carried in the case he'd borrowed from his son-in-law's office, he was still glad to have Gino along to help in the event of trouble. His driver, John, could also help, although he seemed to think these nightly trips were something of a lark, especially after Felix insisted he keep the bribes he'd earned from the newspaper reporters last night.

"Do you think Zimmerman will tell us where Jane is?" Gino asked.

"I think he'll be very grateful to get his money back, and if he isn't, I'll be happy to remind him of his obligation to me. He really owes this Jane nothing by comparison, and we're no threat to her in any case. Why wouldn't he let us speak with her?"

"If he knows where she is at all."

"If she went to him, he would have helped her. He's an honest fellow, if a bit naïve. That's exactly the sort that men like Pollock prey on. I can't tell you how much pleasure it gives me to be able to right his wrong."

"It is a good feeling," Gino said. "That's why I joined the police in the first place. I wanted to see men like Pollock punished."

"And instead, you saw them rewarded," Felix said, remembering only too well his own experiences as a young man.

"Too many times, yes."

"And you hope Frank will establish a detective agency where you can help the people the police don't?"

"I wouldn't have put it like that, but yes, I think so."

Felix hoped his son-in-law would agree. "Young men like you give me hope for the future, Gino."

Gino didn't reply, and Felix realized he had embarrassed him. He quickly changed the subject and started asking Gino about his experiences in Cuba with Roosevelt. Until they reached Zimmerman's house Gino gave Felix what he suspected was a heavily censored version of events.

The maid was surprised to see visitors at this time of night. The family was still at supper, she informed them.

"Please tell Mr. Zimmerman I'm sorry to disturb him, but it's a matter of utmost urgency." Felix handed her his card. "And tell him that I'm here to return his missing property."

"Missing property?" she repeated, as if to make sure she understood correctly.

"That's right."

When she had gone, leaving them standing in the front hall, Gino grinned at him. "Missing property?"

"I didn't think I should mention money. Some people think it's rude to discuss it in polite company."

"I'm guessing Zimmerman won't think it's rude."

The maid returned with an entirely different attitude. She escorted them upstairs to Mr. Zimmerman's library, where he greeted Felix with a warm handshake and welcomed Gino just as eagerly. "It's good to see you again, Mr. Decker, although I didn't expect you back so soon."

"Some things have happened that made me think I should take care of this matter immediately."

"What things?" Zimmerman asked. "Not another murder, I hope."

"As a matter of fact, someone else *has* been murdered. Pollock's partner."

"That's terrible," Zimmerman said, looking like he really thought it was, but then he frowned. "Partner, did you say? I didn't know he had a partner."

"Partner in crime, I suppose I should say. If you didn't know him, then he worked behind the scenes. At any rate, he's dead, and I decided to put an end to this as quickly as possible."

The room might be called the "library," but it held precious few books. A large desk sat against one wall, and the rest of the room was furnished for smoking and conversation. Felix set the case he carried on the desk and opened it. Zimmerman gasped.

"This isn't your entire investment, I'm afraid," Felix said. "Pollock had spent some of it already. I did find a ledger showing the amount of each person's investment, so I'm returning a proportion of the remaining funds, based on each investor's original contribution. I've included the calculations, so you can see how I arrived at the total." He handed Zimmerman the sheet of paper on which he'd determined how much he was due.

"This is amazing. I never expected to see a penny of this money again." He looked truly flummoxed.

"I'm glad you're pleased. If any of the missing money turns up, we'll return it as well, but I'm not holding out much hope of that."

"I don't know how to thank you, Mr. Decker." Zimmerman was almost embarrassingly grateful.

Felix glanced at Gino, giving him silent permission to respond.

"You can thank us by telling us where Jane is, Mr. Zimmerman."

Zimmerman's body jerked with surprise. "Jane?"

"Yes, the maid who wrote to tell you about Pollock's murder."

It was a guess, of course. They didn't know that for sure, but from Zimmerman's reaction, Felix knew they'd guessed correctly

"I . . . I don't know what you're talking about," he tried.

"Mr. Zimmerman, we know that Jane used to work for you," Gino said, surprising Felix because they didn't know anything of the kind, at least for certain. "When Pollock invited you to dinner at his house, she recognized you. Maybe you recognized her, too. That's probably why she felt she should warn you when Pollock was murdered. She knew you were doing business with him. Maybe she even knew you'd given him money that might now be in jeopardy because of his death."

"That's . . . ridiculous," Zimmerman said.

"But it does explain how you knew Pollock was dead

before it was reported in the newspapers," Felix said. "And why you were so certain the person who informed you was not the one who killed Pollock."

"Mr. Zimmerman," Gino said with an authority that impressed Felix, "we need to speak with Jane. We believe she has information that will keep an innocent woman from going to prison."

Felix had to bite back a smile. He didn't want to break the mood, but he certainly was enjoying Gino's performance.

"She's not in any trouble, is she? Jane, I mean. Or any danger?"

"If we don't know where she is, the killer doesn't either," Felix said, "and we aren't going to tell anyone where she is if we do find her. We just need to ask her some questions."

Zimmerman's resolve was fading quickly. Gino's reference to an innocent woman going to prison had really rattled him. "If I have your word no harm will come to her . . ."

"You do," Felix said.

"I . . . Well, she did write to me, as you said. She used to work here until she had a disagreement with one of the other maids and quit. I appreciated learning about Pollock's death, even though it didn't help me in any way. She couldn't have known that, though. Then she came to me the other day. She'd run away from Pollock's house, you see. She seemed frightened, and I couldn't turn her away. We didn't have a place for her here, though, so I couldn't take her on either, so I sent her to Reed."

"Paul Reed?"

"Yes," he said, surprised that Felix had guessed so easily. "Reed always needs help. She'd tried to warn us, even though it didn't help us get our money back, so I felt obligated, you see."

"That was generous of you, Zimmerman," Felix said.

"What are you going to do now?"

"We're going to talk to her."

"Tonight?"

Felix wasn't going to tell him that they were afraid Jane might run again if she had time. "It's very important."

As they left, Felix noticed the case felt much lighter than just the absence of the money would have made it. When the carriage pulled up in front of Reed's house, Felix himself felt lighter, too, as if he'd dropped a decade's worth of aging. This was good work.

"When I was here before, I remember the maid acted oddly," Felix said as they walked up to the house. "She seemed surprised to see me, and then she kept turning her face away and wouldn't look at me."

"She must've recognized you."

"She needn't have worried about that. One hardly notices servants, especially other people's. I don't think I did more than glance at her at Pollock's house."

"I just hope she's still here after seeing you."

Felix hadn't thought of that. He hoped so, too.

He only had another two minutes to wait, because the woman who answered the door was the same one he'd seen yesterday. Once again she registered surprise, and then genuine fear when she saw Gino beside him. She knew Gino as a police officer.

"Jane," Gino said in the gentle voice Felix had heard him use with Catherine. "Don't be afraid. We aren't going to let anything happen to you."

"It's all right, Jane." Reed had come up behind her. "They just need to ask you some questions. If you can help them catch the killer, you won't need to be afraid anymore." He looked up at Felix, who still stood on the stoop. "Zimmerman telephoned me. He wanted to be sure I let you in."

* * *

Maeve was surprised to see Mrs. Decker emerge from Mrs. Malloy's parlor when she arrived back home.

"You're still here?" Maeve asked in surprise. "I hope you're not waiting for me."

"As a matter of fact, I'm waiting for Felix," Mrs. Decker said. "He and Gino decided to deliver some of the money this evening and see if they could find the missing maid. You're back earlier than I expected, though. I guess Una didn't welcome you as warmly as she did her mother. Did she at least let you in the house?"

"She didn't welcome either of us. I don't think we were there ten minutes before she sent us both on our way."

"Her own mother?" Mrs. Decker said.

"I told you, that girl has no heart," Mrs. Malloy said.

"Mrs. O'Neill was heartbroken," Maeve said.

"Why did she want to see her mother at all then?" Mrs. Decker asked.

"She just wanted to know where her mother got the money for her bail and what she'd done with the rest of it."

"So she did know there was more," Mrs. Decker said.

"Yes. Thank heaven we didn't tell Mrs. O'Neill how much we really found. What I can't figure out, though, is why Una is just now realizing it's gone."

"Yes, Felix told her about the robbery practically the first minute she walked in her front door, and she wasn't the least bit upset then. I still think that was odd, even if she hadn't known there was anything of value in the safe."

"And plainly, she did."

"Well, I don't suppose we can solve this standing in the hall," Mrs. Decker said. "You must be frozen. We can make you some hot chocolate."

They'd just settled in the warmth of the kitchen when someone rang the front doorbell. Mrs. Malloy went to answer it. Mr. Decker and Gino were back, and Maeve found herself straining for the first glimpse of Gino as the men filed into the kitchen. He smiled when he saw her, and she smiled back just for an instant, before she caught herself.

"I hope you had better luck than I did," she said.

The men sat down at the table with her, rubbing their hands, their cheeks still rosy from the cold. "I'm not sure we did," Mr. Decker said.

"Didn't you find Jane?" Mrs. Decker asked.

"Yes, and we talked to her." He told her about their conversation with Zimmerman and going to Reed's house while Mrs. Malloy and Mrs. Decker bustled about, serving them all hot chocolate.

"Did she know anything useful?" Maeve asked.

Mr. Decker deferred to Gino. "She told us a few things we didn't know. First of all, the errand Eddie went on the morning Pollock was killed was taking a package to Truett. She even saw it, and from what she described, it was the package of contracts that we found in Truett's apartment."

"Why is that important?" Maeve asked.

"It's probably not," Gino said.

"Why did she run away then?"

"That took a while to get out of her, but she finally admitted that she'd seen Eddie come in and she knew he was there when Pollock was killed. She was also pretty sure nobody else had come into the house, which meant that either Una or Eddie killed Pollock. She was terrified that Eddie would find out she'd seen him, so she finally decided to run away."

"I think her reaction is the one thing that makes sense about all this," Mrs. Decker said with a sigh.

"All right," Maeve said. "Let's go through what happened

step by step to see if there's something we've missed. First of all, on the morning Pollock died, Eddie left the house to take a package to Truett."

"Then Yorke arrives to confront Pollock. They argue, and Yorke leaves. Eddie is just getting back, and they see each other," Gino said.

"Or at least Yorke sees Eddie. We don't know if Eddie saw Yorke," Mr. Decker said.

"That's true," Gino said. "Then we know from the other servants that Pollock started arguing with Una and probably hitting her. The three female servants went down to the kitchen to wait it out, but Eddie was somewhere in the house."

"Maybe he was hiding, too," Maeve said. "Or maybe he went to help her."

"So probably one or the other of them killed Pollock," Gino said. "Either Una was defending herself or Eddie was trying to save her."

"But what happened then?" Mrs. Decker said. "We know Hattie found Una and Pollock's body later. Una was in shock or pretending to be and couldn't remember what happened."

"Or so she said," Maeve said. "She still claims that, too."

"And Eddie must have left again, because he comes back to the house after Pollock is killed, as if he'd just gotten back from his errand, so nobody knows he was there earlier," Gino said.

"Which was a very clever thing for him to do," Mrs. Decker said.

They all considered this for a few moments in silence. Suddenly, Mrs. Malloy cleared her throat and everyone looked up at her expectantly. "Is Eddie smart enough to figure out how to give himself an alibi?"

15

"No, he isn't," Gino said, remembering the sobbing boy he'd seen in the kitchen. "Yesterday, Eddie was crying like a baby in the kitchen because Una had yelled at him that morning about something."

"Do we know what?" Maeve asked with interest.

"No, but why would Una be mad at him all of a sudden?" Gino asked.

"Especially if they were partners, so to speak, in Mr. Pollock's death," Mrs. Decker said.

"Let's keep going, step by step, over everything that happened next, to see if we can figure it out," Maeve said. "Remember, Truett was killed, too, and that has to be part of it."

"So next, after Pollock is killed, the police arrest Una and take her to jail," Mrs. Decker said. She was really getting into the spirit of it. "Mrs. O'Neill finds out and comes here and asks for help."

"The next day, Mrs. Decker and I go with her to the house to pack some clothes and look for some money to pay her attorney. That's when I find the money in the safe," Maeve said.

"And take it," Gino said. "That's important, because the same night somebody breaks into the house and tries to steal it."

"But who would do that? Who even knew the money was in the safe?" Maeve asked.

"Truett probably knew," Mr. Decker said.

"But he didn't even know Mr. Pollock was dead until Friday morning when he went to the house and the servants told him," Mrs. Decker said.

"Unless he was lying about that," Maeve said. "So we need to consider him, at least."

"Right," Gino said. "Who else?"

"The investors who had discovered Pollock's scheme was a fraud could have known about the money," Mr. Decker said.

"That's Zimmerman and Reed. Norwalk was already dead by then," Gino said. "But can you picture either of them breaking into Pollock's house to rob it?"

"And would they even suspect that Mr. Pollock would keep the money in his house?" Mrs. Decker asked. "Even if they knew he hadn't invested it, who keeps that much money in cash?"

"I must admit, I never would have suspected he would do that," Mr. Decker said. "I also wouldn't have the first idea of how to rob a house, and I doubt Zimmerman or Reed would either."

"Una knew the money was there, though," Maeve said. Everyone looked at her in surprise.

"But she couldn't have known. She wasn't at all upset over the robbery," Mr. Decker said.

"That's understandable," Mrs. Malloy said. "Maeve had already taken the money out of the safe."

"But Una didn't know that," Maeve said. "Nobody knew that except us. And tonight she wanted to see her mother because she apparently just realized today that the money is missing, and she remembered her mother had money to pay her bail, and she thought her mother must have taken it."

"Why would she think that? The money has been missing for days and she knew the house had been robbed," Mrs. Decker said, "although I still don't understand why she wasn't upset over the burglary."

"Maybe she knew who the burglar was," Maeve said. "And maybe the burglar finally told her he didn't have it."

Gino had never seen her look so smug, and he'd seen her look pretty smug before now. "How could she know who did it?"

"She and Eddie were partners, remember? If they killed Pollock together somehow—and it looks like they did—and we know Una isn't the kind of person to sacrifice herself when she's got somebody else she can sacrifice, why would she let herself be arrested when she could have just said Eddie killed Pollock?"

"Maybe she really doesn't remember what happened," Mrs. Decker said.

"Or maybe they worked out a plan," Maeve said. "With Pollock dead, the truth about the Panama scheme would probably have come out, and the investors would want their money back. But if Una knew about the scheme, which she must have because she knew about the money, she could claim the money was stolen in the robbery and she wouldn't have to give it back at all."

"But who broke in to steal it?" Mrs. Malloy asked.

"Remember, we thought it might have been Truett," Mr. Decker said.

"Yes, it's possible Truett is the one who broke in to steal the money," Gino said. "That would also explain why somebody broke into his apartment, because they were looking for it. But remember Una wasn't upset about the break-in at her house. She must've thought she knew who'd taken the money and she trusted him. From the way she acted with Truett, I don't think she would've trusted him. And if she thought Truett had the money, I think she would've been a lot more upset that night he came to ask her where it was because she would've realized it was missing."

"Then who else could have done it?" Mrs. Decker asked.

"Eddie," Maeve said with a knowing grin.

"How could he break in if he was already in the house?" Mrs. Decker asked.

"He just made it look like he broke in." Maeve turned to Gino, her dark eyes shining. "Am I right?"

"I think so!" he said, seeing it all now. "The basement window was broken, but that could've been for show. Somebody who just broke in wouldn't know the combination to the safe, although a clever thief might know to look for it written down somewhere."

"The way Maeve did," Mrs. Decker said with a smirk.

"But how would even a clever thief know the money was there in the first place?" Mr. Decker asked, getting into the spirit of it himself.

"He wouldn't," Gino said. "But Una obviously knew the money was there—or she expected it to be there because she didn't know Maeve had rescued it—and she probably knew the combination or where to tell Eddie to find it."

"Then she pretended to be in shock so she couldn't tell the police who killed her husband," Mrs. Decker said. "But did she expect to be arrested?"

"I can't imagine she did," Maeve said. "But once everything was happening, she couldn't accuse Eddie until the money was safely stolen, so she had to keep pretending she didn't remember and go to jail."

"But thanks to Maeve, for advising her mother to hire a good attorney, she got out again," Gino said with a grin.

Maeve groaned. "Why was I so helpful?"

"Because you're a good person, dear," Mrs. Decker said.

"But who killed that other man? What was his name?" asked Mrs. Malloy.

"You mean Truett. Oh yeah. I guess we aren't finished," Gino said. "That was the night Una wouldn't let me stay over till morning. And Eddie was awfully glad to see me leave, too."

"So he'd be free to come and go as he liked," Maeve said.

"You think he went to Truett's apartment and killed him?" Mr. Decker asked. "But why?"

"Oh, I know!" Mrs. Decker exclaimed, making everyone smile. "He must have thought Mr. Truett had the money."

"But how would this Truett have gotten it?" Mrs. Malloy asked.

"The package?" Mr. Decker asked Gino. "The one Eddie delivered to Truett the morning Pollock was killed."

Gino nodded. "That's what I think."

"But there wasn't any money in it," Maeve said. "You said it was just contracts."

"Eddie probably didn't know that, though," Gino said. "All he knew was that there was no money in the safe, even though Una told him it was there, and that he'd taken a package to Truett. Where else could it be?"

"It could be here in Francis's safe," Mrs. Malloy said dryly.

"Yes, but Una and Eddie couldn't possibly know that," Maeve said. "Eddie must've been frantic when the safe was empty. I wouldn't want to have to explain that to Una."

"Do you think she's the one who sent him to Truett's?" Mr. Decker asked.

"She couldn't have been," Gino said. "Truett had been at her place that evening. I think he came to demand she give him the money. When I got there, she was claiming she didn't know anything about any money. If she thought he had it, she would've been frantic when she found out he didn't."

"Where did she think it was, then?" Mrs. Decker asked.

"She thought Eddie had taken it out of the safe and probably hidden it someplace," Maeve said.

"But he hadn't, because it wasn't there. She must have known by then that he hadn't found it," Mrs. Decker said.

Maeve frowned. "I don't think she did. I think she would've been furious when she found out, and I think Eddie would've been afraid to tell her. He was probably hoping to find it at Truett's, so he didn't tell her it wasn't in the safe. She wasn't upset until today, and remember, the servants told Gino she was yelling at Eddie this morning."

"And he was sobbing in the kitchen hours later," Gino said. "He must have just admitted to her that the money wasn't in the safe when he opened it and he didn't find it at Truett's place either."

"But Truett had come to Una looking for the money that night, so she knew he didn't have it. Why didn't she tell Eddie?" Mr. Decker asked.

"Because she didn't know it was missing at that point," Gino said. "If she thought Eddie had it, why bother telling him Truett didn't know where it was? She had no idea he was planning to go to Truett's place to look for it."

"So when Una found out the money was missing, she probably decided her mother must have it," Maeve said. "It was the only logical explanation for how Mrs. O'Neill had been able to post her bond, too. That's the reason she wanted to see her mother," she added for Gino and Mr. Decker. "She wanted to accuse her of stealing the money."

"So of course Mrs. O'Neill told her you're the one who stole it," Gino teased.

"Well, she told her I'm the one who found five hundred dollars in Pollock's office, and that's all I admitted to. She did suggest that I took the money out of the safe, but I pointed out that I can't open a safe unless I have the combination. That seemed to satisfy her of my innocence."

"Poor Una," said Mrs. Decker with a grin. "She greatly under-estimates you."

Maeve returned her grin.

"So," Gino said with some satisfaction, "it appears that Eddie killed Truett and probably killed Pollock, too."

"And if Una finds the money, she will miraculously remember that, and Eddie will be arrested and Una will be free," Maeve said with a sigh.

"So Una must have planned the whole thing, or at least the part about killing Mr. Pollock and robbing the safe," Mrs. Decker said. "Eddie isn't clever enough to figure all that out."

"But if Una says this Eddie killed her husband, surely he'll tell the police about her part in it," Mrs. Malloy said.

Gino glanced at Mr. Decker and saw his own doubts reflected on his face.

"Nobody is going to take the word of a Negro boot boy over a woman as lovely as Una Pollock," Mr. Decker said. "And no jury of twelve men will ever convict her on his testimony. Unless she confesses or there's some other proof, she'll go free and he'll go to the electric chair."

"What other proof could there be?" Mrs. Decker asked. "Maybe we can find it."

Everyone considered the question for a few minutes, but no one came up with any ideas.

"It's too bad I rescued the money," Maeve said at last. "If

Una had it hidden away somewhere, that would at least look bad for her."

"On the other hand, the investors might never get it back," Mr. Decker said. "We don't want to punish the wrong people here."

Maeve sighed. "So what do we do now? Tell the police that Eddie killed Pollock and Truett? If we just wait another day or two, Una will probably tell them that herself."

"Maybe if I go question her and tell her we know exactly what she did, she'll say something to incriminate herself," Gino said.

"Even if she does, nobody will take your word for it," Mr. Decker said. "You're not a police officer anymore."

"They'd take your word, Felix," his wife said. "You could go with him to be a witness."

"And, Gino, you don't have to tell Una you're not with the police anymore. She'll just assume you still are," Maeve added.

"They're right," Gino told Mr. Decker. "It's the only chance we have to prove she's involved. Are you willing to go with me?"

"Of course," he said in surprise.

"Then let's go."

"Now?"

"We'll catch her when her guard is down and she's tired. That's when people tell the most truth. Besides, if we wait until tomorrow, the place will be surrounded by newspaper reporters. Nobody is going to confess to murder with two dozen news hawks outside their door."

"Una was going up to bed when she threw her mother and me out of the house," Maeve said.

"Good," Gino said. "Waking somebody up out of a sound sleep is the best way to get the truth out of them."

"All right then," Mr. Decker said, rising to his feet. "Elizabeth, should we drop you at home on the way?"

She frowned in dismay. She was going to miss all the fun. "I suppose."

Maeve and Mrs. Malloy wished them well and sent them off. Gino only hoped they were doing the right thing.

FELIX WAS GLAD TO SEE THE REPORTERS WERE GONE from the Pollock house. In fact, everyone seemed to be gone from Harlem, or at least gone to their beds. Downtown, the streets got quieter late at night, but they were more dangerous because of the people lurking in the darkness. Here the streets just seemed peaceful. The carriage stopped in front of the Pollock house.

"The lights are on in the parlor," he observed.

"Maybe Una didn't really go to bed after her mother left. That's too bad, but she'll still be tired."

Felix hoped Gino knew what he was doing. He seemed very confident, but sometimes the young were confident because they didn't know how badly they could fail. John climbed down from his seat and opened the door for them. Felix thought he saw the parlor curtain twitch a bit, as if someone was looking out to see who had come.

When they knocked at the door a minute later, it opened almost at once. Hattie smiled, although she looked tired. "Mr. Decker, Officer, it's so nice to see you."

"Let them in, Hattie," Una called from the parlor doorway.

Una looked tired, too, but she had a bright smile for Felix.

Hattie admitted them and took their coats. Una still waited in the parlor doorway. Did she seem anxious or concerned? Felix couldn't tell.

"This is a pleasant surprise, Mr. Decker. Please come in." She didn't acknowledge Gino at all.

She led them into the parlor, and just as she was about to

close the door behind them, Gino said, "Hattie, would you send Eddie in to see us?"

"Why do you want to see Eddie?" Una asked. Her smile vanished.

"It's nothing very important. We'd just like to ask him something," Mr. Decker said.

Una closed the door with a slam. "I can't imagine why you had to come here at this time of night to talk to my boot boy," she said.

"We're sorry to bother you so late, Mrs. Pollock," Felix said, ignoring her tone. "But we had something important to discuss with you."

"If you're going to tell me how to get out of this mess, I'm perfectly willing to sit up all night. Please, sit down."

The two men took the chairs, and Una perched warily on the sofa. Felix noticed a glass sitting on the table beside her with a trace of amber liquid in the bottom. If Una had indeed just found out the money was missing today, she had probably needed a stiff drink.

"What do you want to know?" she asked. "I've had a very long day and I'd like to retire soon."

"Did you have a nice visit with your mother?" Mr. Decker asked.

Her face tightened. "Yes, thank you. Miss Smith was kind to bring her."

"We understand you haven't been able to locate your husband's bank account," he went on as he and Gino had agreed during the trip uptown. "I would be happy to assist you with that. It's easier if you know what bank he dealt with, of course."

"I . . . I'm not sure. Randolph never discussed such things with me."

"A mistake many men make, unfortunately," Felix said.

"And you see where it leads. But I can make some inquiries. I can't believe Pollock left you penniless."

Felix could see her trying to judge his motives. Was he sincere or was he tormenting her?

"You said you had something to discuss with me. I'm very tired."

"Yes, I was concerned, you see, when Miss Smith said you were alarmed over some funds you felt were missing."

She was wary now, taking care with every word. "Yes, as you said, I haven't found my husband's bank account."

"Miss Smith understood that this was money you thought should have been here in the house. In Mr. Pollock's office, in fact, which confused me. When I told you about the robbery the other day, you weren't concerned at all. At that time you didn't think there had been anything of value that might have been taken."

"I . . . I've since reconsidered. I've been under a lot of strain lately, as you know. First Randolph's violent death and then the time I spent in that horrible jail. I don't think you can hold me responsible for anything I might have said the very day I was released from that place."

It was a good argument. Felix felt sure that gentlemen sitting on a jury would be happy to give her the benefit of the doubt. "Miss Smith was quite upset that you accused her of taking this missing money."

"I did no such thing," Una insisted. "If she thought so, then I'm sorry. I'm simply trying to find the truth."

"So are we, Mrs. Pollock."

Mercifully, someone tapped on the door, and Felix gave a sigh of relief. He didn't know how much longer he could keep circling the issue they really wanted to discuss.

Una told whoever it was to enter, and Eddie stepped in.

He looked absolutely terrified, his eyes wide in his handsome face and his hands clutched into fists by his sides.

"Don't be frightened," Una said kindly, or was she really warning him? "You haven't done anything wrong. Mr. Decker just wants to ask you something."

Eddie's gaze darted to Felix and away again. He hung his head and hunched his shoulders as if expecting a blow.

"Come closer, Eddie. We're not going to hurt you," Felix said.

Eddie looked to Una for approval, and she nodded. He stepped forward on stiff legs until he stood at the end of the sofa where Una sat. His gaze kept darting to Una, who tried to smile reassuringly.

Felix glanced at Gino, giving him silent permission to begin. Felix's part had been to put them at ease, although he didn't think he had done a very good job of it. Gino's part was to question them.

"We know what happened to Pollock," Gino said. Una stiffened slightly but Eddie's whole body gave a little jerk.

"Good," Una tried. "I hope you will tell me, because I still have no memory of it."

"I should go back a bit, to explain how we came to this knowledge. You see, we know Pollock used to hit you, Mrs. Pollock. You must have been terrified of him, and who could blame you? You must have been desperate to get away from him but afraid to leave. You knew as long as he was alive, he'd come after you and bring you back, so you enlisted the help of a young man who had fallen in love with you." Gino glanced at Eddie, whose eyes seemed to glow with some intense emotion Felix didn't even want to name.

"This is a fascinating fairy tale," Una said, not sounding the least bit fascinated. "I just hope it has a happy ending."

Unfortunately, Felix knew it didn't. "You asked this young man to kill your husband, because that was the only

way to be free of him. I don't know what you promised him."
Gino watched Eddie carefully, but the boy still refused to
meet his gaze. "Maybe it was money, but more likely it was
other . . . favors."

"Really, Officer, this is very distasteful."

Gino ignored her protest. "You waited until the next time
Pollock started hitting you, and then Eddie rushed to rescue
you. That way he could claim he was only protecting your life.
You decided not to take a chance, though, so afterward you
claimed you were in shock and couldn't remember what happened. That way you wouldn't have to mention Eddie at all.
Except you didn't expect the police to arrest *you* for the crime,
did you?"

"That part is certainly true," Una said with a little of her
usual confidence. "Who would believe a lady could murder
her husband in such a way? It's ridiculous."

"But killing Pollock was only half the plan, wasn't it?"
Gino continued. "The other half was to keep the money he'd
cheated honest people out of for yourself."

"What are you talking about? Randolph didn't cheat
people, and as you already know, I haven't found any of his
money at all."

"But not because you didn't try, eh, Eddie?" Gino asked.

Eddie watched Gino the way you'd watch a poisonous snake
slithering toward you. Felix almost felt sorry for him.

"Yes, Eddie followed your instructions to the letter, didn't
he? He must have been scared when you got arrested, but he
went ahead and set up the fake robbery just like you'd
planned. He broke the basement window, then messed up
the office and opened the safe, using the combination you'd
given him."

"Why would I do a thing like that?" Una asked. "I don't
even know the combination to the safe."

"The person who opened it did, though. How do you suppose they got it?"

"I have no idea!"

"Well, it doesn't matter now, does it, because you went to all that trouble for nothing. The money wasn't in the safe, was it?"

Una was looking a little frantic now. Her gaze darted around the room as if she were looking for a means of escape. "I told you, Mr. Decker," she said, making Felix wonder why she'd chosen to appeal to him, "my husband kept his money in the bank."

Felix just smiled, and Gino went on.

"Eddie, you must have been terrified when you saw the safe was empty. Then you remembered the package you'd taken to Mr. Truett the morning Pollock died, and you thought Pollock must have sent the money to him for some reason. You must have wanted to go to his hotel that very night, but you couldn't because I was here all night, guarding the house. Then, luckily, Mrs. Pollock was released from jail and came home. Did you tell her about the missing money? Is that why she didn't want me to stay the next night?"

Felix saw the hateful glance Una gave Eddie and the way he cringed. Yes, Una was furious about the missing money and blamed Eddie.

"I remember you couldn't wait for me to leave the house that night, Eddie. Then you went to Truett's hotel and snuck in the back door, which you knew wasn't locked because you'd been there many times before. Did you think you could search his rooms without waking Truett or did you plan to kill him all along?"

Eddie had no answer for that, of course, although Felix noticed beads of sweat had formed on his upper lip.

"But you didn't find the money there either, did you? The

package you'd taken to Truett was just a bunch of contracts. And when you told Mrs. Pollock this morning, she was furious." Gino turned to Una. "But maybe you were so furious because that was the first you knew the money was missing at all. We can't blame Eddie for being afraid to tell you it wasn't in the safe, especially because he thought he could still get it from Truett and you'd never have to know."

Felix had to give Una credit. She'd hardly batted an eye in the face of Gino's condemnation.

"This is all very interesting, Officer, but . . . Well, you're right about one thing. My husband was a violent man. He often let his temper get the best of him, and then he would strike me. He was always sorry for it afterward, of course. He didn't mean to hurt me, and I loved him, so I would always forgive him. And now you're saying that the morning he died was one of those times when Randolph . . ." She hesitated, her voice breaking a bit. ". . . when Randolph lost his temper and became violent? And Eddie here—dear, sweet Eddie who has been so devoted to me—decided to come to my defense?"

"Something like that."

"Oh!" Una cried, raising a hand to her head dramatically. "I . . . I just remembered. I remember it all!" She looked wide-eyed at Gino. "You've brought it all back to me. Yes, it was just like you said. Randolph hit me and I was crying and Eddie rushed in. He picked up the Egyptian statue that Randolph loved so much and hit him with it. I was screaming for him to stop, but he wouldn't stop. He kept hitting him and hitting him until Randolph was dead. I crawled over to where my darling lay bleeding on the floor and took his head in my lap. I think I thought I could fix him somehow, but he was too broken. And"—she closed her eyes and sighed—"I'm afraid that's all I remember."

"That's a beautiful story, Mrs. Pollock," Gino said.

"Yes, it is," Felix said. "But we can't help wondering why, if Pollock treated you so badly, you didn't just leave him."

She smiled at that, a grotesque expression that held no trace of happiness. "I couldn't leave him, Mr. Decker, because he'd kill me if I did. Oh, I can see by your face that you don't believe me, but it's true. He told me that every time he beat me, and I believed him because he'd already killed one wife. That's right, little Cecelia. She'd tried to run away, but he caught her and brought her back, and then he choked the life out of her. He told me all about it, every gruesome little detail."

"How could he get away with something like that?" Felix asked, horrified.

"Because nobody knew. He buried her in the cellar and moved out of the house. Her family tracked him down, wanting to know where she was, and he told them she died in childbirth. They didn't believe him, but they had to check anyway, and as soon as they were gone, he left Chicago and came to New York. He thought he'd never see them again, and then the brother showed up here one morning. I've never seen Randolph so angry, and he somehow blamed me for them finding him. He was going to kill me, I'm sure of it, and then Eddie came in and saved me."

That really was a good story, and it might even be true, as far as it went. "Then why did he kill Truett?" Felix asked.

"Because he was yelling at her," Eddie cried.

"Eddie, don't!" Una tried, but she couldn't stop him.

"He came here and started shouting at her. I couldn't let him treat her that way, not when . . ." His eyes widened again as he realized what he'd revealed.

"When what?" Gino asked softly. "When you loved her? When she was your woman?"

"Don't be absurd!" Una snapped.

"You had to go to his apartment anyway, to find the money," Gino said. "You could've gone when he wasn't there, but you didn't. You went there when you knew he'd be home and fast asleep. You wanted to kill him, didn't you, Eddie? Or did she tell you to, like she told you to kill Pollock?"

"No, Mr. Truett was my idea," Eddie said.

"Eddie, stop!" she cried.

"It's no use!" he said. "They already know everything. They even know about the money." Eddie turned to Gino. "We were going to use it to run away. She knows a place that's far away from here where we can get married and no one will care that she's white and I'm not."

"He's lying!" Una said, jumping to her feet. "I never told him any such thing. I can't help it if he fell in love with me. He's been moping around here for months. I felt sorry for him or I would've let him go. But he killed my husband and he killed Truett, and I can't forgive him for that. You need to arrest him and take him away before he harms someone else."

Felix and Gino were on their feet now, too.

"You said you loved me," Eddie said, his face twisting with the agony of her betrayal. "You said we'd get married!"

"I never said any such thing!" she said to Felix, whose opinion she seemed to consider most important. "You must believe me. I couldn't possibly love someone like that!"

Eddie cried out in anguish, and before Felix could guess his intent, he grabbed the empty glass from the table and slammed it into Una's face.

Felix and Gino lunged to stop him, but he'd already hit her again by the time they dragged him off her. Gino grabbed Eddie's hand to get the glass away from him, but it had shattered, and the pieces fell onto the floor. His hand was covered with blood, but before Felix could see where he'd been cut, Una began to scream.

She held both hands to her face as blood poured out between her fingers.

"I've got him," Gino said, so Felix went to where she had collapsed back onto the sofa.

"Dear heaven, what happened?" someone cried.

Felix looked up to see Hattie and another woman had run into the room and were staring in horror at the blood and the sight of Gino still struggling with Eddie.

"Do you know where to find a doctor?" Felix asked.

"And get a policeman if you see one," added Gino.

Hattie nodded and ran out again.

"I'll get some towels," the other woman said. Felix recalled vaguely that she was the cook.

Una was still screaming and holding her face. Felix pulled a handkerchief from his pocket and said, "Here, put this on it."

She instantly stopped screaming and met his gaze with the eye she didn't have covered. "How bad it is?"

"Let me see."

Slowly, she lowered her bloody hands to reveal a terrible gash from her temple nearly to her lips. His stomach lurched, and she must have seen his horrified reaction on his face because she began to scream again. He placed the handkerchief over the wound as gently as he could, but it was almost instantly soaked with blood.

Fortunately, the cook quickly returned with an armload of towels, and she took over, laying Una down on the sofa and tending to the wound as best she could while calming the injured woman.

Felix turned his attention to Gino and Eddie, and found Gino had everything under control. Eddie had ceased struggling, and Gino had hauled him up from the floor to sit in one of the chairs. The boy had begun to weep as the truth of his situation began to sink in. Gino was wrapping his own handkerchief around Eddie's bleeding hand.

Felix stood helpless for a while, watching the others, until he heard someone shouting in the hallway. A police officer had wandered in the open front door.

"Has there been another murder?" he asked with a puzzled frown.

16

Elizabeth had wept when Frank and Sarah Malloy first came in the front door. She couldn't believe how happy she was to see them. Or how happy they looked. Part of it was being glad to see Brian and Catherine, she knew, but it was more than that. They were happy with each other in a way she'd never expected to see again. Between that and the approach of Christmas, the joy in their house was almost unbearable.

For this reason, no one spoke a word about the Pollock case to them for several days, until they'd run out of stories about their travels in France and Italy. But then Frank and Sarah began to notice that Felix and Elizabeth had developed a very close relationship with Gino and Maeve and that nothing was quite the same as when they'd left. Elizabeth could see it in their eyes, the way they watched everyone and then exchanged knowing looks.

Finally, on the night before Christmas Eve, after they'd

tucked the children into bed and finished decorating the Christmas tree in preparation for surprising the children tomorrow and had plugged in the electric lights and were sitting marveling at this wonderful new invention, Frank Malloy finally said, "Now tell me what happened to all of you while we were gone."

"What do you mean?" Elizabeth said with as much innocence as she could muster.

"I think you know what I mean. Gino obviously isn't working for the police department or anybody else anymore. He spends too much time here. And all of you keep smiling at each other like you know a secret that you can't wait to tell." He glanced at Sarah, who nodded in a way that told Elizabeth they'd discussed this already. "So what have you been up to?"

Elizabeth glanced at the others, wondering which of them should start the tale. Felix chose himself.

"Well, Frank, I've been meaning to offer you a business opportunity."

"A business opportunity?"

"Yes," he said. "You see, while you were gone, we've started a private detective agency. We have successfully completed our first case, and we're willing to bring you in as a partner if you're interested."

The expression on Malloy's face was priceless, and everyone burst out laughing. Then they started telling their story. Elizabeth and Felix and Gino and Maeve took turns telling their parts in the tale, often interrupting or talking over one another in the process. Even Frank's mother chimed in once or twice with her opinions. Frank and Sarah would stop them occasionally to ask a question, but for the most part they listened in fascination.

When they were finally finished, Sarah said, "I have to feel a bit sorry for Una. She must have been truly terrified of Pollock. It's no wonder she did such a desperate thing to escape him."

"She shouldn't have involved poor Eddie, though," Elizabeth said. She'd thought a lot about Una's plight in the past few days. "She really was planning to tell the police he killed Pollock and take all the money—which she was going to steal from those people the same way Pollock did—and go off and live a happy life while Eddie went to prison or worse."

"But if Pollock would have really killed her . . . ," Sarah said, shaking her head. "Did they find his first wife?"

"Yes," Elizabeth said. "She was buried in the cellar just like he'd told her. At least Cecelia's family was finally able to mourn her and lay her to rest."

"So Una was right to be scared of him, at least," Sarah said, "although she had no right to ruin that poor boy's life to save her own."

"What's going to happen to Eddie now?" Frank asked.

"He killed two men," Gino reminded them. "He might've claimed he was saving Una's life when he killed Pollock, but he killed Truett for no reason at all."

"Will he go on trial?" Sarah asked.

"Yes, unless his attorney decides he'd be better off to just plead guilty."

"How can he afford to hire an attorney?" Elizabeth asked.

"The Legal Aid Society provided one for him for free," Gino said.

"I had no idea. You mean there are attorneys who will work for free?" she asked.

"Occasionally," Frank said with a small smile. "Is Eddie going to try to blame Una for convincing him to kill Pollock?"

Gino shrugged. "His lawyer doesn't think that's a good idea. Una claims Eddie made the whole thing up and that robbing her and Truett was his idea, too, and the lawyer thinks a jury of white men would believe her instead of him.

Besides, Eddie cut her face pretty badly, and when they see her scar, she'll get a lot of sympathy."

"How bad is it?" Sarah asked.

"It must be awful," Maeve said. "I went to see Mrs. O'Neill, and she could hardly talk about it without crying. Not only does Una have a scar, but the whole side of her face droops down."

"For Una, that's a horrible punishment," Elizabeth said.

"Yes, Eddie got his revenge," Maeve said.

"Where is Una now?" Sarah asked.

"Oh, she lives with Mrs. O'Neill," Maeve said. "I told her once that she could sell the house and the furniture so she could have a little money of her own, but it turns out the house was just rented. She wouldn't even come out of the bedroom when I was there. She still thinks we stole her money."

"It wasn't her money," Felix said. "And it wasn't Pollock's either."

"Did the police ever ask you about it?" Frank asked. "I'm sure Eddie must have mentioned the missing money when he told his story."

"The police wouldn't dream of asking Felix Decker if he stole Pollock's money," Gino reported with a grin. "They did ask *me*, though, and I told them I never saw any money at Pollock's place, which was true. I left them with the impression that Pollock had lied to his wife about having a lot of money."

"And now it's all back where it belongs," Felix said. "None of the investors want anyone to know they were defrauded, naturally, and they're not connected to the murders in any way, so there's no reason to reveal their identities."

"But one good thing came out of all of it," Mrs. Malloy said. "We got a maid and a cook."

Sarah gaped at her. "Are you telling me our new servants worked for Pollock?"

"Yes, and they were very relieved to find new positions so

quickly," Elizabeth said, proud of the way they had solved both Sarah's need for servants and the servants' need for work. "Maeve was afraid Mrs. Malloy wouldn't want someone to take over the cooking, but—"

"—but Maeve was wrong," Mrs. Malloy said, making everyone laugh. "I like being able to sit down and put my feet up when I bring Brian home from school instead of having to cook supper."

"So what do you think about my business proposition, Frank?" Felix asked.

Frank leaned back in his chair. "Tell me again how much money you made from this case."

Felix didn't bat an eye. "We'll be more careful in the future to take clients who can actually pay."

Frank gave Gino a considering look. "And I suppose you're willing to work for this detective agency."

"I already do," Gino told him cheerfully. "But I would like to start getting paid for it."

Frank turned to Maeve. "And what about you? Do we need to hire a new nursemaid for Catherine?"

Elizabeth knew Maeve had given this matter a lot of thought, too, and she was glad to hear her reply. "No, at least not yet. I can't bear to leave Catherine now. She'd be so sad. But I'll help out when you need me."

Then Frank looked at Elizabeth and before she could say a word, he said, "I'm not hiring you no matter what, because your husband would kill me."

Elizabeth smiled serenely. She didn't need to be "hired" to do detective work.

"So we're starting a detective agency?" Sarah asked.

"I suppose we are," Frank said. "Merry Christmas, everyone."

Author's Note

I HOPE YOU ENJOYED THIS GASLIGHT MYSTERY "EXTRA" story. My publisher asked me to do a Christmas story featuring some of the secondary characters from the series; fans have been nagging me to get Gino and Maeve together, and Frank and Sarah were away on their honeymoon, so this seemed like perfect timing. Don't worry, Frank and Sarah are back and better than ever, and they will be leading future investigations as before, only as part of Frank's new "private inquiries" business.

I had fun investigating Christmas traditions in America during this time period. To my surprise, I learned that Christmas wasn't celebrated much at all in America until around the time of the Civil War. The first Christmas tree lot in New York City was set up in 1851. Christmas tree lights first appeared in 1882, but they were too costly for most Americans, who used candles instead. At the turn of the nineteenth century, only about one in five Americans had a Christmas tree. The first department store Santa appeared in 1890 and would wander around the store, greeting children.

I mention the Legal Aid Society, which was established in New York in 1890 to provide legal representation to indigent defendants. Attorneys had been providing pro bono representation for a long time, and this agency merely formalized that process.

Please let me know how you liked this book by contacting me through my website victoriathompson.com or "like" me on Facebook, facebook.com/Victoria.Thompson.Author, or follow me on Twitter @gaslightvt. I'll send you a reminder whenever I have a new book out.